ACCLAIM FOR
THE CAT WHO SERIES
AND *THE NEW YORK TIMES*
BESTSELLING AUTHOR
LILIAN JACKSON BRAUN

"Great fun!"

—Lawrence Block

"Mrs. Braun has a breezy style; the cats are really smart."

—Newgate Callendar,
The New York Times Book Review

"Koko and Yum Yum are delightful sleuths who keep the reader entertained . . . from the opening scene to the final curtain."

—*Daily Press/Newport News (Va.)*

"Ideal to curl up with on a cold winter night!"

—*Cat Fancy*

"*Vive* the cats!"

—New York *Daily News*

The Cat Who Lived High

Lilian Jackson Braun

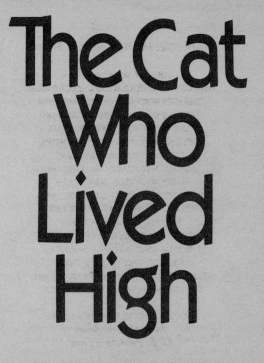

JOVE BOOKS, NEW YORK

This Jove Book contains the complete
text of the original hardcover edition.
It has been completely reset in a typeface
designed for easy reading, and was printed
from new film.

THE CAT WHO LIVED HIGH

A Jove Book / published by arrangement with
the author

PRINTING HISTORY
G.P. Putnam's Sons edition published August 1990
Jove edition / May 1991

ISBN: 0-515-10566-X

Jove Books are published by The Berkley Publishing Group,
200 Madison Avenue, New York, New York 10016.
The name "JOVE" and the "J" logo
are trademarks belonging to Jove Publications, Inc.

PRINTED IN THE UNITED STATES OF AMERICA

10 9

DEDICATED TO
EARL BETTINGER, THE HUSBAND WHO . . .

ONE

THE NEWS THAT reached Pickax City early on that cold November morning sent a deathly chill through the small northern community. The Pickax police chief, Andrew Brodie, was the first to hear about the car crash. It had occurred four hundred miles to the south, in the perilous urban area that locals called Down Below. The metropolitan police appealed to Brodie for assistance in locating the next of kin.

The victim, they said, had been driving through the heart of the city on a four-lane freeway when

1

the occupants of a passing car, according to witnesses, fired shots at him, causing him to lose control of his vehicle, which crashed into a concrete abutment and burned. The driver's body was consumed by the flames, but through the license plates the registration had been traced to James Qwilleran, fifty-two, of Pickax City.

Brodie smashed his leathery fist down on the desk, and his face contorted in grief and anger. "I warned him! I warned him!" he shouted.

Qwilleran had no living relatives; a phone call to his attorney confirmed that fact. His family consisted of two Siamese cats, but his extended family included the entire population of Moose County. The genial personality and quirky philosophy of the retired journalist endeared "Mr. Q" to everyone. The column he wrote for the local newspaper had won him a host of admirers. His luxuriant moustache and drooping eyelids and graying temples were considered sexually attractive by women of all ages. And the fact that he was the richest bachelor in three counties and an unbridled philanthropist made him a civic treasure.

Brodie immediately called Arch Riker, Qwilleran's lifelong friend and current publisher of the Moose County newspaper. "Dammit! I warned him about that jungle!" the chief shouted into the phone. "He's been living up here for three years, and he forgot that life Down Below is like Russian roulette!"

Shocked and searching for something to say, Riker mumbled soberly, "Qwill knew all about that. Before moving up here he lived in cities for fifty years. He and I grew up in Chicago.''

''Things have changed since then,'' Brodie snapped. ''God! Do you know what this means?''

The fact was that Qwilleran had inherited vast wealth from the Klingenschoen estate—on one condition: He must live in Moose County for five years. Otherwise, the Klingenschoen millions—or billions—would go to the alternate heirs out of state.

Riker listened glumly to Brodie's tirade and then phoned Polly Duncan, the woman in Qwilleran's life, who was prostrated by the news. He himself made immediate plans to fly down to the city. By the time the publisher had notified his own news desk and the local radio station, the telephone lines were spluttering with the bad tidings, and Moose County was caught up in a frenzy of horror and grief. Thousands would miss Qwilleran's column on page two of the newspaper. Hundreds would miss the sight of Mr. Q riding his bicycle on country roads and walking about downtown Pickax with a long stride and a sober expression, answering their greetings with a courteous salute. And everyone realized the community would now lose scholarships, grants, and interest-free loans. Why, they asked each other, had he been so rash as to venture Down Below? Only one person thought to worry about the Siamese. His part-time secretary, Lori Bamba, cried, ''What will happen to Koko and Yum Yum?''

There were cats galore in Moose County—barn

3

mousers, feral cats, and pampered pets—yet none so pampered as the two thoroughbreds who lived with Qwilleran, and none quite so remarkable as Kao K'o Kung, whose everyday name was Koko. With his noble whiskers, aristocratic ears, sensitive nose, and inscrutable gaze Koko could see the invisible, hear the inaudible, and sense the unknowable. His companion, Yum Yum, was a charmer who captivated Qwilleran with shameless wiles, reaching out a paw to touch his moustache while squeezing her eyes and purring throatily. They were a handsome pair—fawn-furred, with seal-brown extremities and mesmerizing blue eyes. What would happen to them now? Where were they? Would anyone feed them?

Then came the gripping question: Were they still alive? Had they been in the car when it burned?

About two weeks before the metropolitan police called Brodie with the fateful news, Qwilleran and his two feline companions were spending a quiet evening at home in Moose County—the man, a husky six feet two, sprawled in the second-best easy chair with nothing much on his mind; the cats lounging on the best chair, as was their due, meditating and looking exquisite. When the raucous bell of the telephone disturbed the domestic peace, Qwilleran reluctantly hoisted himself to his feet and went to the phone in the adjoining room. It was a long-distance call from Down Below.

He heard an unfamiliar voice say, "Hello, Mr. Qwilleran. You'll never guess who this is! . . . Amberina, from the Three Weird Sisters in Junktown! Do you remember me?"

"Of course I remember you," he said diplomatically, at the same time thinking fast. The three women had an antique shop, but which of the sisters was Amberina? The giddy young blond or the man-crazy redhead or the unimpressive brunette? "How's everything Down Below?" he asked. "I haven't been there for quite a while—three years, as a matter of fact."

"You'd never recognize Junktown," she replied. "We're being gentrified, like they say. People are buying the old townhouses and fixing them up, and we're getting some first-class restaurants and antique shops."

"Do you still have your shop?"

"No, we gave it up. Ivrene finished art school and got a job in Chicago. Cluthra married money—wouldn't you know?—and moved to Texas. And I'm working for an auction house. From what I hear, Mr. Qwilleran, your life has changed, too, with the inheritance and everything."

"Much to my surprise, yes . . . By the way, did you hear about Iris Cobb?"

"Gosh, were we ever shocked! When she was in Junktown she was such a live wire."

"Does Mary Duckworth still have the Blue Dragon?"

"She sure does! It's the best antique shop on the street—the most expensive, that is. Robert

Maus has opened a classy restaurant, and Charlotte Roop is his manager. You know both of them, I think.''

Why, Qwilleran thought, is this woman calling me after three years? His momentary silence brought her to the point.

Amberina said, "Mary wanted me to call you because she's going out of town. She has something she'd like to suggest to you.''

"Well, fire away!''

"Do you know the big old white apartment building called the Casablanca? It's sort of rundown, but it's a landmark.''

"I vaguely remember it.''

"It's a tall building between Junktown and the reclaimed area where they're putting up the new office towers and condos.''

"Yes, now I know the one you mean," he said.

"Well, to make a long story short, some developers want to tear it down, which would be a crime! That building is really built! And it has a lot of history. Junktown has formed a task force called SOCK—Save Our Casablanca Kommittee—spelled with a K, you know.''

"Does SOCK have any clout?" Qwilleran quipped.

"Not really. That's why we're calling you.''

"What's the proposition?''

She drew a deep breath. "The Casablanca used to be the best address in town. SOCK wants you to buy it and restore it . . . There! I said it! It wasn't easy.''

It was Qwilleran's turn to take a deep breath.

6

"Now wait a minute, Amberina. Let me straighten you out. I'm no financier, and I don't get involved in business ventures. Nothing is further from my mind. In fact, I've turned my inheritance over to the Klingenschoen Memorial Fund. I have nothing to do with it." Actually he made suggestions to the Fund, but he saw no need to mention that.

"We all remember what you did for Junktown when you wrote for the *Daily Fluxion*, Mr. Qwilleran. Your series of articles in the paper really woke us up and started our comeback."

He stroked his moustache as he remembered his memorable winter in that slummy part of town. "I admit my Junktown experience whetted my interest in preservation," he said, "and theoretically I endorse your cause, although I'm in no position to know whether it's feasible."

"Oh, but you should see the Casablanca!" she said with enthusiasm. "The experts tell us it has great possibilities." Qwilleran was beginning to remember her now. Amberina was the least weird of the Three Weird Sisters. "The building used to be very grand," she was saying. "Some changes have been made, but the architects say they're reversible. It could go back to being a fashionable place to live, and that would be a real boost for Junktown. Right now the Casablanca is . . . well, the tenants are a mixed bag. But they're interesting! Mostly singles, but a few couples, not necessarily married. Whites, blacks, Asians, Hispanics . . . yuppies, artists, truck drivers, wealthy widows, college students, a couple of stunning call girls, and a few bums and crazies, but they're harmless.''

''You make it sound irresistible.''

''I live at the Casablanca myself,'' she said with a small hysterical laugh.

Quill now remembered more about Amberina. She had dark hair, very attractive blue eyes (probably wore contacts), and a husband. Yet she now spoke as if she lived alone. ''I'd like to see the place,'' he said.

''Mary said to tell you the penthouse apartment is available for sublet, and it's very well furnished. Maybe you'd like to come down and stay for a while.''

''Well, I don't know . . .''

''You should decide fast, Mr. Qwilleran, because the developers are putting pressure on the owner of the building to sell it to them. SOCK is getting kind of antsy.''

''Who is the owner?''

''We call her the Countess. She's seventy-five years old. She's lived in the building all her life and still has her original apartment. I'm sure you could talk her into selling to your Memorial Fund, Mr. Qwilleran. You're a very charming man.''

''Not always,'' he protested in mock modesty, grooming his moustache. He was well aware of his success in winning over women, especially older ones. ''If I were to drive down there,'' he said slowly and thoughtfully, ''I'd have to take my cats. Are pets permitted?''

''Cats are okay, but not dogs. In fact, there are

cats all over the place.'' Amberina giggled. ''Some people call it the Casablanca Cathouse.''

''Did you say there's a penthouse available?'' he asked with increasing interest.

''You'd love it! It's really very glamorous. There's a large sunken living room with a skylight and indoor trees . . . and a marvelous view . . . and a terrace . . .''

''Let me call you back tomorrow. I'll have to discuss it with my bosses,'' Qwilleran said facetiously, meaning the Siamese.

''Don't lose any time,'' she warned. ''If anything happens to the old lady, Mary says, the building will be sold to the developers so the heirs can be paid off.''

After hanging up the phone he rationalized fast. One: He had been confined to Moose County for three years, except for one flying trip Down Below to have dinner at the Press Club. Two: Winter was on its way, and winters in Moose County were not only cruel but interminable. Three: The imperiled Casablanca would be a convenient excuse to escape the glacial pavements and ten-foot snowbanks of Pickax. At least, he thought, there's no harm in driving down and checking out the building's potential.

First he broke the news to the Siamese. Living alone, he made it a practice to converse with his cats, often reading aloud to them and always discussing his problems and plans. They seemed to enjoy the sound of his voice, whether or not they knew what he was saying. More importantly, verbalizing his thoughts helped him to make decisions.

"Listen, you guys," he called out to them, "how would you like to spend the winter in the Crime Belt instead of the Snow Belt? . . . Where are you?"

His companions had deserted their comfortable chair and were nowhere in view.

"Where did you brats go?" he demanded.

There was not a murmur from either of them, although he could feel their presence, and he could guess where they were. Koko had burrowed under the hearth rug, and Yum Yum was hiding under the rug in front of the sofa. Their silent comment was readily interpreted: They abhorred a change of address, and they sensed what Qwilleran had in mind.

He paced the floor with growing eagerness. Despite the reaction of his housemates, he relished the idea of a winter in the big city. He missed the Press Club. He missed the camaraderie of the staffers at the *Daily Fluxion*, where he had been a popular feature writer. He missed the stage shows, the hockey and pro basketball, and the variety of restaurants. There was one drawback: He would have to forgo the companionship of Polly Duncan. He had become very fond of Pickax City's head librarian. They shared the same interests. She was his own age—an intelligent and loving woman. And since neither had a desire to marry, they were a compatible pair.

Polly was the first one he wanted to consult about his proposed venture, and he phoned her little house in the country, but before he could break the news, she quelched his elation with a cry of distress.

"Oh, Qwill! I was just about to call you. I've had some dreadful news. I'm being evicted!"

"What do you mean?" For years she had been the tenant of a snug cottage in farming country, and he had spent many idyllic weekends surrounded by cornfields and deer habitat and a hemisphere of blue sky.

"I told you the farm had been sold," she said, almost in tears. "Now I learn that the new owner wants my cottage for his married son. Winter's almost here! Where can I go? Landlords don't permit cats, and I can't give up Bootsie! What shall I do?" she wailed. Here was a woman who could devise a swift solution to the most complex problem arising at the public library; her panic over this personal setback was disturbing. "Are you there?" she cried impatiently. "Did you hear me, Qwill?"

"I heard you. I'm thinking," he said. "It so happens that I'm invited to spend the winter months Down Below—in a penthouse apartment. That means . . . you could put your furniture in storage and stay at my place in Pickax while you scout for a new house." Whimsically he added, "I have no objection to cats." There was silence at the other end of the line. "Are you there, Polly? Did you hear me?"

"I'm thinking," she said. "It sounds like an ideal solution, Qwill, and it's certainly very generous of you, and of course it would be handy to the library, but . . ."

"But what?"

"But I don't like the idea of your spending all that time Down Below."

"You went to England for an entire summer," he reminded her. "I didn't care for that idea, either, but I survived."

"That's not what I mean. Cities are so unsafe! I don't want anything to happen to you."

"Polly, may I remind you that I lived in large cities all my life before moving up here."

"What is the penthouse you mentioned?" she asked warily.

"Let's have dinner tomorrow night, and I'll explain."

Next he phoned his old friend, Arch Riker, now publisher of the local paper. He said, "I've just had an interesting call from Down Below. Do you remember the Casablanca apartments on the edge of Junktown?"

"Sure," said Riker. "Rosie and I lived there when we were first married. They'd cut up most of the large apartments into efficiencies and one-bedroom units. We had a few good years there. Then the kids started coming, and we moved to the suburbs. What about the Casablanca? I suppose they're tearing it down."

"You guessed right," Qwilleran said. "Some developers want to take it over."

"They'll need a nuclear bomb to demolish that hunk of masonry. It's built like the Rock of Gibraltar."

"Well, hold on to your hat, Arch. I've been thinking it might be a good public relations ploy for the Klingenschoen Fund to buy it and restore it."

"What! You mean—restore it all the way? That would be a costly operation. You're talking about megamillions!"

"That's what I mean—restore the apartments to their original condition and go condo. The Fund is making money faster than the board of directors can give it away, so what if it's a financial loss? It will be a triumph for the cause of preservation—and a feather in the Klingenschoen cap."

"I have to think about that. Offhand, it sounds like a madcap gamble. Have you suggested it to the board of directors?"

"I heard the news only half an hour ago, Arch. I'll need more particulars, but see what you think of this: If I spend the winter down there, investigating the possibilities, I can write a weekly column for you on the horrors of city living. Moose County readers will lap it up!"

"Are you sure you want to go down there?" Riker asked apprehensively. "It's a dangerous place to live, what with muggings and break-ins and murders."

"Are you telling *me*? I wrote the book!" At the height of his career Qwilleran had written a best-seller on urban crime. "You may remember, Arch, there were muggings and break-ins and murders when you and I worked for the *Daily Fluxion*, and we took them for granted."

"From what I hear and read, conditions are much worse now."

"There's no coward so cowardly as a city dweller who has moved to the boondocks, my friend. Listen to this: I can get the penthouse at the Casablanca, furnished."

"Sounds good, I guess, but don't rush into anything," Riker advised. "Think about it for a couple of weeks."

"I can't wait a couple of weeks. The K Fund will have to sneak in a bid ahead of the wrecking ball. Besides, we can expect snow any day now, and it won't stop snowing until March. I won't be able to get out of here."

"What about the cats?"

"I'll take them with me, of course."

"They won't like living high up. We were on the ninth floor, and our cats hated the elevator."

"They'll adjust. There's a terrace, and where there's a terrace there are pigeons. Koko is a licensed pigeon watcher."

"Well . . . do it if you want to take the gamble, Qwill, but wear a bulletproof vest," Riker warned, and said good-bye.

Qwilleran found it difficult to settle down. He tried reading aloud to the Siamese to calm his excitement, but his mind was not on the printed page. He was impatient to learn more about the Casablanca. Unable to wait until morning, he phoned Down Below.

"I hope I'm not calling too late, Amberina," he said. "I need more information before I can broach the subject to the board of directors."

"Sure," she said distractedly, as if watching something attention-riveting on television.

"First, do you know anything about the history of the building? When was it built?"

"In 1901. The first high-rise apartment building in the city. The first to have an elevator."

"How many stories?"

"Thirteen."

"Who lived there originally? What kind of people?"

"Well, Mary says there were financiers, government officials, railroad tycoons, judges, heiresses—that kind. Also, they had suites for visiting royalty, opera stars, and so forth. After the stock market crash in 1929, more millionaires jumped off the roof of the Casablanca than any other building in the county."

"An impressive distinction," Qwilleran said wryly. "When did the place start to go downhill?"

"In the Depression. They couldn't rent the expensive apartments, so they cut them up, lowered ceilings—anything to cut costs and bring in some rent money."

"What can you tell me about the structure itself?"

"Let's see . . . SOCK put out a brochure that's around here somewhere. If you don't mind waiting, I'll try to find it. I'm not a very well-organized person."

"Take your time," he said. He had been making notes, and while she searched for the brochure, he sketched out his approach to the board of directors, scheduled his departure, and made a list of people to notify.

"Okay, here I am. I found it. Sorry to keep you waiting," Amberina said. "It was with my Christmas cards."

"Aren't you early with Christmas cards?"

"I haven't sent out *last year's* cards yet! . . . Are you ready? It says the exterior is faced with white glazed brick. The design is modified Moorish . . . Marble lobby with Persian rugs . . . Elevators paneled in rosewood . . . Mosaic tile floors in hallways. Apartments soundproof and fireproof, with twelve-foot ceilings and black walnut woodwork. Restaurant with terrace on the top floor. Also a swimming pool up there . . . this is the way it was in 1901, you understand. How does it sound, Mr. Qwilleran?"

"Not bad! You'd better reserve that penthouse for me."

"Mary told me to say that you'll be the guest of SOCK."

"I can afford to pay my own rent, but I appreciate the offer. How's the parking?"

"There's a paved lot with reserved spaces for tenants."

"And what's the crime situation in Junktown?"

"Well, we finally got the floozies and winos and pushers off the street."

"How did you do that?"

"The city cooperated because the Pennimans were behind it—"

"—and the city realized a broader tax base," Qwilleran guessed.

"Something like that. We have a citizens' patrol at night, and, of course, we don't take any chances after dark."

"How about security in the building itself?"

"Pretty good. The front door is locked, and there's a buzzer system. We had a doorman until a year ago. The side door is locked except for emergencies."

"Apparently the elderly woman who owns the building feels safe enough."

"I guess so. She has sort of a live-in bodyguard."

"Then it's a deal. Count on me to arrive next weekend."

"Mary will be tickled. We'll make all the arrangements for you."

"One question, Amberina. How many persons know that SOCK is inviting me to go down there?"

"Well, it was Mary's idea, and she probably discussed it with Robert Maus, but she wouldn't gab it around. She's not that type."

"All right. Let's keep it that way. Don't broadcast it. The story is that I want to get away from the abominable snow and ice up north, and the Casablanca is the only place that allows cats."

"Okay, I'll tell Mary."

"Any instructions for me when I arrive?"

"Just buzz the manager from the vestibule. We

don't have a doorman anymore, but the custodian will help with your luggage. It will be nice to see you again, Mr. Qwilleran.''

"What happened to the doorman?" he asked.

"Well," she said apologetically, "he was shot."

TWO

THE SENIOR PARTNER of the Pickax firm of Hasselrich Bennett & Barter, legal counsel for the Klingenschoen Memorial Fund, was an elderly man with stooped shoulders and quivering jowls, but he had the buoyant optimism and indomitability of a young man. It was Hasselrich whom Qwilleran chose to approach regarding the Casablanca proposal.

Before discussing business, the attorney insisted on serving coffee, pouring it proudly from his paternal grandmother's silver teapot into his maternal grandmother's Wedgwood cups, which rattled in the saucers as his shaking hands did the honors.

"It appears," Qwilleran began after a respectable interval for pleasantries, "that all of the Fund's ventures are on the East Coast, and it might be advisable to make ourselves known in another part of the country. What I have to suggest is both an investment and a public beneficence."

Hasselrich listened attentively as Qwilleran described the gentrification of Junktown, the unique architecture of the Casablanca, and the opportunity for the K Fund to preserve a fragment of the region's heritage. At the mention of the marble lobby and rosewood-paneled elevators, the attorney's jowls quivered with approval. "Many a time I have heard my grandfather extolling that magnificent building. He knew the man who built it," said Hasselrich. "As a young boy I was once treated to lunch in the rooftop restaurant. Unfortunately, I remember nothing but the spinach timbales. I had a juvenile aversion to spinach."

Qwilleran said, "The rooftop restaurant is now a penthouse apartment, and I plan to spend some time there, investigating the possibilities and persuading the owner to sell, if it seems wise. You know what will happen if developers are allowed to acquire the property; the building will be razed."

"Deplorable!" said Hasselrich. "We must not let that happen. This must be added to the agenda for the directors' meeting next week."

"I plan to drive down there in a few days—to beat the snow," said Qwilleran. "If you will be good enough to make the presentation in my absence, I'll supply a fact sheet." He welcomed any excuse to avoid meetings with the board of directors.

"Do you find it quite necessary to attend to this research yourself?" asked the attorney. "There are agencies we might retain to make a feasibility study."

"I consider it highly advisable. The owner is being pressured by the developers, and it will require some personal strategy to persuade the lady to sell to us."

The elderly attorney's lowered eyes and twitching eyelids were making broad inferences.

"She's seventy-five," Qwilleran added hastily, "and if she dies before deciding in our favor, we're out of luck and the Casablanca is doomed."

Hasselrich cleared his throat. "There is one consideration that gives me pause. You have indicated a profound interest in the welfare of Moose County, and that entails a responsibility to remain in good health, so to speak. You understand my meaning, do you not?"

"Moose County's interest in keeping me alive is no greater than my own desire to live, and I might point out another fact," Qwilleran said firmly. "When I go Down Below I am not a naive tourist from the outback; I've been city-smart since childhood."

Hasselrich studied his desktop and shook his

21

jowls. "You seem to have made your decision. We can only hope for your safe return."

That same afternoon, the *Moose County Something*, as the local newspaper was waggishly named, carried the regular Tuesday column headed "Straight from the Qwill Pen," with an editor's note stating that Jim Qwilleran would be on a leave of absence for an indefinite period, pursuing business Down Below, but he would file an occasional column on city living, to appear in his usual space.

As soon as Qwilleran read this he recognized a conspiracy on the part of Arch Riker, the publisher, and Junior Goodwinter, the managing editor. The two guessed what the result of such an announcement would be, and they were right. Qwilleran's telephone started to ring, and the citizens of Moose County tried to dissuade him from braving the perils Down Below. When told that the trip was important and necessary, they offered advice: "Wear a money belt . . . Don't take your best watch . . . Get a burglar alarm for your car . . . Lock yourself in when you drive in the city."

Police Chief Brodie said, "Och, mon, you're a bit daft. I happen to hear a few things that don't get in the papers, but if you insist on going, stay home after dark and buy one of them gadgets that lock the brake pedal to the steering wheel."

From Susan Exbridge, a member of the Theatre Club, there was a melodramatic phone call: "*Darling*, don't *walk* anywhere! Take a taxi, even if you're only going a block. I have friends Down Below, and they tell me it's *hell*!''

Dr. Goodwinter warned of respiratory ailments caused by airborne pollutants, and Eddington Smith, the timid dealer in secondhand books, offered to lend his handgun.

Lori Bamba was concerned chiefly about the cats. ''If you're taking Koko and Yum Yum,'' she said, ''don't let it be known that you have pedigreed animals. Kitnapping is big business Down Below. Also, you should feed them extra B vitamins to combat stress, because they'll sense menacing elements.''

Even Qwilleran's cleaning man was worried. ''It's prayin' I'll be,'' said Mr. O'Dell, ''until you be comin' safe home, Mr. Q.''

Nevertheless, Qwilleran stubbornly shopped for the journey. He bought a cagelike cat carrier that was more commodious and better ventilated than the picnic hamper in which the Siamese had formerly traveled. For their meals en route he laid in a supply of canned crabmeat, boned chicken, and red salmon. He also bought two blue leather harnesses—one medium and one large—with matching leashes. For himself he would take whatever he happened to have on hand. There were two suits in his closet—a gray flannel that he had worn once to a wedding and a dark blue serge that he had worn once as a pallbearer. These—with two white shirts, a couple of ties, and a raincoat—were his concessions to city dressing. Otherwise, he would take flannel shirts, sweaters, and his comfortable tweed sports coat with leather patches on the elbows.

During Qwilleran's final days in Pickax, farewell scenes with friends and associates had the solemnity of a deathbed vigil. Polly Duncan, on their last evening together, was lachrymose and in no mood to be comforted or to quote Shakespeare, although Qwilleran rose to the occasion with "parting is such sweet sorrow."

"Promise you'll call me as soon as you arrive" were her final words. He had hoped for less wifely anxiety and more amorous sentiments.

Even the Siamese sensed that something dire was afoot, and they sulked for twenty-four hours before their departure. When taken for rides in their new carrier, as rehearsal for the trip, they reacted like condemned nobility on the way to the guillotine—stoic, proud, and aloof.

None of this heightened Qwilleran's anticipation of the expedition, but he packed the car on Saturday morning with grim determination. Two suitcases, his typewriter, the unabridged dictionary, and his computerized coffeemaker went into the trunk. On the backseat were two boxes of books, the new cat carrier, and a blue cushion. The cats' water dish and their commode—a turkey roaster with the handles sawed off—were on the floor of the backseat.

The car was a small, energy-efficient, preowned four-door that Qwilleran had bought in a hurry, following his accident on Ittibittiwassee Road. The paint finish, a metallic purplish-blue, was not to his liking, but the used-car dealer assured him it was a color ahead of its time, called Purple Plum, and it would increase in acceptance and popularity.

"It looks better on fruit," Qwilleran remarked. The price was right, however, and the gas mileage was said to be phenomenal, and he had retained thrifty habits despite his new financial status, so he bought it. This was the car he packed for the four-hundred-mile journey, which he intended to stretch over two days for the comfort of the Siamese.

"All aboard the Purple Plum for Lockmaster, Paddockville, and all points south!" he announced to his two reluctant passengers. Grudgingly they allowed themselves to be stuffed into the carrier.

As the three of them pulled away from their home on Park Circle, the pair in the backseat maintained their funereal silence, leaving Qwilleran long, quiet hours to reflect on his sojourn in the north country. Despite the king-size mosquitoes, poison ivy, skunks, and hazardous deer crossings, Moose County afforded a comfortable life among good people. Most of them were rampant individualists and non-stop gossips, but that merely made them more interesting in the eyes of a journalist. How, he questioned, would he adjust to city life with its mask of conformity, guarded privacy, and self-interest?

His ruminations were interrupted by a demanding shriek from the backseat—so loud and so sudden that he gripped the steering wheel to keep the car on the road. Yum Yum was merely making a suggestion. How a creature of such delicacy and gentleness could produce this vulgar screech was beyond his comprehension, but it was effective. At the next crossroads he stopped for a coffee break and released the Siamese from their coop to stretch, peer out the windows, lap a tongueful of water, and examine the gas pedal.

After six hours of driving (Yum Yum objected to speeds in excess of fifty miles per hour), Qwilleran could not fault his passengers. They were behaving like mature, sophisticated travelers. At the motel that night—a less-than-deluxe establishment that welcomed pets—the Siamese slept soundly throughout the night, although Qwilleran was disturbed by barking dogs, slamming doors, and a growling ice machine outside his room. This appliance was located at the foot of wooden steps, up and down which the second-floor guests thumped frequently, shouting to each other:

''Where's the gin?''

''In the trunk under the spare tire!''

''I can't find the peanuts!''

It was Saturday night, and travelers were partying late. They also took an undue number of showers in Qwilleran's estimation. The force of the water hitting the fiberglass tubs in neighboring rooms thundered like Niagara, while he lay awake waiting for the tumult to end.

Meanwhile, the Siamese slept peacefully on top of his feet, and when he wriggled to relieve the numbness, they moved farther up and draped their soft bodies across his knees. Then late arrivals slammed their car doors and ran up the wooden steps, exchanging shouts:

"Bring my zipper bag up with you!"

"Which one?"

"The blue one!"

"Do you have the key?"

"Yes, but I can't find 203."

"Who's going to take Pierre for a walk?"

After that they all took showers, and the cascading water in the rooms above drowned out the television in the rooms on either side. Qwilleran heaved the cats off his knees, and they crawled farther up without opening their eyes.

So it continued until four o'clock in the morning, at which time he managed an hour's sleep before the early risers started taking showers, slamming car doors, and revving motors. He could have been excused for greeting the new day with a colossal grouch, but he exhibited a purposeful and admirable calm. All of Moose County had advised against this trip, and he was determined to prove them wrong from start to finish. He was, he told himself repeatedly, having a good time.

On the second day of driving, the panorama of woods and open fields and farmyards gave way to a scattering of billboards, gas stations, auto graveyards, and party stores, followed by strip malls and housing developments with fine-sounding names, and finally the freeway. Heavy traffic and increased speed began to put the back-seat passengers on their guard, their noses lifting to register the density of emissions, while Yum

Yum complained bitterly. For Qwilleran the sight of sweeping interchanges and incoming jets and the jagged skyline produced an urban high that he had relished in the past and had almost forgotten. Even the Purple Plum looked less offensive in the smoggy atmosphere.

He left the freeway at the Zwinger exit. On this late Sunday afternoon, downtown was virtually deserted. Zwinger Street, formerly a blighted area, was now Zwinger Boulevard—a continuous landscaped park dotted with glass towers, parking structures, and apartment complexes. Then the boulevard narrowed into the nineteenth-century neighborhood known as Junktown, with the Casablanca standing like a sentinel at the approach.

"Oh, no!" Qwilleran said aloud. "It looks like a refrigerator!" The Casablanca was indeed white, although in need of cleaning, and it had the proportions of a refrigerator, with a dark line across the facade at the ninth floor, as if delineating the freezer compartment. Modified Moorish, the SOCK brochure had called it. True, there were some arches and a marquee and two large ornamental lanterns of Spanish persuasion, but on the whole it looked like a refrigerator. Not so in 1901 perhaps, when iceboxes were made of golden oak, but now . . .

Qwilleran made a U-turn and pulled up to the curb, where the city permitted twenty-minute parking. He unloaded the cat carrier and the turkey roaster and then, taking care to lock all four doors, approached the shabby entrance. Broken glass in the two lanterns exposed the light bulbs, and the glass sidelights of the door were walled up with plywood that no one had bothered to paint. Carefully he picked his way up the cracked marble steps and set down the carrier, opening the heavy black door and holding it with his foot while he maneuvered into the dark vestibule.

"Help ya?" called a voice from the gloom. A jogger was about to leave the building.

"How do I ring the manager?" Qwilleran inquired.

"Right over here." A young man with a reddish moustache almost as imposing as Qwilleran's pressed a button on the apartment directory panel. "You moving in?"

"Yes. Where do you jog around here?"

"Around the vacant lots behind the building. Two times around is a mile—and not too much carbon monoxide."

"Is it safe?"

The man held up a small tube and pointed it at Qwilleran. "Zap!" he said, looking wise. "Hey, nice cats!" he added, squinting at the carrier. When a voice finally squawked on the intercom the obliging jogger yelled, "New tenant, Mrs. Tuttle." A buzzer released the door, and he sprang to open it. "Manager's desk straight down the hall, opposite the second elevator."

"Thanks. Good running!" Qwilleran wished him. The inner door slammed behind him, and he found himself in an empty lobby.

It was narrower than he had expected—a tunnel-like hall with a low ceiling and a lingering odor of disinfectant. Fluorescent tubes were spaced too far apart to provide effective light. The floor was well-worn vinyl, but clean, and the walls were covered with something that looked like sandpaper. When he reached the first elevator, however, he stopped and stared; the elevator door was burnished bronze sculptured in low relief, representing scenes from *Don Quixote* and *Carmen*.

As he studied the unexpected artistry, the door slid open, and a man in black tie and dinner jacket stepped out, saying coolly, ''This is a private elevator,'' at the same time flinging a contemptuous glance at the turkey roaster.

With the top handle of the carrier in one hand and the roaster under the other arm, Qwilleran walked slowly toward the rear of the building, observing and sniffing. Someone on the main floor was cooking, and he knew Portuguese garlic soup when he smelled it. Lined up in the tunnel were a cigarette machine, a soft-drink dispenser, and an old wooden telephone booth. Some attempt had been made to brighten the hall by painting apartment doors in jellybean colors, but the paint was scratched and dreary with age.

As he reached the phone booth, a body tumbled out onto the floor. It was a woman of indefinite age, wearing a red cocktail dress, and she was clutching a pint rum bottle, uncapped. ''Oops!'' she said.

Gallantly, Qwilleran set down his baggage and went to her assistance. ''Hurt yourself?''

She slurred an apology as he helped her up,

propped her on the seat of the phone booth, and closed her safely inside, leaving only a puddle on the floor.

He picked up the cat carrier and commode and walked on. As he approached the manager's desk, there was sudden activity within the carrier, which started jiggling and swinging, the reason being that two felines—a calico and a tiger with a chewed ear—had wandered out from nowhere and were eyeing the new arrivals. Although the host cats were not hostile, Qwilleran thought it advisable to place the carrier on the scarred counter where a homemade sign announced: "Mrs. Tuttle, manager. Ring for service." Separating the manager's desk from the tenants' counter was a window of thick, bulletproof acrylic.

He rang the bell, and a large, powerful-looking woman with a broad smile on her ebony face bounded out from the inner office. "Oh, you've got two Siamese!" she exclaimed joyously. Despite her genial greeting, she studied Qwilleran with a stern and forbidding eye, and he imagined that she tolerated no nonsense from the tenants or the resident cats.

"Good afternoon," he said. "Are you Mrs. Tuttle? My name is Qwilleran. The penthouse apartment has been reserved for me."

"Yes, SIR!" she said. "We're expecting you! Glad to have you here. Did you have a good trip?"

"Fine, thank you. Do you also have a parking space for me?"

"Yes, SIR!" She produced a ledger and flipped the looseleaf pages to Q. "First we need one month security deposit and one month rent, and the parking is payable by the quarter . . . What are they called?"

"Uh . . . what?" Qwilleran was concentrating on his checkbook. He considered the rent high, even though utilities were included.

"Do your kitties have names?"

"Uh . . . the larger one is Koko, and the . . . uh . . . female is Yum Yum." He had put the turkey roaster on the floor, and it was being sniffed by the calico and the tiger. "I see you have a welcoming committee down on the floor."

"That's Napoleon and Kitty-Baby," she said. "They live on the main floor. Your kitties will be the only ones on Fourteen."

"Fourteen? I thought the building had thirteen stories."

"They skipped Thirteen. Bad luck, you know. On the top floor there are two apartments, 14-A and 14-B. Yours is the nice one, all furnished. You'll be very comfortable. Here is your receipt and your key to 14-A. And here's your mailbox key; the boxes are through the arch. Mail is delivered around three or four o'clock. Your parking slot is #28 on the west side of the lot. The elevator's right behind you. Ring for the one with the red door. Old Red, we call it. A nice old elevator. Old Green is out of order."

"What's the one with the bronze door, near the entrance?" he asked.

"A private elevator for the owner of the building. Bye-bye, kitties! Glad to have you here, Mr. Qwilleran."

The Siamese had not uttered a sound. He picked up the roaster and the carrier and moved to the elevator bank, accompanied by Napoleon and Kitty-Baby. Two doors, one painted red and one painted green, were closed, displaying an abstract design of scratches and gouges made by impatient tenants carrying doorkeys. He pressed the button, and noises in the shaft indicated that Old Red was descending . . . slowly . . . very slowly. When the car finally arrived, it could be heard bouncing and leveling. Then the door opened with a convulsive jerk, and a tiny Asian woman with two small, doll-like children stepped out and scurried away as if glad to escape safely.

Qwilleran boarded, signaled for the fourteenth floor, and waited for the door to close, while Napoleon and Kitty-Baby stayed in the lobby staring into the car as if they would not be caught dead in Old Red. The Siamese were still ominously silent.

There was a bulletin board on the rear wall of the elevator, where manager and tenants had posted notices, and Qwilleran amused himself while waiting for the door to close by reading the messages. Two signs were neatly lettered with a felt marker and signed "Mrs. T."

IF DOOR IS OPEN, DO NOT JUMP!
ATTENTION ALL CATS! MONDAY IS SPRAY DAY!

There was also a handwritten message on a note card with an embossed W, offering a baby grand piano for sale in apartment 10-F. Scribbled on a scrap of brown paper was an ad for a tennis racquet for twenty-five dollars, spelled T-E-N-I-S R-A-C-K-E-T. Qwilleran was a born proofreader.

Mystified by the first two notices and questioning the market for baby grands in such a building, he failed to notice that the elevator door was still standing open. It was hardly the latest model in automatic equipment, and he looked for a suitable button to press. There was one labeled OPEN and a red button labeled HELP; that was all. The red button, he observed, showed signs of wear. Out in the lobby all was quiet. Mrs. Tuttle had left her post behind the bulletproof window, and the only signs of life were Napoleon and Kitty-Baby.

In Qwilleran's lean and hungry days, when he lived for a brief time at the decrepit Medford Manor, there was a stubborn elevator door that responded to a vigorous kick. He tried it, but Old Red only shuddered. Then he heard running footsteps approaching from the front door and a voice calling "Hold it!" A short man in a yellow satin jacket, with the name "Valdez" on the back, slid into view like a base runner approaching first.

"No hurry," Qwilleran told him. "The door won't close."

The fellow gave him a scornful glance and jumped up and down on the elevator floor. The door immediately closed, and the car proceeded slowly upward, clanking and shuddering as it passed each floor. Valdez got off at Five, and as he left the car he turned and said, "You jump."

Qwilleran jumped, the door closed, and Old Red ascended at the same snail-like pace, with groaning and scraping added to the clanking and shuddering. The Siamese had been patient, but suddenly Yum Yum emitted her ear-splitting screech, and immediately the car stopped dead. According to the floor indicator over the door they were not yet at Fourteen. According to the floor indicator they were not anywhere.

"*Now* what have you done?" Qwilleran scolded.

He pressed the button for his floor, but the car did not budge. He jumped, Valdez-style, and nothing happened. He pressed the button labeled OPEN, and the door slowly obliged, revealing the black brick wall of the elevator shaft.

"Ye gods!" Qwilleran shouted. "We're trapped between floors!"

THREE

THE SIAMESE, who had been more or less uncommunicative for four hundred miles, became vociferous when told they were trapped between floors in the Casablanca elevator shaft. Qwilleran pressed the HELP button and could hear a bell like a fire alarm ringing in some remote precinct of the old building, but the longer he leaned on the red button and the longer the bell pealed, the louder Koko howled and Yum Yum yodeled.

"Quiet!" Qwilleran commanded, and gave the

bell another prolonged ring, but in Siamese cat language "quiet" means "louder."

"Shhhh!" he scolded.

Somewhere an elevator door was being forced open; somewhere a distant voice was shouting.

Qwilleran shouted back, "We're stuck between floors!"

"Where y'at?" came the faint query.

"YOW!" Koko replied.

"Quiet, you dumbbell! I can't hear what he's saying . . . *We're stuck between floors!*"

"What floor?" The voice sounded hollow, suggesting that hands were being cupped for a megaphone effect.

"YOW!"

"I can't hear you!" Qwilleran shouted.

"What floor?" The voice was coming from overhead.

"YOW!"

"Shut up!"

"What you say down there?"

"We're between floors! I don't know where!" Qwilleran bellowed at his loudest.

There was the sound of a heavy door closing, followed by a long period of silence and inactivity.

"You really blew it!" Qwilleran told Koko. "They were coming to our rescue, and you wouldn't keep your mouth shut. Now we may be here all night." He looked around the dismal cell with its soiled walls and torn floor tiles. One of the fluorescent tubes had burned out leaving half the car in shadow. "At least you've got your commode,'' he said to his disgruntled companions, ''which is more than I can say.'' He rang the emergency bell again.

There was another wrenching sound in the shaft above, and a voice overhead—somewhat closer this time—yelled, ''You gotta climb out!''

''YOW!'' Koko replied.

''How?'' Qwilleran shouted.

''What?''

''YOW!''

Qwilleran gave the cat carrier a remonstrative shove with his foot, which only accelerated the howls. ''How do I climb out?''

''Push up the roof!''

In the tan ceiling of the car there was a metal plate, black with fingerprints.

''Push it all the way!'' came the instructions from on high.

Qwilleran reached up, gave the metal plate a forceful push, and it flopped open with a clatter. Through the rectangular opening he could see a bare light bulb, dazzlingly bright in the black shaft, and a ladder slowly descending. He wondered if he could squeeze through the hole in the roof; he wondered if the carrier would go through.

''I've got luggage down here!'' he yelled.

There was another long wait, and then a rope came dangling through the trapdoor.

''Tie it on the handle!'' called the rescuer.

Qwilleran quickly knotted one end to the top handle of the cat carrier and watched it rise off the floor and ascend in jerks that annoyed the occupants. It disappeared into the hole above.

"Anythin' else?"

Qwilleran looked speculatively at the turkey roaster. Its handles had long ago been sawed off to fit on the floor of the car. Furthermore, it contained slightly used kitty gravel.

"Nothing else!" he shouted, kicking the pan into a dark corner of the elevator. Then he started up the ladder. Above him he could see a pale face and a red golf hat clapped on a head of sandy hair.

The custodian was waiting for him at the top. "Sorry 'bout this."

On hands and knees Qwilleran crawled out of the black hole onto the mosaic tile floor of a hallway, a performance that interested the waiting cats enormously; they were always entranced by unusual behavior on his part.

"Where are we?" he asked.

"On Nine. Gotta walk up. We got both cars broke now—Old Red and Old Green. Serviceman don't come till tomorrow. Costs double on Sundays."

Their rescuer was a thin, wiry man of middle age, all elbows and knees and bony shoulders, wearing khaki pants and a bush jacket, its large pockets bulging with a flashlight and other tools of his trade. Judging by his prison pallor, it was doubtful that he had ever bushwhacked beyond the weedy landscaping of the Casablanca. The man picked up the cat carrier and headed for the stairwell.

"Here, let me take that," Qwilleran offered. "It's heavy."

"I seen heavier. Lady on Seven, she's got two cats, must weigh twenty pounds apiece. You in 14-A?"

"Yes. My name's Qwilleran. What's your name?"

"Rupert."

"I appreciate your coming to our rescue."

After that brief exchange, the two men plodded silently up the four long flights to the fourteenth floor, which was really the thirteenth. At the top of the stairs they emerged into a small lobby with a marble floor and marble walls, a relic of the rooftop restaurant in the Casablanca's illustrious past. There were two elevator doors, closed and silent, and two apartment doors with painted numbers.

Qwilleran glanced at his key and opened 14-A. "I guess this is it."

"Yep, this is it," said Rupert. "Doorbell's broke." He touched the pearl button to prove it. "All the doorbells are broke."

They walked into a spacious foyer handsomely furnished in the contemporary style, with doorways and arches leading to other equally lavish areas. This was more than Qwilleran had expected. It explained why the rent was high. A bank of French doors overlooked a large room with a lofty ceiling and a conversation pit six feet deep. "Is that the sunken living room?" he asked. "It looks like a carpeted swimming pool."

"That's what it was—a swimmin' pool," said the custodian. "Not very deep. Didn't do much divin' in them days, I reckon."

An exceptionally long sofa doglegged around one end of the depression, and around the ceramic-tiled rim of the former pool there were indoor trees in tubs, some reaching almost to the skylight twenty feet overhead.

Qwilleran noticed a few plastic pails scattered about the room, and there were waterstains on the carpet. "Does the skylight leak?" he asked.

"When it rains," Rupert said with a worried nod. "Where'd you park?"

"At the front door in a twenty-minute zone. I may have a ticket by now."

"Nobody bothers you on Sunday. Gimme your keys and I'll haul up the rest of your gear."

"I'll go with you," Qwilleran said, remembering the advice showered on him in Pickax. "I suppose we have to walk down thirteen flights and up again."

"If we can find the freight, we'll ride up."

"Then let's go."

The custodian looked at the cat carrier standing in the middle of the foyer. "Ain'tcha gonna let 'em out?"

"They can wait till we get back." Qwilleran always checked the premises for hazards and hidden exits before releasing the Siamese.

The two men began the tedious descent to the main floor, down marble stairs with ornamental iron banisters, each flight enclosed in a grim stairwell. "Good-looking staircases," Qwilleran commented. "Too bad they're enclosed."

"Fire department made 'em do it."

"What's that trapdoor?" In the wall of each

stairwell, toward the top of the flight, there was a small square door labeled DANGER—KEEP OUT.

"That's to the crawl space. Water pipes, heat, electric, and all stuff like that," Rupert informed him.

Halfway down they met the tiny Asian woman shepherding her two small children from one floor to another. She seemed unaware of their presence.

"Are there many children in the building?" Qwilleran asked.

"Mostly kids of the doctors that work at the hospital. From all different countries."

At last they reached the main floor, and as they walked past the manager's desk, Mrs. Tuttle, who was knitting something behind the bulletproof window, sang out cheerfully, "Why didn't you two ride the elevator?" She motioned toward Old Red, which was standing there with its door hospitably open. Qwilleran squinted into the dim back corner of the car and quickly retrieved the turkey roaster, carrying it away triumphantly.

Farther down the hall Valdez, still in his yellow satin jacket, was beating his fists against the soft-drink dispenser, and Napoleon was sniffing a puddle near the phone booth, critically. There was no activity around the elaborate bronze door of the private elevator.

"Quiet on Sundays," Rupert commented.

In front of the building the Purple Plum was still parked at the curb, neither stolen nor ticketed, and Qwilleran drove into the parking lot while Rupert went to the basement for a luggage cart. The lot was an obstacle course dotted with potholes, and his #28 parking slot was occupied by a small green Japanese car.

"Park in #29," Rupert told him. "Nobody cares."

"This lot is in terrible condition," Qwilleran complained. "When was it last paved? In 1901?"

"No use fixin' it. They could tear the place down next week."

Rupert wheeled the suitcases, typewriter, dictionary, books, and coffeemaker into the basement, Qwilleran following with the turkey roaster and the cats' water dish. They rode up in the freight elevator, a rough enclosure of splintery boards, but it worked!

"How come this one works?" Qwilleran asked.

"It's never broke," the custodian said. "Tenants don't get to use it, that's why. They're the ones wreck the elevators. Wait'll you see how they wreck the washers and dryers! There's a coin laundry in the basement."

"What do we do about rubbish?"

"Put it out in the hall at night. Boy picks up startin' at six in the mornin'. Any problem, just ring the desk. Housephone's on the kitchen wall in 14-A."

Qwilleran tipped him liberally. Although frugal by nature, he had developed a generous streak since inheriting money. Now he bolted the door, cat-proofed the rooms, and released the Siamese. "We're here!" he said. They emerged cautiously, swiveling their fine brown heads, pointing their ears, curving their whiskers, and sensing the long broad foyer. Koko walked resolutely to the far wall where French doors led to the terrace; he checked for pigeons and seemed disappointed that none appeared. Meanwhile Yum Yum was putting forth an experimental paw to touch the art rugs scattered about the parquet floor.

Art was everywhere: paintings on the walls, sculpture on pedestals, crystal and ceramic objects in lighted niches. The canvases were not to Qwilleran's liking: splotches of color and geometric studies that seemed meaningless to him; a still life of an auto mechanic's workbench; a bloody scene depicting a butcher block with work in progress; a realistic portrayal of people eating spaghetti.

Then he noticed an envelope with his name, propped against a bowl of fruit on a console table. Nestled among the winesap apples, tangerines, and Bosc pears, like a Cracker Jack prize, was a can of lobster. "You guys are in luck," he said to the Siamese. "But after your shenanigans in the elevator, I don't know whether you deserve it."

The accompanying note was from Amberina: "Welcome to the Casablanca! Mary wants me to take you to dinner at Roberto's tonight. Call my apartment when you get in. SOCK had your phone connected."

Qwilleran lost no time in phoning. "I accept with pleasure. I have a lot of questions to ask. Where's Roberto's?"

"In Junktown, a couple of blocks away. We can walk."

"Is that advisable after dark?"

"I never walk alone, but . . . sure, it'll be okay. Could you meet me inside the front door at seven o'clock? I won't ask you to come to my apartment. It's a mess."

He opened the can of lobster for the Siamese, arranging it on a Royal Copenhagen plate. All the appointments in the apartment were top-notch: Waterford crystal, Swedish sterling, German stainless, and so on. After unpacking his suitcases he wandered about the rooms, eating an apple and marveling at the expensive art books on the library table, the waterbed in the master bedroom, the gold faucets in the bathroom. He looked askance at the painting of the bloody butcher block; it was not something he would care to see early in the morning on an empty stomach, yet it occupied a prominent spot on the end wall of the foyer.

When the Siamese had finished their meal and groomed their paws, whiskers, ears, and tails, he introduced them to the sunken living room. In no time at all they discovered they could race around the rim of the former pool, chase each other up and down the carpeted stairs leading to the conversation pit, climb the trees, and scamper the length of the sofa-back. For his own satisfaction he paced off the length of the dogleg sofa and found it to be an incredible twenty feet. Though few in number, the furnishings were large-scale: an enormous onyx cocktail table stacked with art magazines; an eight-foot bar; an impressive stereo system with satellite speakers the size of coffins.

45

The most dramatic feature was the gallery of paintings that covered the upper walls. They were large still lifes, all studies of mushrooms—whole or halved or sliced, tumbled about in various poses. The jarring effect, to Qwilleran's eye, was not the size of the mushrooms—some two feet in diameter—but the fact that each arrangement was pictured with a pointed knife that looked murderously sharp. He had to admit that the knife lifted the still lifes out of the ordinary. Somehow it suggested a human presence. But he could not imagine why the owner of the apartment had hung so many mushrooms, unless . . . he had painted them himself. Who was this talented tenant? The signature on the work was a cryptic logo: two Rs back-to-back. Why did he specialize in mushrooms? Why did he leave? Where had he gone? When would he return? And why was he willing to sublet this lavishly furnished apartment to a stranger?

There were no windows in the room—only the skylight, and it admitted a sick light on this late afternoon in November. Apart from the potted trees and the green and yellow plastic pails strategically placed in case of rain, the interior was monochromatically neutral. Walls, upholstered sofa, and commercial-weave carpet were all in a pale gray-beige like the mushrooms.

He checked his watch. It was time to dress for dinner. At that moment he heard a door slam in the elevator lobby; the occupant of 14-B was either coming in or going out. He soon discovered which.

When 14-A had been carved out of the former restaurant, space was no object, and the master bathroom was large enough to accommodate a whirlpool bath for two, a tanning couch, and an exercise bike. The stall shower was large enough for three. At the turn of a knob, water pelted Qwilleran's body from three sides, gentle as rain or sharp as needles. He was luxuriating in this experience when the water abruptly turned ice cold. He yelped and bounded from the enclosure. Dripping and cursing and half-draped in a towel, he found the house telephone in the kitchen. Mrs. Tuttle's businesslike voice answered.

"This is Qwilleran in 14-A," he said in a politely shocked tone. "I was taking a shower and the water suddenly ran cold, ice cold!"

"That happens," she said. "It's an old building, you know. Evidently your neighbor started to take a shower at the same time."

"You mean I have to coordinate my bathing schedule with 14-B?"

"I don't think you need to worry about it too much," she said soothingly.

That's right, he thought. The building may be torn down next week. "Who is the tenant in 14-B?"

Mrs. Tuttle said something that sounded like Keestra Hedrog, and when he asked her to repeat the name, it still sounded like Keestra Hedrog. He huffed into his moustache and hung up.

After toweling and donning his old plaid bathrobe in the Mackintosh tartan (his mother had been a Mackintosh), he was in the process of eating another apple when he heard incredible sounds from the adjoining apartment—like a hundred-piece orchestra tuning up discordantly for Tchaikovsky's *1812 Overture*. The cats' ears swiveled nervously, the left and right ears twisting in opposite directions. He realized that they were hearing a composition for the synthesizer, a kind of music he had not yet learned to appreciate. He also realized that the walls between 14-A and 14-B were regrettably thin—one of the Casablanca's Depression economies. By the time he had finished dressing, however, the recording ended, a door slammed again, and his neighbor apparently went out for the evening.

He checked out the cats as he always did before leaving and found Yum Yum in the bedroom, sniffing the waterbed, but Koko was not in evidence. He called his name and received no response. For one sickening moment he wondered if the cat had discovered a secret exit. Hurrying from room to room he called and searched and worried. It was not until he went down into the conversation pit that he found the missing Koko.

The eight-foot bar in the pit was situated rather conspicuously in the middle of the floor, and Koko was sniffing this piece of furniture, oblivious of everything else. Qwilleran himself had not touched alcohol for several years, and when he served spirits to his guests, Koko showed no interest whatever unless he happened upon a stray anchovy olive. So why was he so intent upon investigating this leather-upholstered, teak-topped liquor dispensary? Koko always had a sound reason for his actions, although it was not always obvious.

Qwilleran opened the drawers and cabinets of the bar and found decanters, glassware, jiggers, corkscrews, muddlers, napkins, and so forth. That was all.

"Sorry, Koko," he said. "No anchovies. No mice. No dead bodies."

The cat ignored him. He was sniffing the base of the bar, running his twitching nose along the line where the furniture met the carpet, as if some small object had found its way underneath. Qwilleran touched his moustache questioningly, his curiosity aroused. It was a heavy bar, but by putting his shoulder against one end of it he could slide it across the tightly woven carpet. As it began to move, Koko became agitated, prancing back and forth in encouragement.

"If this turns out to be an anchovy-stuffed olive," Qwilleran said, "you're going to be in the doghouse!" He shoved again. The ponderous bar moved a few inches at a time.

Then Koko yowled. A thin dark line had appeared on the pale carpet. It widened as Qwilleran lunged with his shoulder—wider and wider until a large dark stain was revealed.

"Blood!" Qwilleran said.

"Yow!" said Koko. He arched his back, elongated his legs, hooked his tail, and pranced in a circle. Qwilleran had seen the dance before—Koko's death dance. Then from the cat's innards came a new sound: less than a growl yet deeper than a purr. It sounded like "Rrrrrrrrrr!"

FOUR

BEFORE LEAVING FOR dinner with Amberina, Qwilleran made a long-distance phone call. It was Sunday evening, and Polly Duncan would be at home waiting for news. He deemed it advisable to keep the report upbeat: Yes, he had enjoyed the trip . . . Yes, the cats behaved well . . . The manager and custodian were helpful. The apartment was spacious and well-furnished, with a magnificent view of the sunset. He mentioned nothing about the malfunctioning elevator nor the leaking skylight nor the bulletproof window at the manager's desk nor the bloodstain on the carpet, and he especially avoided reference to his dinner date with Amberina. Polly was a wonderful woman but inclined to be jealous.

Then he said goodbye to the Siamese, having placed their blue cushion on the bed in the small bedroom. "Be good kids," he said. "Have a nap and stay out of trouble. I'll be back in a couple of hours, perhaps with a doggie bag." He turned off all the lights except the one in the bathroom, where they had their commode, thinking that the darkness would encourage them to nap and stay out of mischief.

Leaving 14-A, he spotted a namecard tacked on the door of 14-B, and he sauntered close enough to read it. His neighbor's name was indeed Keestra Hedrog, as Mrs. Tuttle had said. It looked like something spelled backward and he considered tacking a namecard to his own door: Mij Narelliwq.

What, he asked himself, had happened to nomenclature in recent years? Strange new words had entered the language and strange new names were popping up in the telephone directory. Mary, Betty, and Ann had been replaced by Thedira and Cheryline. Even ordinary names had tricky spellings like Elizabette and Alyce, causing inconvenience to all concerned, not to mention the time lost in explaining and correcting. (His own name, spelled with the unconventional QW, had been the bane of editors, typesetters, and proofreaders for thirty years, but that fact escaped him.)

He signaled for the elevator and heard evidence of mechanical torment in the shaft—noises so threatening that he chose to walk downstairs. Feeling his way through the poorly lighted stairwells, he encountered bags of trash, unidentified odors and—between the seventh and sixth floors—a shrouded figure standing alone on the stairs and mumbling.

On the main floor he passed two elderly women in bathrobes, huddled in conference. One of them was saying in a croaking voice, "I've been mugged five times. How many times have you been mugged?"

"Only twice," said the other, shrilly, "but the second time they knocked me down."

Both of them squinted suspiciously at Qwilleran as he passed.

He found Rupert hanging around the manager's desk, still with the red golf hat on the back of his head, while three boisterous students practiced karate chops in front of the elevators.

"Knock it off," Rupert warned them, "or I'll tell Mrs. T."

The youths clicked their heels, clasped their hands prayerfully, and bowed low, then made a dash for Old Red when it arrived.

"Crazy college kids," Rupert explained to Qwilleran. "Everything okay on Fourteen?"

"So far, so good." He started for the front door but returned. "There's something I wanted to ask about, Rupert. In my living room there's a huge piece of furniture—a serving bar—right in the middle of the floor. Do you happen to know why?"

"Mrs. T said to put it there," said the custodian. "I didn't ask no questions. Me and the boy had to move the thing. It's mighty heavy."

"How long have you been working here, Rupert?"

"Twenty years next March. Good job! Meet lotsa people. And I get an apartment in the basement thrown in."

"What will you do if they tear down the building?"

"Go on unemployment. Go on welfare, I reckon, if I can't find work. I'm fifty-six."

Qwilleran had a long wait for Amberina, but the time was not wasted. While standing at the front door he watched a circus parade of tenants and visitors coming in and going out. He tried not to stare at the outlandish clothing on the young ones, or the pathetic condition of some of the old ones, or the exotic beauty wearing a sari, or the fellow with a macaw in a cage.

When two well-dressed young men arrived, carrying a small gold tote bag from the city's most exclusive chocolatier, he watched them go to the burnished bronze door and ring for the private elevator, and he began to conjecture about the "Countess." The mysterious seventy-five-year-old who was visited by men wearing dinner jackets or bearing gifts sounded like Lady Hester Stanhope in Kinglake's *Eothen*, a book he had been reading aloud to the Siamese. Lady Hester lived in a crumbling middle-eastern convent, subsisting on milk and enjoying the adulation of desert tribes. Was the Countess the Lady Hester of the crumbling Casablanca?

His flights of fancy were interrupted when Amberina came running down the hall. "Sorry I'm late. I lost my contact lens, and I couldn't seem to get myself together."

He said, "Who are the well-dressed men who ride up and down on the Countess's elevator?"

"Her bridge partners," she explained. "She loves to play cards."

Amberina had changed since their last meeting three years before. Her strikingly-brunette hair was a different color and a different style—lighter, redder, and frizzier. She had put on weight and her dimples were less beguiling. He was disappointed, but he said, "Good to see you again, Amberina. You're looking great!"

"So are you, Mr. Qwilleran, and you look so countrified!" He was wearing his tweed coat with leather patches and his chukka boots.

They left the building and zigzagged down the broken marble slabs with care. "These steps should be repaired before someone trips and sues the Countess," he remarked.

"No point in making repairs when the whole place may be torn down next week," she said with a touch of bitterness. "We're all keeping our fingers crossed that nothing terrible will happen. Mary says the city would love it if the elevator dropped and killed six tenants, or a steam boiler blew up and cooked everyone on the main floor. Then they'd condemn the place and start collecting higher property taxes on a billion-dollar hotel or something. I do hope your people decide to buy the Casablanca, Mr. Qwilleran.''

Now they were strolling down Junktown's new brick sidewalks, recently planted with small trees and lighted with old-fashioned gaslamps.

Qwilleran said, ''This is exactly what C. C. Cobb wanted three years ago, and the city fought him every step of the way.''

The jerry-built storefronts that previous landlords had tacked on to the front of historic townhouses had been removed. One could never guess where the old fruit and tobacco stand had been, or the wig and fortune-telling shop. New owners had miraculously restored the original stone steps, iron railings, and impressive entrance doors. A brightly lighted coffee house occupied the premises of the former furniture-refinishing shop in an old stable, now named the Carriage House Café.

''Tell me about this restaurant we're going to. What is Roberto's?'' Qwilleran asked.

''You know—don't you?—that Robert Maus wanted to open a restaurant when he gave up the law business. Well, he went to Italy and worked in a restaurant in Milan for a year. When he came home he was cooking Italian and had changed his name to Roberto.''

''I hope he didn't change his last name to 'Mausolini.' ''

Amberina let out an involuntary shriek. ''Wait till Mary hears that! She won't think it's funny. She's very serious, you know.''

''I know. So is he.''

"Well, anyway, he opened this Italian restaurant in one of the old townhouses—Mary talked him into it, I think—and he lives upstairs. I've never eaten there—too expensive—but Mary says it's fabulous food."

"Everything Robert prepares is fabulous. Will he be there tonight?"

"You're supposed to call him Roberto, Mr. Qwilleran. No, he's off on Sundays, and they're closed on Mondays, but he personally supervises the kitchen five nights a week. Imagine! A law degree! And he's cooking spaghetti!"

An unobtrusive sign on the iron railing of a townhouse announced "Roberto's North Italian Cuisine." As they climbed the stone steps Qwilleran knew what to expect. He had lived in Junktown long enough to be familiar with old townhouses. Even though they became rooming houses they had high ceilings, carved woodwork, ornate fireplaces (boarded up), and gaslight chandeliers (electrified)—all of these in various degrees of shabbiness. With Robert Maus's taste for English baronial he would add red velvet draperies and leather chairs studded with nailheads. *Ecco!* North Italian!

Qwilleran was shocked, therefore, when they entered the restaurant. The interior had been gutted. Walls, ceiling, and arches were an unbroken sweep of smooth plaster in a custardy shade of cream. The carpet was eggplant in hue; so was the upholstery of the steel-based chairs. Silk-shaded lamps on the tables and silk-shaded sconces on the walls threw a golden glow over the cream-tinted table linens.

Before he could splutter a comment, a white-haired woman armed with menus approached in a flurry of excitement. "Mr. Qwilleran! Do you remember me? I'm Charlotte Roop," she said in a reedy voice.

She had been his neighbor three years before on River Road—a strait-laced, spinsterish woman obsessed with crossword puzzles—but she had changed drastically. Where was her disapproving scowl? Her tightly pursed lips? Had she had a face-lift? Could she possibly have found love and happiness with a good man? Qwilleran chuckled at the idea. Instead of her usual nondescript garb smothered in costume jewelry, she was wearing a simple beige dress with a cameo at the throat— a cameo brought from Italy by her new boss, Qwilleran assumed.

"Of course I remember you!" he exclaimed. "You're looking . . . you're looking . . . What's a six-letter word for beautiful?"

"Oh, Mr. Qwilleran, you remembered!" she cried with pleasure, adding in a lower voice, "But I don't do crossword puzzles anymore. I have a gentleman friend." She flushed.

"Good for you! He's a lucky fellow!"

Miss Roop touched the cameo self-consciously. "I'm the one who's lucky. I have a lovely apartment at the Casablanca and a lovely job with our wonderful Roberto. Let me show you to our best table."

"This is a handsome place," Qwilleran said.

"Very warm, very friendly, yet surprisingly modern."

"Roberto wanted it to be the color of zabaglione. He brought Italian artisans over to do the plastering." She handed them menus and recommended the *tagliatelle con salmone affumicato* and the *vitello alla griglia*. Her boss, always a perfectionist, had coached her on the pronunciation. She added, "Roberto wishes you to be our guests tonight. Would you like something from the bar?"

Considering Miss Roop's former attitude toward anything stronger than weak tea, this was a right-about-face. She suggested Pinot Grigio as an apéritif. Amberina shrugged and accepted. Qwilleran asked for mineral water with lemon. Meanwhile, a waiter displaying professional éclat draped napkins across their laps—*heated* napkins.

"Real flowers," Amberina whispered as she fingered the rosebuds in a Venetian glass vase. "I wonder how many of these vases they lose."

There was little general conversation as they adjusted to the elegance of the room and the awesomeness of the menu. Finally she said, "Tell me honestly, Mr. Qwilleran. What do you think of the Casablanca?"

"It's a dump! Does anyone really think it's worth restoring? Does anyone think it's even *possible* to restore such a ruin?"

"SOCK is positive," she replied earnestly. "Mary Duckworth and Roberto are officers, and you know they don't waste their time on a lot of baloney. They've had an architect make a study for SOCK, and he knows exactly what has to be done and how to do it and how much it will cost. I don't have the exact facts, but Mary can fill you in on that stuff.''

''Where is she?''

''Right now she's flying back from Philadelphia. There was a big antique show there, and she took a double booth. Her porters drove a truckload down, and she expected it would return empty. Mary has that snooty manner, you know, and she can sell anything and get a good price for it. People *believe* her! I wish I had her class. But that's the way it goes! The rich get richer. Her family is in banking, you know.''

''Does she still wear kimonos embroidered with dragons when she waits on customers?''

''No, she's gone back to being preppy, pearls and everything . . . EEK! Did you see these prices?'' she squealed when she saw the right-hand side of the card. ''I'm glad I'm not paying for this! I'm going to order the most expensive thing on the menu. The chances are I'll never come here again.''

They each ordered an antipasto, soup, and a veal dish. Then Qwilleran said, ''I have a few questions to ask, Amberina. Is the elevator service always as bad as it was today?''

''I wish you'd call me Amber,'' she said.

''And you seem to have forgotten that you used to call me Qwill.''

''I didn't forget,'' she said sheepishly, ''but now that you've got all that money, I thought I should call you mister . . . What were we talking about?''

''The elevators.''

''Oh, yes . . . You just happened to hit a bad weekend. Usually they break down one at a time, and that's not so bad. Or if it happens during the week, we're in luck, because the serviceman comes right away—if it's during the day. It's time and a half after five o'clock, you know, and the management doesn't go for that.''

''I should have taken an apartment on a lower floor,'' Qwilleran said. ''Another question: What's the meaning of the notice in the elevator about cats and spraying? It doesn't sound good.''

''Oh, *that*! Mrs. Tuttle posts a notice every time the exterminator is scheduled. He sprays the hallways, plus any apartments that request it, so people keep their cats locked up on Spray Day.''

''My cats never go out under any circumstances.''

''That's a good idea. They can get on the elevator and just . . . disappear. There's a big turnover in cats at the Casablanca.''

''Do you have one?''

''No, I have fish. They're cheaper and they don't have to go to the vet. They just die.''

''Frankly, I fail to understand the roving-cat policy at the Casablanca.''

''It's for rodent control.''

''Does the building have rats in addition to everything else?''

''Only around the back street, where they keep the dumpsters. I've had mice in my apartment, though. I don't know how mice get up to the eighth floor.''

"On Old Red," Qwilleran suggested.

The antipasti were served: breaded baby squid with marinara sauce, and roasted red peppers with anchovies and onion.

"I wish my sisters could see me now!" said Amber. "Eating squid at Roberto's with a millionaire!"

"Getting back to the notices in the elevator," he said, "is there a large market for baby grand pianos at the Casablanca?"

"You'd be surprised! There's still some money floating around the building—and a few good-sized apartments. We have elderly widows who are *loaded*! They don't move out because they've always lived here."

"Who's selling the piano? The sign says apartment 10-F."

"That's Isabelle Wilburton. Her rooms are crammed with family heirlooms, and she sells them off one at a time to buy booze."

"What does she look like? I saw a middle-aged woman in a cocktail dress, tippling in the phone booth when I moved in."

"That's our Isabelle! Her family made a killing in the furniture business, and they pay her basic living expenses, so long as she stays out of their sight. I warn you! Don't let Isabelle latch onto you! She'll drive you crazy."

The antipasto plates were whisked away, and the proficient waiter—who was always there when needed and absent when not—served the soup, a rich chicken broth threaded with egg and cheese.

"What do they call this?" Amber asked Qwilleran. "I wish I had written it down so I can tell my sisters."

"*Stracciatella alla romana*. What will happen to tenants like Isabelle if the building is restored to its original grandeur?"

"What will happen to any of us?" said Amber with a shrug. "I'll have to find a rich husband and move to the country. Maybe he'll set me up in a shop of my own." She had a suggestive twinkle in her eyes, which he ignored.

He said, "You had a husband the last time I saw you."

She twisted her lips in an unattractive smirk. "Husbands come and go like the Zwinger Boulevard bus."

"You've changed your hair color, too."

"This is my natural color. I dyed it for him because he liked brunettes. I suppose you're having a tough time staying single now that you've got all that money."

"So far I've been successful without trying very hard," he said, and then added to keep the record straight, "but I have a good friend up north who shares my interests and tastes. I hope she'll come down for a visit while I'm here."

"That must be nice," said Amber. "We weren't so compatible. I don't know why we ever happened to get married. I'm a slob around the house, but my ex liked everything *just so*. A place for everything and everything in its place, you know. If he repeated that remark *once more*, I swore I'd shoot him, and I didn't want to go to prison, so I filed for divorce. I hope he marries a computer. Mary tells me you're divorced."

"Right." He popped a chunk of crusty roll into his mouth to preclude further elaboration.

Amber was not easily put off, however. "What happened?"

"Nothing worth mentioning." He gobbled another morsel. "What do you do at the auction house?"

"Just clerical work. It doesn't pay much, but I'm working with antiques, so I like it. You should come to one of our auctions. Last month a painting went for $2.3 million—right in your class, Qwill."

He huffed into his moustache and ignored the remark. "Here comes the veal."

She had ordered the top-price rib chop with wine and mushroom sauce, and now she asked for a bottle of Valpolicella, explaining, "What I don't drink, I can take home."

As Qwilleran knifed his medium-priced *vitello alla piccata*, sautéed with lemon and capers, he inquired about Mrs. Tuttle. "She seems to have a remarkable blend of motherly concern and military authority."

"Oh, she's wonderful! Can you believe that she was actually born in the Casablanca basement?" Amber replied. "Her father was the custodian. They lived in the basement, and she grew up playing in the boiler room and on the stairs. By the time she was twelve she knew the building inside out, and it was always her ambition to be manager. She's very obliging, as long as you

don't break the rules. Ask her for anything you
need. You may not get it, but she'll smile a lot.''

''I might need some more pails. The skylight
leaks. Also, the hot water in the shower is unpredictable.''

''We all have that problem,'' said Amber. ''You
get used to it.''

''Do you know the person in 14-B?''

''No, she's new, but I've seen her on the elevator—sort of wild-looking.'' Amber was gob-
bling her food hungrily.

''I hope she doesn't take too many showers,''
Qwilleran said. ''What can you tell me about the
Countess?''

''I've never met her. I've never even seen her!
I'm not in her class. Mary knows her. Mary gets
invited to the twelfth floor because her father is a
banker and she went to one of those eastern col-
leges.'' Amber was well into her bottle of Valpolicella and was losing what little reticence she had.
''When you lived here before, Qwill, we all
thought you had a thing for Mary and couldn't
get anywhere because you worked for a newspaper and she thought she was too good for you.''

''It's gratifying to know that all the gossips
aren't in Pickax City,'' he said. ''Shall we have
dessert? I recommend gelato and espresso.'' Then
he launched the subject that was uppermost in
his mind. ''Why is the penthouse apartment being sublet—with all those valuable furnishings?''

''The former tenant died, and the estate is going through the courts,'' Amber said. ''Mary had

to pull strings to get you in there. If it wasn't for all your money—"

"Who was the tenant?"

"An art dealer—part owner of a gallery in the financial district, Bessinger-Todd."

"Apparently he was very successful, although I don't concur with his choice of art."

"It was a woman, Qwill. Dianne Bessinger. We called her Lady Di."

"Why was she living in a broken-down place like the Casablanca?"

"I guess she thought the penthouse was glamorous. She was the one who founded SOCK."

"Did you ever see her apartment? It's filled with mushroom paintings."

"I know. She gave a party for SOCK volunteers once, and I asked her about the mushrooms. I don't pretend to know anything about art. She said mushrooms are sexy."

"What happened to her?"

"She . . . well, she died unexpectedly." For the first time that evening, Amber was speaking guardedly.

"At what age?"

"In her forties. Forty-five, I think it said in the paper."

"Was it drugs?"

"No." Amber was fidgeting nervously. "It's something we don't like to talk about. Ask Mary when you see her."

Ah! It was AIDS, Qwilleran thought, but immediately changed his mind. That would hardly explain the large bloodstain on the carpet, and people never died "unexpectedly" of AIDS. Or did they? "You say she was the founder of SOCK?" he said.

"Yes, she felt very strongly about the Casablanca," said Amber, relieved to veer away from the unmentionable subject. "Anybody who's ever lived here feels that way—kind of emotional about the old building."

"And what happened to your doorman? You said he was shot. What were the circumstances? Was he mixed up in something illegal?"

"No, nothing like that," she said, relaxing over her cup of espresso. "Doesn't this have a wonderful aroma?"

"So what happened to him? What's the story?"

"Well, he was a nice old joe who had lived in the basement forever. Then he went on social security, and we really didn't need a doorman any longer, but he liked to put on his old uniform once in a while and open car doors and collect a few tips. It was a long coachman's coat down to his ankles—made him feel important, I guess. But it had turned green with age, and the gold braid was tarnished, and some of the buttons were missing. Also he'd forget to shave. We called him Poor Old Gus. He was a sad sight, but he sort of fitted the Casablanca image, you know—a character! People used to drive past and laugh. He was written up in the *Daily Fluxion* once. Then one night some kids—high on something, I guess—drove by and shot Poor Old Gus dead!"

Qwilleran frowned and shook his head in abhorrence.

"Is everything all right?" asked an anxious voice at his elbow.

"The food and service were perfection, Miss Roop," he assured her. "Give my compliments to Roberto."

"Oh, thank you. That will make him very happy. Do you still have your kitties, Mr. Qwilleran?"

"I certainly do! And I brought them to the Casablanca with me."

"Would they like a treat from our kitchen?"

"I feel safe in saying that they would be overjoyed."

Qwilleran and Amber walked home under the gaslights—she carrying a half-empty bottle of wine and he carrying a foil package folded decorously into a cream-colored napkin. They walked along a street almost deserted except for a woman airing a pair of Dobermans and two men walking together with purposeful stride, swinging long-handled flashlights.

"That's our Junktown patrol," Amber said. "They're volunteers. You might like to take a turn some night, just to see what it's like."

"Be glad to," said Qwilleran, recognizing a subject for his newspaper column. "Are they ever called upon to handle any . . . incidents?"

"I don't think so. Mostly they discourage crime just by being there. They shine their flashlights, you know, and blow their whistles, and talk on their portable phones."

When they reached the Casablanca and entered through the heavy black doors, Qwilleran noticed the black paint-covered brass fittings that the management no longer cared to keep polished. Only the bronze door of the Countess's elevator retained its original burnished beauty.

Amber said, "I'd invite you in for a nightcap, but my apartment's a disaster area. I'm ashamed of it."

"Thanks anyway," he said. "I've had a long hard day on the road and in the elevator shaft, and I'm ready to turn in." He was glad of an excuse; he had had enough of Amber's company for one evening. He would have preferred the preppy Mary, or the mysterious Countess, or even the affable, dictatorial Mrs. Tuttle. He pictured her as a subject for his column.

Old Red was in operation, and it took them to the eighth floor, where he walked Amber to her door and said a courteous goodnight, thanking her for her company and the indoctrination.

"Sorry I couldn't give you much information," she said, "but Mary will call you tomorrow. We're awfully glad you're here, Qwill." She gave him a lingering look that he pretended not to notice.

He walked up the remaining flights, and when he arrived at Fourteen (which was really Thirteen), the door of Old Red was slowly closing. Someone was going down . . . or had just come up. Unlocking his door and reaching for the light switch, Qwilleran discovered that the foyer and other rooms were already lighted, although he distinctly remembered leaving the apartment in darkness, except for the bathroom.

"Who's here?" he demanded.

Koko and Yum Yum came running. They showed no symptoms of terror, no indication that an intruder had threatened them. They were simply aware that Qwilleran was carrying a packet of veal, scallops, and squid. Yum Yum rubbed against his ankles voluptuously, while Koko stood on his hind legs and pawed the air.

Ignoring them, he moved from room to room, warily. In the library both the desk lamp and a floor lamp were unaccountably lit—as were a pair of accent lamps on the foyer console, the buffet lamp in the dining room, and the bedlamps in both sleeping rooms. The French doors to the living room were closed, as he had left them, and the area was in darkness, likewise the kitchen. He examined closets, then went out on the terrace and explored its entire length, passing the French doors of 14-B. His neighbor's blinds were closed, but light glowed through dimly. The huddled mass in a dark corner of the terrace turned out to be a cluster of large empty plant pots.

Qwilleran stroked his moustache in puzzlement and returned to 14-A. Who could have entered—and why? Did someone know he was being taken to dinner by SOCK? Did they have a key to his apartment? But why would they leave all the lights blazing? . . . unless they were interrupted and made a quick getaway.

At that moment he heard the door of 14-B open and close. He rushed out to the elevator lobby, but there was no one there—merely the evidence that Keestra Hedrog had put her rubbish container outside the door.

Mystified, Qwilleran returned to the kitchen to give the Siamese a taste of squid; the chef had wrapped enough food for three days. But he was too late. The cream-colored napkin lay on the floor, and the foil wrapper was open and licked clean, while two satisfied gourmands sat nearby, washing up, with not the slightest indication that they felt any guilt. On the contrary, they seemed proud of themselves.

FIVE

"YOU GUYS HAD a picnic last night!" Qwilleran said grudgingly on Monday morning as he opened a can of boned chicken for the Siamese. "After stuffing yourselves with all that food, you don't deserve breakfast!"

Yet, Koko was prowling as if he had fasted for a week, and Yum Yum was clawing Qwilleran's pantleg.

"What I want to know is this: Which one of you two turned on all the lights?"

While he was dining at Roberto's with Amber,

Koko or Yum Yum or both of them had discovered that most of the lamps in 14-A had touch-switches, and the scamps had run from one to the other making them light up. No doubt they expected to make this a nightly romp, but Qwilleran foiled them. Before retiring he cat-proofed all the lamps by turning off thumb-switches or disconnecting plugs, at the same time making the observation that touch-switches were not practical in households dominated by felines.

After that he had some difficulty in falling asleep. He was not accustomed to a waterbed, and he lay there expecting to drown . . . listening to the periodic clanking of the radiators as the boilers sent up another burst of steam . . . hearing the drone of traffic on the nearby freeway . . . counting the number of police and ambulance sirens . . . wondering why the helicopter was hovering overhead . . . recognizing an occasional gunshot. He had lived too long in the country.

Eventually he fell asleep and slept until the yowling outside his bedroom door told him to shuffle out into the kitchen and open that can of boned chicken. While searching for the can opener, he discovered a Japanese slicer with a tapered blade and light wood handle, similar to those in the mushroom paintings. He carried it into the gallery—as he preferred to call the sunken living room—to compare, and he was right. Koko followed him and sniffed the bloodstain, opening his mouth and showing his teeth.

"Get away from that!" Qwilleran ordered, and put his shoulder to the bar once more to cover the stain. Then he changed his mind. It was an awkward location for a bar. He nudged it back again into a more suitable position and covered the stain with a rug from the library—an Indian dhurrie in pale colors that blended with the mushroom carpet. Shooing the cat from the gallery, he closed the French doors.

Yum Yum was now batting some small object about the floor of the foyer. Koko might have a notably investigative nose, but Yum Yum had a notably meddlesome paw. Rings, watches, and coins—as well as bottle caps and paper clips—were within her realm of interest, and any sudden activity that gave her pleasure was suspect. This time it was an ivory-colored tile less than an inch square—not exactly square but slightly rectangular, and not ivory or ceramic but a lightweight wood in a smooth, pale finish. Qwilleran confiscated it, to Yum Yum's disappointment, and dropped it in his sweater pocket.

While waiting for the computerized coffeemaker to perform its morning magic, he ate a tangerine and speculated that the bowl of fruit had been Mary Duckworth's idea; she remembered that winesaps were his favorite apple and that lobster sent the Siamese into orbit. Did she have romantic memories of their previous association? Or was this thoughtful gesture a political move on behalf of SOCK? He could never be sure about that woman. Circumstances had thrown them together in Junktown three years before, and she was haughty and aloof at first, but she had relaxed briefly on one unforgettable Christmas Eve.

After that they went their separate ways. At what point they would resume their acquaintance remained to be seen. Three years ago he had been a stranger in town, down on his luck and trying to make a comeback. Now he was in a position to buy the entire inventory of her antique shop, as well as the Casablanca and most of Zwinger Boulevard.

When she phoned him that morning, however, there was no hint that she entertained sentimental memories. She greeted him in the crisp, impersonal way that was her normal manner of speech.

"Good to hear your voice, Mary," he said. "How was your Philadelphia trip?"

"Immensely successful. And your journey down here, Qwill?"

"Not bad. It's hard to get used to the smog, though. I'm used to breathing something called fresh air."

"In Junktown," she said loftily, "we don't call it smog. We call it opalescence. Are you comfortably settled in your apartment?"

"Settled but not necessarily comfortable. More about that later. But the cats and I appreciate your welcoming gift, and I don't need to tell you that dinner at Roberto's was superb."

"Yes, Roberto is a perfectionist. He uses only the best ingredients and takes infinite pains with the preparation. He actually imports water from Lake Como, you know, for baking the rolls."

"I noticed the distinction," Qwilleran said, "but I traced it to one of the Swiss lakes. That

74

shows how wrong one's palate can be." He said it facetiously, knowing that the literal antique dealer would take him seriously, and she did.

She said, "You're wonderfully knowledgeable about food, Qwill."

"When can you and I get together, Mary. I have a lot of questions to ask."

"The sooner the better. Could you come to my shop this afternoon around four o'clock? We can have a private talk. The shop is closed on Mondays, so we won't be interrupted."

Qwilleran agreed. That would give him time to buy supplies for the cats, reorient himself in the city, and have lunch at the Press Club. But before leaving the apartment, he brushed the silky fawn-colored coats of the Siamese, all the while plying them with compliments on their elegantly long brown legs, their gracefully slender brown tails, their incredibly beautiful blue eyes, and their impressively alert white whiskers. They listened with rapture displayed by their waving tails.

Then he tuned in the radio to check the weather prediction. In doing so he learned that four houses on a southside block had been torched by arsonists over the weekend; a co-ed had been strangled backstage at the university auditorium; and a man had killed his wife and three children. The weather would be clear but chilly.

"They call this clear?" Qwilleran said scornfully as he peered out the window at the smog-filtered sunlight.

He walked to the Carriage House Café for ham and eggs, wearing a Nordic sweater and field jacket and his Aussie hat. Its brim had a dip in the front that complemented his large drooping moustache and made women turn to look at him.

At the restaurant he found not a single familiar face. The patrons—gulping breakfast or reading the *Morning Rampage* with their coffee—were all strangers, and they were better-dressed than the former denizens of Junktown. Much had changed in three years, but that was typical of inner cities. In Moose County nothing ever changed unless it blew away in a high wind. The same families went on for generations; the same storekeepers managed the same stores; and everyone knew everyone else. Not only that, but the eggs tasted better up north, and when Qwilleran paid his check at the Carriage House he noted that ham and eggs cost two dollars less in Pickax.

On one of the side streets he found a grocery store where he could buy a ten-pound bag of sterilized gravel for the cats' commode, gourmet canned goods for their meals, and white grapejuice for Koko—further evidence that Junktown had upscaled.

He was becoming accustomed to surprises, but when he walked back to the Casablanca he was shocked to see a painted sign on the vacant property across the street where a row of old buildings had been demolished. The sign featured an artist's rendering of a proposed building spanning Zwinger Boulevard—actually two towers connected by a bridge across the top, somewhat like the Bridge of Sighs in Venice.

"Site of the new Gateway Alcazar," the sign

proclaimed. "Offices, stores, and hotel. Space now leasing."

One of the two towers obviously occupied the Casablanca site, and Qwilleran considered it an example of gross nerve! He made a note of the firm promoting the project: Penniman, Greystone & Fleudd. He knew of the wealthy Pennimans and the civic-minded Greystones, but Fleudd was a new name to him. He could not even pronounce it.

At the Casablanca a stretcher was being loaded into an ambulance, and Qwilleran inquired about it at the manager's desk.

"An old gentleman on Four had a heart attack," said Mrs. Tuttle as if it were a routine occurrence.

"May I leave my groceries here while I go for a walk?"

"Certainly," she said. "Be careful where you go. Stay on the main streets."

Qwilleran had acquired the walking habit up north, and he headed for downtown on foot, proceeding at a studious pace in order to evaluate the streetscape. Ahead of him stretched the new Zwinger Boulevard with its trendy buildings: glass office towers like giant mirrors; an apartment building like an armed camp; the new Penniman Plaza hotel like an amusement park. The thought crossed his mind that the Klingenschoen Fund could buy all of this, tear it down, and build something more pleasing to the eye.

He was, of course, the only pedestrian in sight. Traffic shot past him in surges, barreling for the next red light like race horses bursting out of the gate. At one point a police car pulled up. "Looking for something, sir?" asked an officer.

If Qwilleran had said, "I'm thinking of buying all of this and tearing it down," they would have sent him to the psychiatric ward, so he flashed his press card and told them he was reporting on the architecture of inner cities in the northeast central United States.

Next, discovering an office building with shops on the main floor, he bought a handbag for Polly and had it gift-wrapped and shipped with an affectionate enclosure. It was called a "Paris bag," something not to be found in Moose County, where a "Chicago bag" was considered the last word.

He also entered a bookstore called "Books 'n' Stuff," that stocked more videos and greeting cards than books. Furthermore, its supermarket lighting and background music discouraged browsing. Qwilleran had his own ideas about the correct ambiance for a bookstore: dim, quiet, and slightly dusty.

Downtown he passed the *Daily Fluxion* and would have dropped in to banter with the staffers, but the formidable new security system in the lobby was inhibiting. He kept going in the direction of the Press Club.

This venerable landmark on Canard Street had been remodeled and redecorated. It was no longer the hangout where he and Arch Riker used to lunch almost every day at the same table in the same corner of the bar, served by the same waitress who knew exactly how they liked their burgers. None of the old crowd was there. Everyone seemed younger, and there was a preponderance of ad salesmen and publicity hacks on expense accounts—a suit-and-tie crowd. He was the only one in the place who looked as if he had arrived on horseback. He ate at the bar, but the corned beef sandwich was not as good as it used to be. Bruno, the bartender, had quit, and no one remembered Bruno or knew where he had gone.

As Qwilleran was leaving the bar, he recognized one familiar face. The portly and easygoing Lieutenant Hames of the Homicide Squad was lunching with someone who was obviously a newsman and probably the new reporter on the police beat; Qwilleran could identify the breed instantly. He stopped at their table.

"What brings you down from the North Pole?" the detective asked in his usual jocular style.

"The developers are evicting me from my igloo," Qwilleran replied. "They're building air-conditioned condos."

"Do you guys know each other?" Hames introduced Matt something or other from the *Fluxion*'s police bureau. The name sounded like Thiggamon.

"Spell it," Qwilleran requested as he shook hands with the young reporter.

"T-h-i-double g-a-m-o-n."

"What happened to Lodge Kendall?"

"He went out west to work on some new magazine," said Matt. "Aren't you the one who gave the big retirement bash for Arch Riker? I missed it by two days.''

''You're entitled to a raincheck.''

''What are you doing here anyway?'' asked Hames.

''Spending the winter with crime and pollution instead of snowdrifts and icebergs. I'm staying at the Casablanca.''

''Are you nuts? They're getting ready to bulldoze that pile of rubble. Do you still have your smart cat?''

''I sure do and he's getting smarter every day.''

''I suppose you still indulge his taste for lobster and frog legs.''

Qwilleran said, ''I admit that he lives high, for a cat, but he saved my neck a couple of times, and I owe him.''

Hames turned to the new reporter. ''Qwill has this cat that can dig up clues better than the whole Homicide Squad. When I told my wife about him, she bugged me until I got her a Siamese, but ours is more interested in breaking the law than enforcing it. Pull up a chair, Qwill. Have some coffee. Have dessert. The *Fluxion*'s picking up the tab.''

Qwilleran declined, saying that he had an appointment, and went on his way, thinking about the proliferation of Hedrogs and Thiggamons, like names out of science fiction. Moreover, the bylines at the *Fluxion* were getting longer and more complicated. Fran Unger had been replaced by Martta Newton-Ffiske. At the *Morning Rampage* Jack Murphy's gossip column was now written by

Sasha Crispen-Schmitt. Try saying that fast, he thought: Try saying it three times.

In a critical and slightly grouchy mood he pushed through the lunch-hour crowds on the street, finding most of the pedestrians to be in a mad rush, tense, and rude. The women he evaluated as chic, glamorous, and self-consciously thin, though not as pretty or as healthy-looking as those in Moose County.

Returning to the Casablanca too early for his appointment with Mary Duckworth, he went for a ride, extricating the Purple Plum from the parking lot's tire-bashing cracks and craters and driving to River Road, his last address before moving up north. His old domicile and the tennis club next-door had been replaced by a condo complex and marina, and he could hardly remember how either of the original buildings looked. Too bad! He chalked up another score for the developers and drove back to the Casablanca, hoping it would still be there. What he found was a revised situation in the parking lot. His official slot, #28, was still occupied—not by the green Japanese car but by a decrepit station wagon with a New Jersey license plate. Someone else had pulled into #29, so he wheeled the Purple Plum into #27. After a morning of disappointment, indignation, and other negative reactions, Qwilleran was none too happy when he left for Mary Duckworth's antique shop.

The Blue Dragon still occupied a narrow townhouse, handsomely preserved, and a large blue porcelain dragon (not for sale) still dominated the front window bay. That much had not changed. Nor had the entrance hall with its Chinese wallpaper, Chippendale furniture, and silver chandeliers. There was a life-size ebony carving of a Nubian slave with jeweled turban that had not yet sold, and Qwilleran glanced at the price tag to see if it had been marked down. It had gone up another two thousand dollars, Mary's credo being: If it doesn't sell, raise the price.

As for Mary herself, she still had the sleek blueblack hair and willowy figure that he remembered, but the long cigarette holder and the long fingernails were no longer in evidence. Instead of an Oriental kimono, she wore a well-tailored suit and pearls. She shook his hand briefly and glanced at his Nordic sweater and Aussie hat. "You look so *sportif*, Qwill!"

"I see you haven't sold the blackamoor," he said.

"I'm holding it back. Originally it stood in the lobby of the Casablanca, and it will appreciate in value, no matter what happens to the building."

"Do you still keep that unfriendly German shepherd?"

"Actually," said Mary, "I don't feel the need for a watchdog, considering the new atmosphere in Junktown. I was able to find him a good home in the suburbs, where he's really needed. Come into the office." She motioned him to sit in a wing chair.

Its tall, narrow proportions labeled it an antique, and he glanced at the price tag. He looked twice. At first reading he thought it was $180.00, then realized it was $18,000. He sat down carefully.

"Before we say another word," he began, "would you explain the dark line that makes the Casablanca look like a refrigerator? It's just above the ninth floor."

"There was a projecting ledge there," she said, "and the city ordered it removed. Portions of it were falling down on the sidewalk and injuring passersby. Our architect maintains it can be safely restored, and it should be restored, being an integral part of the design. Meanwhile, the building management is reluctant to spend money on cosmetic improvements because—"

"Because the building may be torn down next week," Qwilleran interrupted. "Everyone chants that excuse like a Greek chorus, and they may be right. This morning I saw the sign announcing the Gateway Alcazar. The developers seem to be supremely confident."

"Aren't you appalled?" Mary said with a shudder. "The audacity of those people is unthinkable! They've even contrived a publicity story in the *Morning Rampage* comparing their arched monstrosity to the Arc de Triomphe!"

"Well, the Pennimans own the *Rampage*, don't they?"

"Nevertheless, Roberto wrote a letter to the editor calling it the 'Arc de Catastrophe.' If your Klingenschoen Fund comes to our rescue, we shall be eternally grateful."

"What do you know about Penniman, Grey-

stone and F-l-e-u-d-d? I don't know how to pronounce it.''

''Flood.''

''What's their track record?''

''Fleudd has recently joined them, but the Penniman and Greystone firm has been in real-estate
development for years. They're the ones who
wanted to tear down the Press Club.''

''The media clobbered that idea in a hurry,''
Qwilleran recalled. ''Has the *Daily Fluxion* come
to the support of SOCK?''

''Not with any conviction. They merely fuel the
controversy. The mayor and the city council have
made statements in favor of the Gateway Alcazar,
but the university and the art community support
SOCK.''

''How about your father? What does he think
about saving the Casablanca?''

Mary raised her eyebrows expressively. ''As
you know, he and I are always at odds on every
issue, and his bank has already agreed to lease
space for a branch office in the Gateway building.
Ironic, isn't it?''

''Tell me about the Countess,'' he said. ''So far
no one has mentioned her name.''

''She is Adelaide St. John Plumb. Her father
was Harrison Wills Plumb, who built the Casablanca in 1901. She was born on the twelfth floor
of the Casablanca seventy-five years ago, with a
midwife, a nurse, and two doctors in attendance,
according to the story she tells and tells and tells.
She's inclined to be repetitive.''

''Did she ever marry?''

"No. She was engaged at an early age but broke it off. She adored her father, and they were very close."

"I see . . . How does she react to all this brouhaha over her birthplace?"

"That's a curious situation," Mary admitted. "I believe she enjoys being the center of attention. The promoters make her large offers and ply her with gifts, while SOCK appeals to her better instincts and makes pointed references to her father—her 'dear father.' She procrastinates, and we stall for time, hoping to find an angel. Do you play bridge?"

Jolted by this non sequitur, Qwilleran said, "Uh . . . no, I don't."

"How about backgammon?"

"Frankly, I've never liked games that require any mental effort. What is the reason for this interrogation, may I ask?"

"Let me explain," said Mary. "The Countess has one interest in life: table games—cards, Parcheesi, checkers, mah-jongg, anything except chess. Roberto and I stay in her good graces by playing once a week."

"Does much money exchange hands?"

"There's no gambling. She plays for the pleasure of competition, and she's really very good. She should be! She's been playing daily all her life, beginning as a young child. Did Amber tell you that the Countess is a recluse?"

"No, she didn't." Qwilleran's vision of Lady Hester Stanhope flashed across his mind.

"Yes, she lives in a world of her own on the twelfth floor, with three servants."

"Surely she goes out occasionally."

"She never leaves the building or even her own apartment, which occupies an entire floor. Her doctors, lawyers, hairdresser, dressmaker, and masseuse all make house calls."

"What's her problem? Agoraphobia?"

"She claims to have trouble breathing if she steps outside her door . . . You don't play dominoes?"

"No! Especially not dominoes."

"Scrabble?"

He shook his head. "Does this woman know I'm here—and why?"

"We told her you're a writer who inherited money and retired to the country, and you're spending the winter here to escape the bad weather up north."

"What was her reaction?"

"She asked if you play bridge."

"Does she know I used to write for the *Fluxion*?"

"There was no point in mentioning it. She never reads newspapers. As I said before, she has created a private world."

Qwilleran was convinced he had discovered Lady Hester in the flesh. He said, "Does anyone know of my interest in buying the Casablanca?"

"Only Roberto and myself and the architect. And we confided in Amber, of course, when I had to leave town."

"Since the Klingenschoen board of directors

won't even hear about this until Thursday, I don't want my possible involvement to leak out.''

"We understand that.''

"I'll be filing stories for the Moose County paper while I'm here, and I'm thinking that a column on the Casablanca would make a good kickoff. Will the Countess object to being interviewed?''

"I'm sure she'll enjoy the attention, although she'll want to talk mostly about her dear father.''

"Who handles the business end of the Casablanca?''

"A realty firm, with her lawyers as intermediaries.''

"Is she interested in the tenants?''

"Only if they have good manners and good clothes and play bridge. To break the ice, I'd like to take you to tea on Twelve. She pours every afternoon at four.''

"First," Qwilleran said, "I want to know your architect's appraisal of the building. As of this moment I don't believe it shows much promise.''

Mary handed him a bound copy of a report. "There it is! Two hundred pages. Most of it is technical, but if you read the first and last chapters, you'll have all the necessary information.''

Qwilleran noted the name on the cover: Grinchman & Hills, architects and engineers. It was a well-known firm. Magazines had publicized their projects around the country: an art museum, a university library, the restoration of a nineteenth-century government building. "Not a bad connection," he said. "I'll study this thing, and if I have any questions, whom do I call? Grinchman or Hills?''

''They're both deceased,'' Mary said. ''Only the name remains, and the reputation. The man who prepared the report for SOCK, virtually gratis, is Jefferson Lowell. He's totally sympathetic to the cause. You'll like him.''

Qwilleran rose. ''This discussion has been enjoyable and enlightening, Mary. I'll let you know when I'm ready for tea with the Countess.''

''Time is of the essence,'' she reminded him. ''After all, the woman is seventy-five, and anything can happen.'' She accompanied him to the door, through a maze of high-priced pedigreed antiques. ''Do you still have your Mackintosh coat of arms?''

''I wouldn't part with it. It's the first antique I ever bought, and it's incorporated into my apartment up north.'' He drew a small object from his pocket. ''Can you identify this?''

''Where did you get it?''

''My cat was batting it about the floor in the penthouse.''

''It's a blank tile from a Scrabble set. Blanks are wild in Scrabble. The former tenant was an avid player.''

''She was an art dealer, I understand, and that explains some of the peculiar artwork, but why so many mushrooms? Who painted them? They're signed with a double R.''

Mary's eyes wavered as she replied, ''He was a young artist by the name of Ross Rasmus.''

''Why did he put a knife in every picture?''

88

She hesitated momentarily. "Roberto says there's sensuous pleasure in slicing a mushroom with a sharp knife. Perhaps that's what it's all about."

With a searching look Qwilleran said, "I hear she died unexpectedly. What was the cause of death?"

"Really, Qwill, we avoid talking about it," Mary said uncomfortably. "It was rather—sordid, and that's not the image we want for the Casablanca."

"You don't have to be cagey with me, Mary. Since I'm subletting the apartment, I deserve to know."

"Well, if you insist . . . I have to tell you that she was . . . murdered."

He stroked his moustache smugly. "That's what I surmised. There's a sizable bloodstain on the carpet. Someone had placed a piece of furniture over it for camouflage, but Koko found it."

"How is Koko?" Mary asked brightly.

"Never mind Koko. Tell me what happened to the art dealer."

The words came out reluctantly. "She . . . her throat was cut."

"By the mushroom artist?"

She nodded.

"That figures. He was obsessed with knives. When did this happen?"

"On Labor Day weekend."

"Why is so much of this Ross fellow's work hanging in the apartment?"

"Well," said Mary, selecting her words with

care, "he was a young artist . . . and she thought he had promise . . . and she promoted him in her gallery. He was her protégé, you might say."

"Uh-huh," said Qwilleran knowingly. "Where is he now? I assume he was convicted."

"No," Mary said slowly. "He was never brought to trial . . . You see, he left a confession . . . and took his own life."

SIX

QWILLERAN FELT IN better spirits when he left the Blue Dragon. Koko's discovery was pertinent: 14-A had been the scene of a murder. That cat had an infallible sense when it came to turning up evidence of criminal activity.

Carrying the Grinchman & Hills report Qwilleran headed for home with a brisk step, eager to start reading. Instead of wasting time on dinner in a restaurant, he stopped at the Carriage House Café to inquire about take-out food.

"We don't usually . . . do . . . take-outs," said

the cashier in a distracted way. She was staring at Qwilleran's oversized moustache. ''Are you on television?''

Regarding her with mournful eyes under drooping lids, he said in a rich, resonant tone reserved for such occasions, ''At this moment I am live—in person—talking with an attractive woman behind a cash register, regarding the possibility of a take-out dinner.''

''I'll see what I can do,'' she called over her shoulder as she hurried into the kitchen. Immediately a man with long hair and a chef's hat peered through the small window in the kitchen door. Qwilleran gave him a cordial salute.

The cashier returned. ''We don't have take-out trays, but the cook will put together a serving of today's special, if you don't mind carrying a regular plate. You can bring it back tomorrow. Are you driving?''

''I'm walking but I don't have far to go. What is your special?''

''Beef Stroganoff.''

''It sounds most appetizing.''

''We'll put some coleslaw and a dinner roll in foil,'' the cashier volunteered.

While retrieving his bill clip from his pocket, Qwilleran placed the Grinchman & Hills report on the counter and noticed the cashier trying to read it upside down.

''Grinch . . . man . . . and . . . Hills,'' she read aloud. ''Is that the script for a movie?'' she asked, wide-eyed.

''Yes, but keep it quiet,'' he replied in a low

voice with a swift glance to either side. "It's going to be a buddy movie like *Bonnie and Clyde* or *Harold and Maude*. I'm playing Grinchman."

Leaving a sizable tip for a happy and flustered cashier, he departed with the bulky report under one arm and a plate of hot food covered with foil, on top of which were balanced two foil packets. "Your coleslaw and buttered roll," the cashier told him with an expansive display of hospitality. "Open the door for him," she called to the busboy.

Qwilleran covered the distance to the Casablanca quickly, and a young man held the two heavy doors for him, saying, "Somebody's gonna eat tonight."

On the main floor there was activity suitable for late afternoon on a Monday. The person seated in the phone booth was telephoning and neither swigging nor snorting. An elderly man using a walker moved down the hall slowly and with extreme concentration. Kitty-Baby, having picked up the scent of the beef Stroganoff, was dogging Qwilleran's feet. In the vicinity of the desk a young man was swinging a mop across the floor, while Mrs. Tuttle sat at her post, knitting, and Rupert lounged about in his red hat. Despite the tools in his jacket pocket, he never seemed to do much work. Among the persons waiting for the elevator were employed tenants with gaunt end-of-day expressions, the Asian mother with her children, elderly souls complaining about Medicare, and students with an excess of youthful energy, talking loudly about bridges, professors, and final exams. Probably engineering students, Qwilleran guessed.

Rupert caught his eye and nodded toward the elevators. "Both workin' today."

"A cause for celebration," Qwilleran replied.

While the passengers waited in suspense, reassuring knocks and whines could be heard in both elevator shafts. Old Green was the first to appear, immediately filling with passengers and going on its way. Then the door of Old Red opened, and two of the waiting students rushed aboard. Qwilleran stood back, allowing a white-haired woman with a cane to go next. Slowly, one faltering step at a time, she approached the car, and just as her head and one foot were inside, the heavy door started to close.

"Hold it!" he yelled.

One student lunged for the door; the other lunged at the woman, pushing her from danger. As she toppled backward, Qwilleran dropped everything and caught her, while Old Red closed its door and took off.

Instantly Mrs. Tuttle and Rupert were on the scene, the custodian retrieving the woman's cane and the manager saying, "Are you all right, Mrs. Button?"

Set back on her feet but shaking violently, the woman raised her cane as if to strike and screamed in a cracked voice, *"That man grabbed me!"*

"He saved you, Mrs. Button," explained the manager. "You could have fallen and broken your hip."

"He grabbed me!"

"Wheelchair," Mrs. Tuttle mumbled, and Rupert quickly brought one from the office and took the offended victim upstairs in Old Green, while Qwilleran surveyed the gooey hash on the floor.

"I'm so sorry, Mr. Qwilleran," said Mrs. Tuttle. "Is that your dinner?"

"It *was* my dinner. Anyway, the plate didn't break, but I'm afraid I messed up your floor."

"Don't worry about that. The boy will take care of it."

"I don't think that will be necessary," he said. Kitty-Baby had been joined by Napoleon and two other cats, and the quartet was lapping it up, coleslaw and all.

"At least let me wash your plate," Mrs. Tuttle offered.

"It looks as if Old Red is my nemesis," said Qwilleran as he nodded his thanks to a child who handed him his buttered roll and a man who picked up the Grinchman & Hills report, straightening its rumpled pages.

"Could the boy go out and bring you something to eat?" the manager suggested.

"I think not, thank you. I'll go upstairs and feed the cats and then go out to dinner."

When he opened the door of 14-A, Koko and Yum Yum came forward nonchalantly.

"How about showing some concern?" he chided them. "How about displaying a little sympathy? I've just had a grueling experience."

They followed him into the kitchen and watched politely as he opened a can of crabmeat.

They were neither prowling nor yowling nor ankle-rubbing, and Qwilleran realized that they were not hungry.

"Has someone been up here?" he demanded. "Did they give you something to eat?"

When he placed the plate of food on the floor, the cats circled it and sniffed from all angles before consenting to nibble daintily. Then Qwilleran was sure someone had been feeding them. He inspected the apartment for signs of intrusion and found no evidence in the library or in either bedroom. The doors to the terrace were locked. Both bathrooms were undisturbed. Only in the gallery was there anything different, and he could not imagine exactly what it was. The Indian dhurrie still covered the bloodstain on the carpet; no artwork was missing; the potted trees had all their leaves, but something had been changed.

At that moment Koko entered the gallery and embarked on a businesslike program of sniffing. He sniffed at the foot of the stairs, alongside the sofa, on the gallery level between trees, and in front of the stereo.

"The pails!" Qwilleran shouted. "Someone took the pails!" He hurried to the housephone in the kitchen and said to a surprised Mrs. Tuttle, "What happened to my pails?"

"Your what?" she asked.

"This is Qwilleran in 14-A. There were plastic pails standing around my living room to catch drips when the skylight leaks. What happened to them? It might rain!"

"Oh, I forgot to tell you," she apologized. "The

man was here to fix the skylight today, so Rupert collected the pails. I forgot to tell you during the trouble with Mrs. Button.''

''I see. Sorry to bother you.'' He tamped his moustache. He would have to speak firmly to Rupert about feeding the animals. But his annoyance at the custodian was erased by his admiration for Koko. That cat had known the exact location of every pail!

Now Qwilleran was twice as hungry. Carrying the clean plastic plate he returned to the Carriage House Café.

''Oh, it's you again!'' cried the cashier in delight. ''How did you like the special? You didn't need to bring the plate back right away.''

''It was so good,'' Qwilleran said, ''that I'd like to do it all over again, including that delicious coleslaw and perhaps two rolls if you can spare them.'' He sat on a stool at the counter, and the cashier insisted on serving him herself, while the cook waved a friendly hand in the small window of the kitchen door and later sent out a complimentary slice of apple pie.

Thus fortified, Qwilleran returned to the Casablanca, where he found the red-hatted Rupert sitting at the manager's desk, reading a comic book. ''I notice that the skylight's been repaired,'' he said to the custodian.

''Yep. No more leaks.'' The man held up crossed fingers.

''How did you get along with the cats when you picked up the pails?''

"Okay. I gave 'em a jelly doughnut. They gobbled it up."

"Jelly doughnut!" Qwilleran was aghast.

Rupert, misunderstanding his reaction, excused the apparent extravagance by explaining that it was a stale doughnut that had been lying around the basement for several days.

Controlling himself, Qwilleran said in a friendly way, "I'd rather you wouldn't give the cats any treats if you have occasion to enter the apartment, Rupert. They're on a strict diet because of . . . because of their kidneys."

"Yeah, cats always have trouble with their kidneys, seems if."

"But thanks for collecting the pails, friend. You're right on the ball!"

Then Qwilleran rode up to Fourteen on Old Red and confronted the Siamese. "Stale jelly doughnut!" he said in indignation. "You ate a stale jelly doughnut! And yet you guys turn up your nose at a fresh can of salmon if it's pink! You hypocrites!"

Changing into a warm-up suit, he locked himself into the library to study the Grinchman & Hills report. It appeared to be a formidable task, and he wanted no one sitting on his lap or purring in his ear.

The introduction described the original structure, as Amber had quoted from the SOCK brochure. Then came the chapter on necessary improvements, which Qwilleran condensed on a legal pad as follows:

- Clean and repair exterior and restore ornamentation.
- Restore grassy park on west side and porte cochere on the east.
- Acquire property behind building for parking structure.
- New roof and skylight.
- New triple-glazed windows throughout, custom-made.
- Mechanical update: elevators, heating and air-conditioning, plumbing, wiring, TV cables, and intercom.
- Remove superimposed floorings, false walls, and dropped ceilings.
- Restore former apartment spaces with maids' rooms.
- Update bathrooms in the character of the original.
- Restore marble, woodwork, paneling, mosaic tile.
- Duplicate original light fixtures, custom-made.
- Furnish lobby as before: Spanish furniture, Oriental rugs, oil paintings.
- Reinstate restaurant on Fourteen, converting pool area into sidewalk café.
- Landscape terrace in 1900 style.
- Update basement apartments for staff.
- Redesign kitchen and laundry facilities.
- Preserve owner's apartment on Twelve as refurbished in 1925.

After compiling this ambitious list, Qwilleran blew into his moustache—an expression of incredulity. Turning to the final chapter he had greater cause for disbelief; the bottom line was in nine digits. He emitted an audible gulp! Such a sum was beyond his comprehension. Despite his inheritance, he still bought his shirts on sale and telephoned long distance during the discount hours. Nevertheless, he knew that the Klingenschoen Fund was accustomed to disbursing hundreds of millions without blinking, and he managed not to blink, although he gulped audibly.

As he mused on the possibilities and problems of such an extensive restoration, the hush of the library was broken by the sound of drumbeats. They were coming through the wall from 14-B. *Thump thump thump dum-dum thump dum-dum thump BONG!* The final beat reverberated like a Chinese gong. Then he heard a shrill voice, although the words were inaudible, followed by a repetition of the drumbeats.

He went out on the terrace and walked past the French doors of 14-B, but the blinds were closed as before. Next he went out to the elevator lobby and listened at his neighbor's door. He could hear a voice chanting, then more thumps and a BONG! He was standing with his ear close to the door when noises in the elevator shaft alerted him, and he sprang back just as Old Red debouched a creature with spiky hair, wearing black tights, black boots, a black poncho, and black eye makeup.

"Good evening," he said to the creature, giving his greeting a neighborly inflection.

Without replying, he or she darted past him, hammered on the door of 14-B, and was admitted amid birdlike shrieks.

The charivari had no effect on the Siamese, who were sleeping soundly somewhere, full of crabmeat and stale jelly doughnut. Qwilleran spent the next two hours in the gallery, however, with the French doors closed and the stereo volume turned to high.

Toward the end of the evening, when the thumps and bongs had subsided, he heard a commotion in the hall: the door of 14-B slamming, a cacophony of shrill voices. He grabbed his wastebasket and opened his front door on the pretext of putting out his rubbish. As he did so, he caught sight of more creatures in black, chattering and shrieking like inhabitants of a rain forest as they boarded Old Red. When they saw him, they fell silent and stared with black-rimmed eyes. The elevator door closed and Old Red descended. Qwilleran told himself with a chuckle that they were members of some kind of satanic cult, and Old Red was taking them down to the infernal regions.

Perhaps it was the sudden silence that roused the Siamese, or their internal clock told them it was time for their eleven o'clock treat. Whatever alerted them, they wandered out from wherever they had been sleeping and performed the ritual of yawning and stretching, first two forelegs and then one hind leg. Koko jumped to the desktop and nosed the Grinchman & Hills report. Yum Yum stood on her hind legs and placed her paws on the edge of the wastebasket, peering into its depths in hope of finding a crumpled paper or piece of string.

"I don't know about you," Qwilleran said to the pair, "but I've had a most interesting evening. If we do what the architects suggest, this building will no longer look like a refrigerator, and it won't be a sore thumb on Zwinger Boulevard. The lobby will be a showplace; the apartments will be palatial; the rooftop restaurant will be exclusive; and they'll no longer allow cats. How do you react to that?"

"Yow," said Koko, who was now examining the library sofa. It was covered with fake leopard, and he knew it was not the real thing. Industriously, with vertical tail, he sniffed the seams, pawed the button tufting, and reached down behind the seat cushions. Some of his memorable discoveries had been made behind seat cushions: cocktail crackers, paper clips, folding money, pencils, and small articles of clothing. Now he was scrabbling so assiduously that Qwilleran went to his aid. He removed one of the seat cushions, and there—tucked in the crevice between the seat platform and the sofa-back—was an item of gold jewelry.

"Good boy!" he said. "Let me see it."

Engraved discs were linked together to make a flexible bracelet, but the clasp was broken. One disc was engraved in cursive script: "To Dianne." Another was inscribed: "From Ross." The remainder bore the numerals: 1-1-4-1, 5-1-1-1, 4-1-3-5, etc. Obviously it was a secret code between the two.

"Okay, this is enough excitement for tonight," Qwilleran said, "but tomorrow we do a little research on the Labor Day incident."

On Tuesday morning Qwilleran called Jefferson Lowell at Grinchman & Hills, inviting him to lunch at the Press Club, and the architect accepted. There was a certain mystique about the Press Club, and most persons jumped at an invitation.

Before going out to breakfast, he checked the weather report on the radio and learned that the Narcotics Squad had rounded up fifty-two suspects in a drug bust; a judge had been indicted for accepting bribes; and a cold front was moving in.

On his way out of the building Qwilleran was flagged by the manager. She said, "I'm sorry about that commotion last night. Mrs. Button is very old and a little confused at times."

"I understand, Mrs. Tuttle."

"Last year she had an attack, and the paramedics gave her CPR. The next day she accused them of rape. It even went to court, but of course it was thrown out."

"I'm glad you warned me," Qwilleran said. "Next time I'll let her fall."

If Mrs. Tuttle appreciated his sly humor, she gave no indication. "I also wanted to tell you, Mr. Qwilleran, that some of our tenants do cleaning—

those that are on social security, you know. They like to keep active and earn a little extra. Let me know if you need help with your apartment.''

''I'll take you up on that,'' he said, ''but don't send me Mrs. Button.''

Then he walked downtown. It was a good day for walking—by urban standards; a light breeze diluted the emissions from cars and trucks and diesel vehicles. En route he stopped for pancakes and sausages, observing that they were twice the price of a similar breakfast in Pickax, and the sausages were not half so good. Moose County had hog farms, and independent butchers made their own sausages. He was spoiled.

At the *Daily Fluxion* he braved the security cordon and gained admittance to the library, where he asked to see clips on the Bessinger murder. The film bank produced three entries, the first dated the day after Labor Day. Although the victim's name was spelled differently in each news item, that was not unusual for the *Daily Fluxion*.

MURDER-SUICIDE JOLTS ART WORLD

The violent deaths of an art dealer and an artist Sunday night, apparently murder and suicide, have shocked the local art world and the residents of the Casablanca apartments.

The body of Diane Bessinger, 45, co-owner of the Bessinger-Todd Gallery, was found in her penthouse apartment Monday morning. Her throat had been cut. The body of Ross Rasmus, 25, a client of Bessinger, was found earlier atop a car in the parking lot below the murdered woman's terrace.

Rasmus apparently jumped to his death after leaving a contrite confession daubed on a wall. His body landed on the roof of a car owned by a Casablanca tenant, who found it at 12:05 A.M. Monday and notified the police.

"I went out for some smokes and beer," said Jack Yazbro, 39, "and the top of my car was all bashed in. He wasn't that big of a guy, but it's a long way down."

Bessinger died between 11 P.M. and midnight Sunday, according to the medical examiner, although the body was not discovered until Monday morning when her partner, Jerome Todd, phoned and was unable to get an answer.

"I heard about Ross's suicide on the radio and tried to call her," Todd said. "When she didn't answer, I got worried and called the building manager."

The gallery had mounted a one-man exhibit of Rasmus's mushroom paintings in June. "They sold poorly," said Todd, "and Ross blamed us for not publicizing the event enough."

Rasmus rented a loft apartment adjoining Bessinger's lavish penthouse at the Casablanca. Jessica Tuttle, manager of the building, called him a good tenant. "He was a nice, quiet, serious young man," she said. "We rented to him at Ms. Bessinger's recommendation."

It was Tuttle who found the murdered woman's body. ''Mr. Todd called me about not getting an answer on the phone. He was sure she was home, because she had guests coming for a holiday brunch. So I took my keys and went up there. Her body was on the living room floor, and there was a lot of blood on the carpet.''

Bessinger had been in the news frequently in connection with the Save Our Casablanca Kommittee, of which she was founder and leader.

Following the news item, a brief obituary had been published in the Wednesday edition of the *Fluxion*, with a half-column photo of the deceased, a vivacious-looking woman with dark shoulder-length hair. Diane had become Diana.

BESSINGER, DIANA

Diana Bessinger, 45, of the Casablanca apartments died Sunday at her home. She was co-owner of the Bessinger-Todd Gallery, founder of the Save Our Casablanca Kommittee, an officer of the Turp and Chisel Club, and an active worker in local art projects.

A native of Iowa, she was the daughter of the late Prof. and Mrs. Damon Bessinger. She is survived by one brother and two daughters.

Private services will be held Thursday. Memorials may be made to the Turp and Chisel scholarship fund.

The following Sunday, the art page of the *Fluxion* carried a commentary by art writer Ylana Targ, with yet a third spelling of the victim's name. A photo taken by a *Fluxion* photographer at the Rasmus opening in June showed a smiling "Dianne" Bessinger and a shy Ross Rasmus, posed with one of the mushroom paintings. The byline, Qwilleran noted, was another one of those names that was just as logical spelled backward or forward.

MUSHROOM MURDER HAS NO ANSWERS
by Ylana Targ

There is only one topic of conversation in the galleries and studios as Dianne Bessinger is tearfully laid to rest and the ashes of the "mushroom painter" are shipped ignominiously to his hometown—somewhere.

Why did he do it? What caused this talented, thoughtful artist to turn violent and commit such a heinous crime? His suicide is easier to explain; it was the only possible escape from intolerable guilt. Desperate remorse must have driven him over the parapet of the Casablanca terrace.

"Lady Di" was his patron, his enthusiastic press agent, his best friend, who saw merit in his work when no other gallery would take a chance on his monomania for mushrooms. Once, when asked why he never painted broccoli or crook-neck squash, Ross said meekly, ''I haven't said all I have to say about mushrooms.''

Granted, mushrooms are erotic, and he captured their mushroomness succinctly. Pairing the fleshy fungus with the razor-edge knife, as he did, bordered on soft porn.

Dianne said in an interview last June, ''There have been artists who painted softness, crispness, silkiness, or mistiness sublimely, but only Rasmus could paint sharpness so sharp that the viewer cringes.''

The knife he portrayed in the paintings was always the same—a tapered, pointed Japanese slicer with a pale wooden handle and a provocative shapeliness of its own. One shudders to think too much about the actual crime. The motive is all one can safely or sanely contemplate, and that is a question that will never be answered.

Dianne Bessinger was the founder and president of SOCK. It was a passion with her, and she would not want her worthwhile cause to be overshadowed by the notoriety surrounding her tragic death. She would say, ''Let the matter fade away now, and get on with the business of saving the Casablanca.''

Qwilleran finished reading the clips and patted his moustache. It would be a challenge, he thought, to uncover that hidden motive. It might be buried in 14-A.

SEVEN

ON AN IMPULSE, after reading the murder-suicide clips in the *Fluxion* library, Qwilleran walked to the Bessinger-Todd Gallery in the financial district. It had the same address as the old Lambreth Gallery that he knew so well, but the interior had changed dramatically. At that morning hour the place had a vast emptiness, except for a business-suited man supervising a jeans-clad assistant perched on a stepladder. He turned in surprise as Qwilleran entered, saying, ''We're closed. I thought the door was locked.''

"Am I intruding? I'm Jim Qwilleran, formerly of the *Daily Fluxion*. I used to cover the art beat when Mountclemens was the critic."

"How do you do. I'm Jerome Todd. I've heard about Mountclemens, but that was before my time here. I'm from Des Moines."

"I've been away for three years. I see you've enlarged the gallery."

"Yes, we knocked out the ceiling so we could exhibit larger works, and we added the balcony for crafts objects."

Qwilleran said, "I'm retired now and living up north, but I heard about the tragic loss of your partner and wanted to extend my condolences."

"Thank you . . . Is there anything I can do for you?" Todd asked in an abrupt change of subject. He was a tall, distinguished-looking man with one disturbing mannerism—the habit of pinching his nose as if he smelled an unpleasant odor.

Qwilleran was adept at inventing impromptu replies. "I happen to be staying at the Casablanca," he said, "and I would like to propose a memorial to Ms. Bessinger that would help the cause she championed."

Todd looked surprised and wary in equal proportions.

"What I envision," Qwilleran went on smoothly as if he had been planning it for months, "is a book about the historic Casablanca, using old photos from the public library. For text I would rely on interviews and research."

"That would be costly to put together," said

the dealer, withdrawing slightly as he began to anticipate a touch for money.

"There are grants available for publishing books on historical subjects," Qwilleran said coolly, "and revenue from the sale of the books would go to the Bessinger Memorial Fund. My own services would be donated."

Instead of being relieved, Todd showed increased wariness. "Who would be interviewed?" he asked sharply.

"Local historians, architects, and persons who have recollections of the early Casablanca. You'll be surprised how many of them will come forward when we broadcast a request. My own attorney remembers eating spinach timbales in the rooftop restaurant as a boy."

"I wouldn't want anyone to go digging into the circumstances of my partner's death. There's been too much notoriety and gossip already," the dealer said, pinching his nose.

"There would be nothing like that, I assure you," said Qwilleran. At that moment a glimpse of movement overhead caused him to look up; a Persian cat was walking along the railing of the balcony. "By the way," he said, "I'm subletting Ms. Bessinger's apartment while the estate is in probate, and I admire her taste in furniture and art."

Todd nodded in silent agreement.

"How long were you in partnership, Mr. Todd?"

"Eighteen years. We came here to take over the

Lambreth Gallery when Zoe Lambreth moved to California.''

''Do you happen to have any Rasmus paintings?''

''I do not! And I'm weary of the talk about that fellow! There are plenty of *living* artists.'' Todd pinched his nose again.

''The only reason I asked is that I'm in the market for large-scale art for a house I'm building up north.'' Qwilleran was exercising his talent for instant falsehood.

''Then you must come to our opening on Friday night,'' said the dealer, visibly relieved as he anticipated cash flow. ''We're in the process of mounting the show, so the walls are vacant, but you'll see some impressive works at the vernissage.''

''I'm converting a barn into a residence,'' said Qwilleran, embroidering his innocent lie, ''so I'll have large wall spaces, and I was hoping for a mushroom painting. Mushrooms seem appropriate for a barn.''

Stiffly Todd said, ''All his work sold out immediately after his suicide. If I'd had my wits about me, I would have held some back, but I was in shock. They didn't sell well at all in June. He's worth more dead than alive. But if you come here Friday night you'll see the work of other artists you might like. What kind of barn are you remodeling?''

''An apple barn. Octagonal.'' The barn on the Klingenschoen property had indeed stored apples, and it really was eight-sided.

"Spectacular! You might consider contemporary tapestries. Do you know the sizes of your wall spaces?"

"Actually, the job isn't off the drawing board as yet," said Qwilleran, being completely truthful.

"Come anyway on Friday. There'll be champagne, hors d'oeuvres, live music, and valet parking."

"What are the hours?"

"From six o'clock until the well runs dry."

"Thank you. I'll be here." Qwilleran started toward the door and turned back. "Tell me frankly. How do you feel about the future of the Casablanca?"

"It's a lost cause," said Todd without emotion.

"Yet your partner was convinced it could be saved."

"Yes . . . but . . . the picture has changed. The building is being razed to make way for the new Gateway Alcazar, which will be the missing link between the new downtown and the new Junktown. I'm moving the gallery there. I've signed up to lease space twice the size of what I have here."

Qwilleran consulted his watch. It was time to meet the architect at the Press Club. "Well, thanks for your time, Mr. Todd. I'll see you on Friday."

As he walked to the Press Club he told himself that the book project, born on the spur of the moment, was not a bad idea. As for converting the apple barn, that sounded good, too. It would be ten times roomier than his present apartment in

Pickax, and the Siamese could climb about the overhead beams.

The Press Club occupied a grimy stone fortress that had once been the county jail, and as a hangout for the working press it had maintained a certain forbidding atmosphere for many years. The interior had changed, however, since Qwilleran's days at the *Daily Fluxion*. It had been renovated, modernized, brightened and—in his estimation—ruined. Yet it was a popular place at noon. He waited for the architect in the lobby, observing the lunch-time crowd that streamed through the door: reporters and editors, advertising and PR types, radio and TV personalities.

Eventually a man with a neatly clipped beard entered slowly, appraising the lobby with curiosity and a critical set to his mouth. Qwilleran stepped forward and introduced himself.

"I'm Jeff Lowell," said the man. "So this is the celebrated Press Club. Somehow it's not what I expected." He gestured toward the damask walls and gilt-framed mirrors.

"They redecorated a couple of years ago," said Qwilleran apologetically, "and it's no longer the dismal, shabby Press Club that I loved. Shall we go upstairs?"

Upstairs there was a dining room with tablecloths, cloth napkins, and peppermills on the tables instead of paper placemats and squeeze bottles of mustard and ketchup. They took a table in a secluded corner.

"So you're interested in the Casablanca restoration," said the architect.

"Interested enough to want to ask questions. I've done my homework. I spent last evening reading the Grinchman & Hills report. You seem quite sanguine about the project."

"As the report made clear, it will cost a mint, but it's entirely feasible. It could be the most sensational preservation project in the country," Lowell said.

"What is your particular interest?"

"For one thing, I lived in that building for a few years before I was married, and there's something about the place that gets into a person's blood; I don't know how to explain it. But chiefly, my firm is interested because the Casablanca was designed by the late John Grinchman, and we have all the original specs in our archives. Naturally that facilitated the study immeasurably. Grinchman was a struggling young architect at the turn of the century when he met Harrison Plumb. Plumb had a harebrained scheme that no established architect would touch, but Grinchman took the gamble, and the Casablanca made his reputation. In design it was ahead of its time; Moorish didn't become a fad until after World War One. The walls were built two feet thick at the base, tapering up to eighteen inches at the top. All the mechanical equipment—water pipes, steam pipes, electric conduits—were concentrated in crawl spaces between floors, for easy access and to help soundproof the building. And there was another feature that may amuse you: The occupants could have *all the electricity they wanted*!"

"What do you know about Harrison Plumb?" Qwilleran asked.

"His family had accumulated their fortune in railroads, but he was not inclined to business. He was a dreamer, a dilettante. He studied for a while at L'Ecole des Beaux Arts, and while he was in Paris he saw the nobility living in lavish apartments in the city. He brought the idea home. He dreamed of building an apartment-palace."

"What was the reaction from the local elite?"

"They tumbled for it! It was a smash hit! For families there were twelve-room apartments with servants' quarters. There were smaller apartments for bachelors and mistresses. Horses and carriages were stabled in the rear and available at a moment's notice, like taxis. Curiously there were no kitchens, but there was the restaurant on the top floor, and the residents either went upstairs to the dining room or had their meals sent down."

"What about the swimming pool?"

"That was for men only—and somewhat of a conceit. On the main floor they had a stockbroker, jeweler, law firm, and insurance agency. In the basement there were laundresses and cobblers. Barbers, tailors, seamstresses, and hairdressers were on call to the apartments."

"And Plumb kept the best apartment for himself?"

"The entire twelfth floor. It was designed to his specifications in Spanish style and then redesigned in the 1920s in the French Modern of its day. If the building is restored, the Plumb suite could eventually be a private museum; it's that spectacular!''

Qwilleran said, ''Suppose the Klingenschoen Fund undertook to restore the Casablanca to its original character, would there be a demand for the apartments?''

''I have no doubt.''

''I suppose you've met Harrison Plumb's daughter?''

''Only twice,'' said Lowell. ''The first time was when I asked permission to make the study. I buttered up the old girl, invoked the memory of her dear father, indulged in some architectural double-talk, and got her okay. The second time was when I presented her with a copy of the report—leather-bound, mind you—which I'm sure she hasn't opened, even though we bound in a photo of her father, arm in arm with John Grinchman. Unfortunately, I'm not a bridge player, so I was never invited back.''

''I have yet to meet the lady,'' said Qwilleran. ''What is she like?''

''Nice enough, but an absurd anachronism, living in a private time capsule. She doesn't give a damn if the front steps are pulverizing and the tenants' elevators are shot. If someone doesn't shake some sense into her, she'll hang on to the place until she dies, and that'll be the end of the Casablanca. I don't want to be there on the day they blast.''

They ordered the Press Club's Tuesday special, pork chops, and talked about the metamorphosis of Zwinger Boulevard, the proposed Gateway Alcazar, and the gentrification of Junktown. Then over cheesecake and coffee they reverted to the subject of the Casablanca.

"Let's draw up the battlelines," said Qwilleran. "On the one side, the developers and the city fathers want to see it demolished."

"Also the financial backers for the Gateway Alcazar. Also the realty firm that manages the Casablanca. The building is a headache for them; in spite of the low rents, it's only half-occupied, and the mechanical equipment is constantly breaking down because of age and mishandling."

"Okay. And on the other side we have SOCK and G&H, right?"

"Plus the art and academic sector. Plus an army of former tenants in all walks of life who've contributed to SOCK for the campaign. Strange as it may seem, there are people who are sentimental about the Casablanca in the same way they love the memory of—say—Paris. It has almost a living presence. It's too bad what happened to Di Bessinger. She had a lot of drive and—as you probably know—she was set to inherit the building."

"That's news to me," Qwilleran said.

"You might say she had a vested interest in the Casablanca. That's not to discount her genuine love for it, of course."

"Are you telling me that the Countess had named Bessinger in her will?"

"Yes, Di spent a lot of time up on Twelve, and it must have been appreciated by the older woman, who—let's face it—lives a lonely life."

"Tell me this," said Qwilleran. "If the Klingenschoen Fund makes an offer—and at this point I'm not sure they will—can we be certain that the Countess will sell?''

''That I can't answer,'' said the architect. ''Mary Duckworth thinks the woman is craftily playing cat and mouse with both sides. She can't possibly want to see her home demolished, and yet she's related to the Pennimans on her mother's side, and they're financial backers for the Gateway. Do you know the Pennimans?''

''I know they own the *Morning Rampage*,'' said Qwilleran, ''and as an alumnus of the *Daily Fluxion* I don't think highly of their paper.''

''Also they're big in radio, television, and God knows what else. Penniman is spelled P-O-W-E-R in this town. It would give me personally a lot of satisfaction to see that crew get their blocks knocked off.''

''This is going to be an interesting crusade,'' said Qwilleran. ''You understand, of course, that the Klingenschoen board doesn't meet till Thursday, and at this point it's just pie in the sky.''

The two men shook hands and promised to keep in touch.

From the Press Club Qwilleran wandered over to the public library, one of the few buildings in town that had not changed, except for the addition of a parking structure. It was forty times the size of the library in Pickax, and he wondered if Polly Duncan had ever seen it. She crossed his mind more often than he imagined she would. What would she think of the Casablanca elevators? The tenants? The conversation pit? The mushroom paintings? The gold faucets? The waterbed? He doubted that she had the objectivity to appreciate a building that looked like a refrigerator.

Browsing through the library's local history collection, he was gratified to find abundant material on the Casablanca in the years when Zwinger Boulevard was crowded with horses and carriages—later with Stanley Steamers and Columbus Electrics. Photos in sepia or black and white depicted presidents, financial wizards, and theater greats standing on the front steps of the building, or stepping from a Duesenberg with the assistance of a uniformed doorman, or dining in the Palm Pavilion on the roof. Women in satin hobble skirts and furs, escorted by men in opera cloaks and top hats, were shown departing for a charity ball. In the grassy park adjoining the building a bevy of nursemaids aired infants in perambulators, and overdressed children batted shuttlecocks with battledores. There was even a photo of the undersized swimming pool with male bathers wearing long-legged bathing suits.

What interested Qwilleran most were the pictures of Harrison Plumb with his little moustache, probably a souvenir of his Paris days. He was shown sometimes with his friend Grinchman, often with visiting dignitaries, frequently with his wife and three children, the boys in knee pants and little Adelaide with ringlets cascading below the brim of a flower-laden hat. In later photos Adelaide and her father posed in a Stutz Bearcat or at a tea table on the terrace. Qwilleran recalled hearing that the personalities and events of the past seep into the brick and stones and woodwork of an old building, giving it an aura. If true, that accounted for the Casablanca magic that Lowell had tried to describe.

Following his two-hour immersion in the gentle, elegant past, Qwilleran found the whizzing traffic hard to take. He walked home briskly because a cold breeze was blowing, and Zwinger Boulevard, with its high buildings, functioned as a wind tunnel. It had been called Eat Street by the *Fluxion* food editor, and Qwilleran counted a dozen ethnic restaurants not to be found in Moose County: Polynesian, Mexican, Japanese, Hungarian, Szechuan, and Middle Eastern, to name a few. He intended to try them all. He wished Polly were with him.

It was the end of the day, and tenants were converging on the Casablanca by car, bus, and taxi. Qwilleran, the only one to arrive on foot, checked the parking lot, hoping that his space might be vacant, but this time a 1975 jalopy was parked in #28.

As he joined the miscellaneous crew trooping through the front door, a man with a reddish moustache hailed him. "Hi! Did you move in?"

"Yes, I've joined the happy few," Qwilleran acknowledged.

"What floor?"

"Fourteen."

"Does the roof still leak?"

"I'll know better when it rains, but they claim to have fixed it yesterday."

"You must have connections. They never fix anything around here." He ran ahead to catch the elevator, and only then did Qwilleran realize that he was the friendly jogger who had helped him on his arrival Sunday afternoon.

In the lobby were workmen in coveralls carrying six-packs, boisterous students with bookbags, women dressed for success and carrying briefcases, and elderly inmates with canes and bandages and swollen legs. Together they created the atmosphere of a bus terminal and a hospital corridor.

Most tenants stopped in the mailroom to unlock their mailboxes, after which they looked sourly at what they found there. Upon entering the crowded cubicle, Qwilleran had to dodge a large hairless man wearing a T-shirt imprinted "Ferdie Le Bull." Next, a middle-aged woman in a sequin-studded black cocktail dress, looking anxiously at a handful of envelopes, collided with him.

"Sorry," he mumbled.

"Well, hello!" she said in a girlish voice, regarding his moustache appreciatively. "Where have they been hiding *you*?"

There was no mail in Qwilleran's box. It was too soon to hear from Polly, and other letters were being intercepted by his part-time secretary.

Rupert was standing by as if expecting an emergency, his red hat having the visibility of a fire hydrant. Mrs. Tuttle was sitting behind her desk, knitting, but keeping a stern eye on the engineering students. And among those waiting for the elevator was Amber, carrying a bag of groceries and looking tired.

Qwilleran asked her, "Is there an engineering school in the vicinity? These kids are always talking about bridges."

"They're from the dental school," she said. "Qwill, meet my neighbor on Eight, Courtney Hampton. Courtney, this is Jim Qwilleran. He's got Di's apartment on Fourteen."

The young man she introduced had square shoulders, slim hips, and a suit of the latest cut. He glanced at Qwilleran's boots and tweeds and said with a nasal twang, "Just in from the country?"

Amber said, "Courtney works at Kipper & Fine, the men's clothing store. What have you been doing all day, Qwill?"

"Walking around. Getting oriented. Everything has changed."

"The Casablanca will be the next to go," her neighbor predicted. "Don't unpack your luggage."

"I wonder what's on TV tonight?" Amber said with a weary sigh.

"As for me," said Courtney with a grandiose flourish of eyebrows, "if anyone is interested, I . . . am playing bridge . . . with the Countess tonight."

"La di da," said Amber.

Both elevators arrived simultaneously, and the crowd surged aboard, separating Qwilleran from the other two. As Old Green reluctantly ascended, it performed a sluggish ritual at each floor, first bouncing to a stop, then listlessly opening its door to unload a passenger, after which it waited a long minute, closed its door in slow motion, and crept upward to the next floor. No one spoke. Passengers were holding their collective breath.

It had been a long day, and Qwilleran was glad to be home, but when he opened the door of 14-A he was met by a blast of heat. The radiators were hissing and clanking, and both cats were stretched full-length on the floor, panting.

"What happened?" he demanded. "It must be 110 in here!" He hunted for a thermostat and, finding none, grabbed the housephone. "Mrs. Tuttle! Qwilleran in 14-A. What happened to the furnace? We're suffocating! The cats are half cooked! I expect the window glass to melt!"

"Open the windows," she said calmly. "Your side of the building heats up when a cold wind comes from the east. We don't have much control over it. The apartments on the east side are freezing, and the furnace works overtime to try to get them a little heat. Just open all your windows."

He did as he was told, and the Siamese revived sufficiently to sit up and take a little nourishment in the form of a can of red salmon. As for Qwilleran, he lost no time in going out to dinner. It occurred to him that he should invite Amber; she looked too tired to thaw whatever was in her grocery bag, and the temperature in her apartment might be insufferable, whether she lived on the frigid or sweltering side of the building. Yet, he disliked her line of conversation, and he believed that too soon an invitation might encourage her. In his present financial situation he had to be careful. Women used to be attracted to his ample moustache; now he feared they were attracted to his ample bank account.

Feeling guilty, he went to the nearest restaurant on Eat Street, which happened to be Japanese—a roomful of hibachi tables under lighted canopies, against a background of shoji screens and Japanese art. Each table seated eight around a large grill, and Qwilleran was conducted to a table where four persons were already seated.

He often dined alone and entertained himself by eavesdropping and composing scenarios about the other diners. At the hibachi table he found a young couple sipping tea from handleless gray cups and giggling about the chopsticks. The man was cloyingly attentive, and his companion kept admiring her ring finger. Newlyweds, Qwilleran decided. From the country. Honeymooning in the big city. They ordered chicken from the low end of the menu.

At the opposite end of the table two men in business suits were drinking sake martinis and ordering the lobster-steak-shrimp combination. On expense accounts, Qwilleran guessed. (He himself ordered the medium-priced teriyaki steak.) Upon further study, pursued surreptitiously, he decided that the man wearing a custom-tailored suit and ostentatious gold jewelry was treating the other man to dinner, his guest being a deferential sort in a suit off the rack and a shirt too loose around the neck. Also, he had a bandage on his ear. They were a curious pair—employer and employee, Qwilleran thought, judging by their respective attitudes. He had a feeling that he had seen that ear patch at the Casablanca—in the lobby or in the elevator. The man in question suddenly glanced in Qwilleran's direction, then mumbled something to his host, who turned to look at the newcomer with the oversized moustache. All of this Qwilleran observed from the corner of his eye, enjoying it immensely.

Conversation at the table halted when the Japanese chef appeared—an imposing figure in his stovepipe hat, two feet tall, and his leather knife holster. He bowed curtly and whipped out his steel spatulas, which he proceeded to wield with the aplomb of a symphony percussionist. The audience was speechless as he manipulated the splash of egg, the hill of sliced mushrooms, and the mountain of rice. Steaks, seafood, and chicken breasts sizzled in butter and were doused with seasonings and flamed in wine. Then the chef drew his formidable knife, cubed the meat and served the food on rough-textured gray plates. With a quick bow he said, ''Have a nice evening,'' and disappeared.

Qwilleran was the only one who used chopsticks, having acquired virtuosity when he was an overseas correspondent.

Watching him in admiration, the bride said, ''You're good at that.''

''I've been practicing,'' he said. ''Is this your first time here?''

"Yes," she said. "We think it's neat, don't we, honey?"

"Yeah, it's neat," said her groom.

When Qwilleran left the restaurant it was dark, and he took the precaution of hailing a taxi. It was mid-evening now, and the main floor of the Casablanca was deserted. Most of the tenants were eating dinner or watching TV. The students were doing their homework, and the old folks had retired for the night.

As Qwilleran waited for Old Red, the door opened. The young woman who stepped out could only be described as a vision! She had a model's figure and an angel's face, enhanced by incredibly artful makeup. He stared after her and confirmed that she had also a model's walk and an heiress's clothing budget. He blew copiously into his moustache.

After Old Red, scented with expensive perfume, had transported him to Fourteen, which was really Thirteen, he greeted the Siamese in a daze, saying, "You wouldn't believe what I've just seen!"

"Yow!" said Koko, rising on his hind legs.

"Sorry. No samples tonight. How's the temperature? A little better? I apologize for the sauna. How would you guys like a read?"

Shedding his street clothes gratefully and getting into his pajama bottoms, Qwilleran intended to read another chapter of Kinglake's *Eothen*. It may have been his imagination, but the Siamese seemed to enjoy the references to camels, goats, and beasts of burden. Their ears always twitched and their whiskers curled. It was uncanny.

So the three of them filed into the library, Koko leading the way with tail erect as a flagpole, followed by Yum Yum slinking sinuously, one dainty foot in front of the other, exactly like that girl in the lobby, Qwilleran thought. He brought up the rear, wearing the bottoms of the Valentine-red pajamas that Polly had given him the previous February.

The library was the most livable room in the apartment, made friendly with shelves of art books and walls of paintings. The furniture was contemporary teakwood and chrome created by big-name designers whose names Qwilleran had forgotten. He dropped into an inviting chair and turned to chapter ten, while Yum Yum turned around three times on his lap and settled down with chin on paw. Koko had just assumed his posture of eager listener when a slight noise elsewhere catapulted both cats out of the library and into the foyer. Qwilleran followed and found Koko scratching at something under the door. An envelope had been pushed halfway underneath.

There was no name on it, but it contained a sheet of heavy notepaper embossed with a W, and the following message had been written with an unsteady hand:

"Welcome to the Casablanca. Come down and have a drink with me—any time." It was signed by Isabelle Wilburton of apartment 10-F, the one who wanted to sell her baby grand piano.

Qwilleran growled into his moustache and

tossed the note into the wastebasket, being careful not to crumple it. Crumpled paper was like catnip to Yum Yum, and she would retrieve it in three seconds. All his life it had been his compulsive habit to crumple paper before discarding it, but those days were gone forever. Amazing, he thought, how one adjusts to living with cats. A few years before, if anyone had suggested such a thing, he would have called that person a blasted fool.

Back in the library he turned once more to chapter ten, but a slight quiver on his upper lip caused him to put the book down. He passed a hand over his moustache as if to calm the disturbing sensation. "Let's sit quietly and think for a while," he said to the waiting listeners. "We've been here for forty-eight hours and I'm getting some vibrations."

The fact that someone had been murdered on the premises did not bother Qwilleran; it was Koko's interest in the incident that alerted him. That cat knew everything! First he found the bloodstain under a heavy piece of furniture, and then he found the gold bracelet buried in the upholstery of a sofa. Koko had an instinct for sinister truths hidden beneath the surface.

Qwilleran himself, after reading the newspaper accounts, questioned the motive of the "nice, quiet, young man" who brutally knifed his benefactor, his "best friend," to whom he had given a gold bracelet inscribed with an intimate code. Ross may have blamed the gallery because his paintings failed to sell, but that was a weak excuse for murder. It was Todd who gave the *Fluxion* that frail scrap of information, Todd with his nervous habit of nose-pinching. What did *that* signify?

The news that Di Bessinger had been named heir to the Casablanca also raised suspicions in Qwilleran's mind. Many powerful interests opposed her. It was definitely to their advantage to have her out of the picture. Even her own partner disagreed with her on the preservation of the old building and was now planning to move the gallery to the Gateway Alcazar. But none of this explained the role of Ross Rasmus as the hit man.

"What's your opinion, Koko?" Qwilleran asked.

The cat was not listening. He was craning his neck and staring toward the foyer. A moment later there was a frantic banging on the front door. Qwilleran hurried to the scene and yanked the door open, catching a wild-eyed woman with fists raised, ready to pound the door panels again. She screamed, "The building's on fire!"

EIGHT

JUST AS THE woman from 14-B screamed "Fire!" Qwilleran smelled smoke and heard the sirens.

"Don't take the elevator!" she cried as she dashed for the stairwell in a terrycloth robe.

He jammed the cats unceremoniously into their carrier, grabbed his pajama top, and started down the stairs, assuming that the boilers had over-heated in their battle with the bitter east wind. Other tenants joined the downward trek at every floor, most of them grumbling and whining.

"Why are we doing this? The building's fire-proof," one protested.

"My husband's watching football on TV, and he won't budge," said a woman. "I say: Let him burn!"

"Smells like burning chicken to me," said another.

"Did they ring the firebell? I didn't hear it. My neighbor banged on my door. They're supposed to ring the firebell."

"Betcha ten bucks the Countess ain't walkin' down."

By the time the disgruntled refugees reached the main floor, the lobby was filled with a hubbub of voices raised in alarm or indignation, while Mrs. Tuttle tried to calm them. They were a motley assemblage in various states of undress: women with hair curlers and no makeup; hairy-legged men in nightshirts; old tenants without their dentures; bald tenants without their hair-pieces. Qwilleran was conspicuous in his red pajamas. A few persons were clutching treasured possessions or squawling cats, and the Siamese in their carrier yowled and shrieked in the spirit of the occasion. Among the refugees was a man in a washed-out seersucker robe that might have been purloined from a hospital. He had thinning hair, a pale face, and a white patch where his right ear should be; Qwilleran recognized his fellow diner from the hibachi table.

Fortunately for the underclad residents, the lobby was on the warm side of the building. Those from the cold side were threatening to bring their mattresses and sleep on the lobby floor. Mrs. Tuttle was doing a heroic job of controlling the crowd.

Then an elevator door opened, and firemen in black rubber coats and boots, carrying red-handled axes, stepped out. "Go back to bed, folks," they said, grinning. "Only a chicken burning."

The tenants would have been happier if it had been a real fire.

"What! I walked down six flights for a chicken?"

"I knew it was a chicken. I know burning chicken when I smell it."

"Somebody put it in the oven to thaw and went out to the bar and forgot it."

"Whoever done it, they should kick 'em out."

"They're gonna kick us all out pretty soon."

The crowd began to disperse, some boarding the elevators and some heading for the stairwells, while others hung around the lobby, welcoming the opportunity for social fellowship.

The Siamese, following their rude experience among angry tenants and complaining cats, were understandably upset. Qwilleran, too, was restless and perhaps slightly lonesome, although he would not have admitted it. He considered it too late to call Polly but took a chance on phoning Arch Riker. "How's everything in Pickax?" he asked his old friend.

"I wondered when you were going to report in," said the editor. "Everything's just the way you left it—no snow yet."

"Any world-shaking news?"

"We had some excitement today. One of the conservation officers spotted a bald eagle near Wildcat Junction."

"What did you do? Put out an extra?"

"I'll blue-pencil that cynical remark. You talk like city folks."

"Have you seen Polly?"

"Yes—at a library meeting tonight. She showed slides of her trip to England. She told me she'd heard from you."

"What's happening at the paper?"

"Hixie sold a full-page ad to Iris Cobb's son. He's going into business up here."

"Watch her! He's happily married," Qwilleran said.

"And we ran a notice in the sick column that old man Dingleberry is in the hospital for observation."

"Of the nurses, no doubt. That old roué is ninety-five and thinks he's twenty-five."

"What about you?" asked Riker. "What have you been doing?"

"Nothing much. Dropped into the *Flux* office today . . . Had lunch twice at the Press Club . . . Bumped into Lieutenant Hames. There's a whole string of new restaurants on Zwinger that you'd like, Arch. So far I've tried North Italian and Japanese. Why don't you fly down for a few days?"

"Can't right now. There's a special edition coming out for deer season, and we're sponsoring a contest for hunters. What do you think of the Casablanca?"

"Not bad for an old building, and the sunsets from the fourteenth floor are spectacular."

"That's one thing the city does well," said Riker. "Sunsets! That's because of the dirt in the atmosphere."

"My apartment has a skylighted living room, a terrace, a waterbed, gold faucets, and a library of art books that you wouldn't believe."

"How do you do it, Qwill? You always luck out. How do the cats react to the altitude?"

"No complaints, although I think Koko is disappointed by the scarcity of pigeons."

"Have you decided about the restoration?"

"I've done some research and had a couple of conferences. Today I met with the architect, and next I'm going to meet the owner of the building, so it's coming right along. You know, Arch, what we have here is King Tut's tomb, waiting to be excavated."

"Well, stay out of trouble, chum," said Riker, "and don't forget to send us some copy."

After delivering this upbeat report, Qwilleran felt better, and he retired, allowing the Siamese to share the waterbed because of their disturbed state of mind. Yum Yum particularly liked the sensation.

On Wednesday morning he telephoned Mary Duckworth. He said, "I've read the Grinchman report and I'm ready to meet the Countess. When can you arrange it?"

"How about this afternoon at four?"

"How do I dress?"

"I'd suggest a suit and tie. And she doesn't permit smoking."

"No problem. I've given up my pipe," Qwilleran said. "I found out the smoke is bad for the Siamese."

"I've given up cigarettes," she said. "My doctor finally convinced me the smoke is bad for antique furniture. Have you talked to Jefferson Lowell?"

"We had lunch. Nice guy."

"Are you convinced, Qwill?"

"I don't know as yet. Where shall we meet?"

"At the front door a few minutes before four. One is always prompt when calling on the Countess."

Before having his hair cut, his moustache trimmed, his good gray suit pressed, and his shoes shined, Qwilleran checked the weather on the radio and learned that a woman shopper had been abducted from a supermarket parking lot; a jogger had been beaten by hoodlums in Penniman Park; and rain was predicted, clearing in midafternoon. He taxied around town to do his errands, had a quick lunch at the Junktown deli, and returned to 14-A early enough to spend a little quality time with the Siamese. He proposed another chapter of *Eothen*, and the cats followed him into the library, but Koko had other ideas. He jumped to the library table and started pawing furiously.

Koko was known to be a bibliophile, and on the six-foot library table there were large-format art books reproducing the work of Michelangelo,

Renoir, Van Gogh, Wyeth, and others, although the cat usually preferred small volumes that he could easily knock off a bookshelf.

"What are you doing, you crazy animal?" Qwilleran said.

Koko had found a long flat box among the art books. It looked like leather, and it was labeled "Scrabble." The blank tile found by Yum Yum had obviously strayed from this box. Opening it, Qwilleran found a hundred or so small tiles, each with a single letter of the alphabet. The sight was like a B-12 shot to one who had won all the spelling bees in grade school and had been an orthographic snob ever since. He sat down at the desk, opened the game board, and read the rules out of sheer curiosity.

"This is easy," he said. Scooping up a handful of tiles at random he spelled words like QADI and JAGIR. Years of playing a dictionary game with Koko had given him a vocabulary of esoteric words that he had little opportunity to use. Soon he was building a crossword arrangement on the board. It began with CAD, grew to CADMIUM, and intercepted with SLUMP. This connected with EGRETS and OLPE.

The Siamese watched, patiently waiting for their quality time, but Qwilleran was fascinated by the lettered tiles and the small numerals that gave the value of each letter. All too soon it was time to put on his gray suit and meet Mary Duckworth on the main floor. Before leaving the apartment, he slipped a piece of fruit in his suitcoat pocket.

"You look splendid!" she said when they met, although she gave a brief qualifying glance at the bulge in his pocket.

They rang for the private elevator at the bronze door and rode up to Twelve in a carpeted car with rosewood walls and a velvet-covered bench. The ride was no faster than Old Red or Old Green, but it was smoother and quieter.

On the way up, Qwilleran mentioned, "You knew that Di Bessinger was going to inherit the Casablanca?"

Mary nodded regretfully.

"Who gets it now?"

"Various charities. Qwill, I don't know what you're expecting, but the Plumb apartment may come as a surprise. It's done in vintage Art Deco."

They stepped off the elevator into a large foyer banded in horizontal panels of coral, burgundy, and bottle green, defined by thin strips of copper, and the floor was ceramic tile in a metallic copper glaze. Everything was slightly dulled with age. A pair of angular chairs flanked an angular console on which were two dozen tea roses reflected in a large round mirror.

Mary pressed a doorbell disguised as a miniature Egyptian head, and they waited before double doors sheathed in tooled copper. When the doors opened, they were confronted by a formidable man in a coral-colored coat.

"Good afternoon, Ferdinand," said Mary. "Miss Adelaide is expecting us. This is Mr. Qwilleran."

"Sure. You know where to go." The houseman waved a hamlike hand toward the drawing room. He had the build of a linebacker, with beefy shoulders, a bull neck, and a bald head. The Countess's live-in bodyguard, Qwilleran guessed, doubled as butler. "She was late gettin' up from her nap," the man said, "and then she had to have her hair fixed. She fired the old girl that fixed it, and the new girl is kinda slow."

"Interesting," said Mary stiffly.

The drawing room was more than Qwilleran could assimilate at a glance. What registered was a peach-colored marble floor scattered with geometric-patterned rugs, and peach walls banded in copper and hung with large round mirrors.

Mary motioned him to sit in a tub-shaped chair composed of plump rolls of overstuffed black leather stacked on chrome legs. "You're sitting in an original Bibendum chair from the 1920s," she said.

His gaze went from item to item: The tea table was tortoiseshell; all lamps had bulbous bases; the windows were frosted glass crisscrossed with copper grillwork. Everything was somewhat faded, and there was a sepulchral silence.

Ferdinand followed them into the drawing room. "You never been here before," he said to Qwilleran.

"This is my first visit."

"You play bridge?"

"I'm afraid not."

"She likes to play bridge."

"So I have heard," said Qwilleran with a glance at Mary. She was sitting tight-lipped and haughty.

"She likes all kinds of games," said the houseman. "Is it still raining?"

"It stopped about an hour ago."

"We had some good weather this week."

"Very true."

"I used to wrestle on TV," said the big man.

"Is that so?" Qwilleran wished he had brought his pocket tape recorder.

"I was Ferdie Le Bull. That's what they called me." The houseman unbuttoned his coral coat and exhibited a T-shirt stenciled with the name. "You never saw me wrestle?"

"I never had that pleasure."

"Here she comes now," Ferdinand announced.

Adelaide St. John Plumb was a small unprepossessing woman who carried her head cocked graciously to one side and spoke in a breathy little-girl voice. "So good of you to come." Brown hair plastered flat against her head in uniform waves contrasted absurdly with her pale aging skin, a network of fine wrinkles. So did the penciled eyebrows and red Cupid's-bow mouth. She was wearing a peach chiffon tea gown and long strands of gold beads.

Her guests rose. Mary said, "Miss Plumb, may I present James Qwilleran."

"So happy to meet you," said their hostess.

"*Enchanté!*" said Qwilleran, bending low over her hand in a courtly gesture. Then he drew from his pocket a perfect Bosc pear with bronze skin and long, curved stem, offering it in the palm of his hand like a jewel-encrusted Fabergé bauble. "The perfect complement for your beautiful apartment, Mademoiselle."

The Countess was a trifle slow in responding. "How charming . . . Please be seated . . . Ferdinand, you may bring the tea tray." She seated herself gracefully on an overstuffed sofa in front of the tortoiseshell tea table. "I trust you are well, Mary?"

"Quite well, thank you. And you, Miss Adelaide?"

"Very well. Did it rain today?"

"Yes, rather briskly."

The hostess turned to Qwilleran, inclining her head winningly. "You have recently arrived from the east?"

"From the north," he corrected her. "Four hundred miles north."

"How cold it must be!"

Mary said, "Mr. Qwilleran is spending the winter here to escape the snow and ice."

"How lovely! I hope you will enjoy your stay, Mr . . ."

"Qwilleran."

"Do you play bridge?"

"I regret to say that bridge is not one of my accomplishments," he said, "but I have a considerable aptitude for Scrabble."

Mary expressed surprise, and the Countess expressed delight. "How nice! You must join me in a game some evening."

Ferdinand, wearing white cotton gloves, placed

a silver tea tray before her—cubistic in design with ebony trim—and the hostess performed the tea ritual with well-practiced gestures.

"Mr. Qwilleran is a writer," said Mary.

"How wonderful! What do you write?"

"I plan to write a book on the history of the Casablanca," he said, astonishing Mary once more. "The public library has a large collection of photos, including many of yourself, Miss Plumb."

"Do they have pictures of my dear father?"

"Quite a few."

"I would adore seeing them." She tilted her head prettily.

"Do you have many recollections of the early Casablanca?"

"Yes indeed! I was born here—in this very suite—with a midwife, a nurse, and two doctors in attendance. My father was Harrison Wills Plumb—a wonderful man! I hardly remember my mother. She was related to the Pennimans. She died when I was only four. There was an influenza epidemic, and my mother and two brothers were stricken. All three of them died in one week, leaving me as my father's only consolation. I was four years old."

Mary said, "Tell Mr. Qwilleran how you happened to escape the epidemic."

"It was a miracle! My nurse—I think her name was Hedda—asked permission to take me to the mountains where it would be healthier. We stayed there—the two of us—in a small cabin, living on onions and molasses and tea . . . I shudder to think of it. But neither of us became ill. I returned to my home to find only my father alive—a shattered man! I was four years old.''

Ferdinand's clumsy hands, in white gloves the size of an outfielder's mitt, passed a silver salver of pound cake studded with caraway seeds.

The Countess went on. ''I was all my father had left in the world, and he lavished me with attention and lovely things. I adored him!''

''Did he send you away to school?'' Qwilleran asked.

''I was schooled at home by private tutors, because my father refused to allow me out of his sight. We went everywhere together—to the symphony and opera and charity balls. When we traveled abroad each year we were entertained royally in Paris and always dined at the captain's table aboard ship. I called Father my best beau, and he sent me tea roses and cherry cordials . . . Ferdinand, you may pass the bonbons.''

The big hands passed a tiny footed candy dish in which three chocolate-covered cherries rested on a linen doily.

Qwilleran took the opportunity to say, ''You have a handsomely designed apartment, Miss Plumb.''

''Thank you, Mr . . .''

''Qwilleran.''

''Yes, my dear father designed it following one of our visits to Paris. A charming Frenchman with a little moustache spent a year in rebuilding the entire suite. I quite fell in love with him,'' she said, cocking her head coquettishly. ''Artisans came from the Continent to do the work. It was an exciting time for a young girl.''

''Do you remember any of the people who lived here at that time? Do you recall any names?''

''Oh, yes! There were the Pennimans, of course. My mother was related to them . . . and the Duxbury family; they were bankers . . . and the Teahandles and Wilburtons and Greystones. All the important families had complete suites or *pieds-à-terre.*''

''How about visiting celebrities? President Coolidge? Caruso? The Barrymores?''

''I'm sure they stayed here, but . . . life was such a whirl in those days, and I was only a young girl. Forgive me if I don't remember.''

''I suppose you dined in the rooftop restaurant.''

''The Palm Pavilion. Yes indeed! My father and I had our own table with a lovely view, and all the serving men knew our favorite dishes. I adored bananas Foster! The captain always prepared it at our table. On nice days we would have tea on the terrace. I made my debut in the Palm Pavilion, wearing an adorable white beaded dress.''

''I enjoy that same view from my apartment,'' Qwilleran said. ''I'm staying where Dianne Bessinger used to live. I understand you knew her well.''

The Countess lowered her eyes sadly. ''I miss her a great deal. We used to play Scrabble twice a week. Such a pity she was struck down so early in life. She simply passed away in her sleep. Her heart failed.''

Qwilleran shot a glance at Mary and found her frowning at him. Furthermore, Ferdinand was standing by with arms folded, looking grim.

Mary rose. ''Thank you so much, Miss Adelaide, for inviting us.''

''It was a pleasure, my dear. And Mr. Qwillen, I hope you will join me at the bridge table soon.''

''Not bridge,'' he said. ''Scrabble.''

''Yes, of course. I shall look forward to seeing you again.''

Ferdinand followed the two guests to the foyer and whipped out a dog-eared pad and the stub of a pencil. ''Friday, Saturday, and Sunday is full up,'' he said. ''Nobody's comin' tomorrow. She needs somebody for tomorrow.'' He looked menacingly at Qwilleran. ''Tomorrow? Eight o'clock?'' It sounded less like an invitation and more like a royal command.

''Eight o'clock will be fine,'' Qwilleran said as they stepped into the waiting elevator. Once in its rosewood and velvet privacy they both talked at once.

He said, ''Where did she find that three-hundred-pound butler?''

Mary said, ''I thought you didn't play games, Qwill.''

''Her hair is like Eleanor Roosevelt's in the Thirties.''

''I almost choked when you handed her that pear.''

"She doesn't even know that Dianne was murdered!"

As they stepped out of the rosewood elevator on the main floor, the workaday crowd was pouring through the front door. They stared at the privileged pair.

Qwilleran said, "I'll walk out of the building with you, Mary. I want to check the parking lot. I've been here since Sunday, and five different cars have been parked in my space." As they approached the lot he asked, "May I ask you a question?"

"Of course."

"What do you think was the artist's motive for killing his patron?"

"Jealousy," she said with finality.

"You mean he had a rival?"

"Not just one," she replied with a knowing grimace. "Di liked variety."

"Were you friendly with her?"

"I admired what she was trying to accomplish, and I admit she had charisma, or people would never have rallied around SOCK the way they did."

Qwilleran stroked his moustache. "Could there have been anything political about her murder?"

"What do you mean?"

They had arrived at the entrance to the parking lot, and Mary was looking at her wristwatch.

"We'll talk about it another time. Perhaps we could have dinner some evening," he suggested.

"If we arrange it for a Sunday or Monday," she

said, adopting her usual businesslike delivery, "I'm sure Roberto would like to join us."

Qwilleran said it would be a good idea. He had lost his personal interest in Mary. Yet, it was a remarkable fact that she was the only woman Koko had ever actively approved. The cat discouraged Melinda, antagonized Cokey, and feuded openly with Rosemary. As for Polly, he tolerated her because she had a soothing voice, but he endorsed Mary Duckworth because she was an opportunist, and so was he! Koko knew a kindred spirit when he sniffed one. Also in her favor was the entire case of canned lobster she had given the Siamese three years before. That's the way it was with cats!

While Mary returned to the Blue Dragon, Qwilleran zigzagged his way through the parking lot, avoiding potholes filled with rainwater. To his surprise, slot #28 was finally vacant. Now he could move the Purple Plum into its rightful space. He pulled out his car keys, but there was something wrong with the purplish-blue metallic four-door parked in #27. It appeared to have sunk into the ground! Actually, it had four flat tires.

NINE

WHETHER THE TIRES of the Purple Plum were slashed or the valves were loosened, it made no difference to Qwilleran. In high dudgeon he strode toward the building entrance. Halfway there he stopped and considered: If he left the scene, someone could pull into the lot and turn into his legal parking space. He returned to #28 and stood between the yellow lines—or lines that had been yellow once upon a time. He took up his position with a belligerent stance and folded arms and fierce expression made more intimidating by his rambunctious moustache.

The first car to pull into the lot was a BMW. Hmmm, Qwilleran murmured to himself. What was a BMW doing in the Casablanca parking lot? The driver parked several slots away and walked slowly toward the building entrance. It was a woman. She walked seductively. She was dressed exquisitely. She was the vision he had seen in the lobby the night before.

"Excuse me, miss," he said in his richest, most mellifluent tones. "Are you going into the building?" He was glad he was wearing a suit and tie.

"That was my intention," she replied in a silky voice.

He had no time for pleasurable reactions. "Kindly do me a favor," he asked. "Tell Mrs. Tuttle to send Rupert out here. Someone has slashed my tires." He gestured toward the dejected vehicle slumped in the adjoining slot.

"Who would have the temerity to perpetrate such a reprehensible act?" she replied.

Qwilleran thought, She's not real; she's a robot; she's programmed; she's from outer space. Calmly he said, "I was parked in his—or her—space because my own was occupied by someone else, and I suppose he—or she—resented it. Have you had any trouble like that?"

"Fortunately I seem immune to hostility," she replied. "I shall be happy to send the custodian to your assistance."

"Watch out for the puddles," he advised. "They're a foot deep."

She gave him a languid smile and walked toward the building. In a state of transfixion Qwilleran watched her go, breathing lustily into his moustache.

When Rupert arrived a few minutes later, it was determined that the tires were not slashed. Someone had tampered with the valves, and Rupert knew a garage that would come right over with portable airtanks.

"Who pays for #27?" Qwilleran demanded.

"I dunno."

"Well, as soon as the tires are inflated, I'm going to move my car into my own slot and leave it there for the rest of the winter. I'll walk, or take the bus . . . By the way, who is the woman who drives the BMW?"

"Winnie Wingfoot," said Rupert. "She's a model. Lives on Ten."

"Is that her real name?"

"I dunno. I guess so."

If Qwilleran entertained any thoughts of revenge against the reprehensible perpetrator, they were mollified by thoughts of Winnie Wingfoot. He floated up to Fourteen on Old Red, changed absentmindedly into red pajamas instead of his gray warm-up suit, and fed the cats twice. For his own dinner he phoned for pizza.

"Casablanca? What floor?" asked the order taker.

"Fourteen."

"We don't deliver in that building any higher than Three."

"Send it over. I'll meet the delivery man at the front door," Qwilleran said.

He walked down to the main floor for the sake of the exercise and encountered the jogger between Eleven and Ten. The man was running up the stairs. Between aerobic gasps he explained, "Too muddy . . . round the . . . vacant lots." Then he added, "You going . . . to bed early?"

Only then did Qwilleran realize his Freudian slip. He returned to the penthouse and changed from red pajamas into gray warm-ups.

In the lobby a white-haired man was taking his constitutional by walking briskly the length of the hallway and back, swinging his arms and taking exaggerated strides. A few stragglers were picking up their mail. The Asian woman was coming in with her two children, and Amber was on her way out.

"I've been trying to get you on the phone," she said. "Courtney wants me to bring you to dinner at his place Saturday night. You remember—the Kipper & Fine salesman."

"What's the occasion?"

"Nothing. He just likes to show off. He can be a nerd sometimes, but the food's always good—better than I cook—and he knows all the gossip."

"I accept," said Qwilleran without further deliberation.

"Cocktails at six. Come as you are," she said. "Are you waiting for someone?"

"The pizza man. By the way, Amber, I'm ashamed to admit I don't know your last name."

She said something like "Cowbell."

"Spell it."

"K-o-w-b-e-l. Here comes your pizza, Qwill. Gotta dash. I'm late."

The pizza was good—better than any he had found in Moose County, he had to admit. He gave the Siamese a taste of the cheese and a nibble of the pepperoni. Then he pushbuttoned a pot of coffee and carried it into the library. He intended to study his Scrabble—particularly the scoring rules and the value of the various letters—in preparation for his forthcoming joust with the Countess. He unfolded the board and deployed the tiles on the teakwood-and-chrome card table, then started building crosswords, playing for premium squares as well as high-value words. Koko was on hand, watching the process in his nearsighted way. Abruptly the cat lifted his head and listened. A minute or so later, there was a knock at the apartment door.

No one had buzzed from the vestibule, so it was obviously a resident, and a fantasy flashed through Qwilleran's mind: It was the beauteous Winnie Wingfoot! Then again, he reflected, it might be Rupert. Nevertheless, he gave the mirror a quick glance, smoothed his moustache, and finger-combed his hair before opening the door.

A woman was standing there, wearing a fur coat, and it was not Winnie Wingfoot. It was Isabelle, the middle-aged tippler, and she was carrying a bottle. He regarded her without speaking.

"Hello," she said.

"Good evening," he replied coolly.

"Like a drink?" she asked, looking flirtatious

and waving the bottle. Her other hand clutched the coat, and he hesitated to guess what she might have under it, if anything.

"No thanks, I'm on the wagon, but thanks for the offer," he said in a monotone intended to discourage her.

"Can I come in?" she asked.

"You must forgive me, but I'm working and I have a deadline."

"Don'cha wanna take your mind off your work?" She opened her coat, and Qwilleran's wildest surmise was confirmed.

He said, "You'd better bundle up before you catch cold." Gently he closed the door, hearing a vulgar remark as he did so.

Huffing into his moustache, he returned to the library. "That was Isabelle," he told Koko. "Too bad it wasn't Winnie. She has a better vocabulary."

At that moment he felt an uncomfortable desire to talk with Polly Duncan in Moose County, even though the eleven o'clock discount was not yet in effect. He dialed anyway.

"I'm so glad you called, Qwill," she said. "I was just thinking about you. How is life in the wicked city?"

"You'd be surprised how wicked," he said. "Today someone let the air out of my tires, and tonight a female flasher presented herself at my door."

"Oh, no! Qwill, you must have been encouraging her!"

"All I did was pick her up off the floor when

she fell out of the phone booth. How are things in Moose County?''

''I'm starting to pack things to go into storage. Bootsie is helping me by jumping into every carton. He's adorable, but he's a monomaniac about food, Qwill—tries to steal it right off my fork!''

''He's growing. He'll get over it. Koko and Yum Yum have gone through all kinds of phases.''

''How do they like it down there?''

''Yum Yum has discovered the waterbed and gets some kind of catly thrill out of it. Koko and I are learning to play Scrabble. I have a Scrabble date with the Countess tomorrow night.''

''Is she very glamorous?'' Polly inquired anxiously.

''Not exactly. She's a gracious hostess but out of touch with reality. I don't know how I'm going to talk real-estate business with her.''

''Is the Casablanca as wonderful as you thought?''

''Yes and no, but I'd like to write a book about its history. I wish you were here, Polly, so we could discuss it.''

''I wish I were, too. I miss you, Qwill.''

''There are some interesting restaurants we could explore.''

''Qwill, something has been worrying me. Suppose I move into your apartment—''

''Hold it!'' he shouted into the phone. ''I can't hear you!'' There was a prolonged wait during which a helicopter circled overhead. ''Okay, Polly. Sorry. What were you saying? A helicopter was hovering over the building and creating pandemonium. The cats hate it!''

''What's happening?'' she asked.

''Who knows? They're up there every night, sometimes shining their searchlight into my window.''

''Why, that's terrible! Isn't that unconstitutional?''

''Now what were you saying about moving into my apartment?''

''Suppose I move in, and then the Casablanca project falls through and you decide to come home!''

''We'll cross that bridge when we come to it,'' Qwilleran said. ''Call me if anything interesting happens, or even if it doesn't.''

''I will, dearest.''

''A bientôt,'' he said with feeling.

''A bientôt.''

Sometimes he wished he could find the words to express what he wanted to say to Polly. Though a professional wordsmith, he was tongue-tied with this woman of whom he was so fond, but she understood. Feeling suddenly bereft of human companionship, he considered calling Amber Kowbel but decided he was not as bereft as all that.

On the Scrabble table Koko was sitting tall in his impudent pose, with ears askew and whiskers tilted. He had been up to some kind of mischief; Qwilleran could read the signals. A brief search revealed a scattering of Scrabble tiles on the floor under the table.

155

"You joker! You think that's funny!"

"Rrrrrrrrrrrr," said the cat.

"What's this new noise you're making? It sounds like a Scrabble tile stuck in your throat."

Qwilleran stooped to gather up the tiles, and at the same instant Koko jumped from the table with a flip of his tail that struck the man on the cheek, stinging like a whip.

"Please! Watch your tail!"

Koko walked stiff-legged from the room, turning once to look scornfully over his shoulder. Koko's scorn had an edge like a knife.

Qwilleran wondered, Did I say something wrong? Is he trying to tell me something?

Compulsively he tried to make a word out of the tiles that Koko had dislodged: H, R, O, S, B, X, and A. On the first try he came up with SOAR, but that was worth only four points. BOAR was good for six. (He was beginning to think in terms of scoring.) HOAR was even better—seven points—but HOAX added up to fourteen. Qwilleran congratulated himself; he was getting the hang of it.

Out in the foyer Koko was warbling his new tune: "Rrrrrrrrrrr!"

TEN

ON THURSDAY MORNING, when Qwilleran was brushing the Siamese and giving them their daily dose of flattery, he was interrupted by a phone call from Jeff Lowell of Grinchman & Hills. "I hear you're going to do a book on the Casablanca," he said.

"News travels fast."

"I saw Mary Duckworth last night. The reason I'm calling—we have photographs in our archives of both exterior and interior, taken in 1901. You're welcome to use them. We even have shots of Harrison Plumb's Moorish suite on Twelve with its carved lattices and decorative tiles and iron gates—fantastic!''

"Was the Art Deco renovation ever photographed?''

"Not to my knowledge. Our firm wasn't involved with that.''

"It should be photographed. Could you recommend someone to do it?''

"Sure could!'' He mentioned a name that sounded like Sorg Butra.

"Spell it,'' Qwilleran asked.

"S-o-r-g B-u-t-r-a. Want me to tell him you're interested?''

"Just give me his phone number. I haven't broached the subject to the Countess as yet. Did Mary mention anything else I discussed? About the Bessinger murder?''

"No, I just saw her briefly in a theater lobby.''

"I have a theory I'd like to try out on you, whenever we can get together.''

"Well, I'm leaving for San Francisco right now, but I'll get in touch when I get back. Enjoyed lunch on Tuesday, Qwill.''

"So did I. Have a good trip, Jeff.''

"Nice guy,'' he said to the cats when he resumed the brushing. "I never met an architect I didn't like.''

"Ik ik ik,'' said Koko.

"Now what does that mean?''

The phone rang again, and this time it was from the *Daily Fluxion* police bureau.

"Sure, Matt, I'm always interested in ideas,''

Qwilleran said. "What's on your mind? . . . Well, I don't know about that. Hames is a smart cop, but he goes overboard about Koko . . . Yes, I admit he's a remarkable cat, but . . . Okay, Matt, let me think about it. Why don't we have lunch? . . . See you at the Press Club at noon."

"That was Matt Thiggamon," he explained to the cats afterward. "He wants to do a story on you, Koko—on your sleuthing. How does that grab you?"

Koko rolled over, thrust one leg skyward, and proceeded to groom the base of his tail.

"I assume you're giving him the leg. I agree with you. We don't want any publicity, but I'm taking him to lunch anyway. I wonder what the weather is going to be."

He tuned in the newscast and learned that a law clerk who had been fired returned and shot his boss and the boss's secretary; a city councilman was found to have more than a hundred unpaid parking tickets; and the weather would be cold and overcast with a slight chance of showers. In Pickax, he reflected, WPKX would be announcing that a bow-hunter had bagged an eight-point buck, and a fourteen-year-old girl had won the quilt contest.

To create a stir at the Press Club, Qwilleran wore a plaid flannel shirt, a field jacket, and his Aussie hat. Matt said enviously, "You're really living the life, Qwill!"

They sat at a table in a far corner of the bar. "I wish I had a nickel," Qwilleran remarked, "for every time Arch Riker and I had lunch at this table.''

''I hear he was a great guy,'' said Matt. ''He left just before I joined the staff. What's he doing now?''

''He's editor and publisher of our small newspaper up north. It's called the *Moose County Something.*''

''And what do you do up there?''

''I'm busier in my retirement than I was when I wrote for the *Fluxion*. Merely keeping up with the local gossip can be a full-time occupation in a small town.''

They ordered French onion soup and roast beef sandwiches, and Qwilleran specified horseradish. There had been a time when every waitress in the club knew that Qwilleran liked horseradish with beef, but those days were past.

Matt said, ''Is that your cat's picture in the lobby?''

''Yes, that's Koko. He's a lifetime member of the Press Club, and he has his own press card signed by the chief of police.''

''Hames says he's psychic.''

''All cats are psychic to a degree. If you pick up a can opener, they know whether you're going to open a can of catfood or a can of green beans. They can be sound asleep at the other end of the house, but all you have to do is *think about salmon*, and they're right there! I have to admit, though,'' Qwilleran said with thinly veiled pride, ''that Koko goes the average cat one better. Perhaps you've heard about the pottery murders on River

Road. Koko solved that case before the police knew a crime had been committed. Prior to that there was a major theft in Muggy Swamp, and then a shooting at the Villa Verandah, and later a high death rate among antique dealers in Junktown. Koko investigated all those incidents successfully—not that he did anything uncatlike. He just sniffed and scratched and shoved things around, coming up with pertinent clues. I don't want him to have any publicity, however; it might go to his head and cause him to give up sleuthing. Cats are perverse and unpredictable, like wives."

"Are you married?" Matt asked.

"I was at one time."

"For how long?"

"Long enough to become an authority on the subject."

The young reporter said, "I just got married last June and I think it's the only way to live."

"Good for you!"

The roast beef sandwiches were served, and Qwilleran had to ask for horseradish a second time. He said to Matt, "Where are you living?"

"Happy View Woods."

All young couples, Qwilleran had discovered, were paying mortgages in Happy View Woods, raising families, and worrying about crabgrass in their lawns. He himself had always preferred to live in apartments or hotels, being somewhat of a gypsy at heart. He said, "I'm staying in the penthouse apartment at the Casablanca. Does that ring a bell?"

''That's where the art dealer was murdered a couple of months ago.''

''Did you see the scene of the crime?''

''No, the coverage was cut-and-dried,'' said the police reporter. ''The murderer left a confession and killed himself. Also, there was a major airline crash at the airport on the same day, and that took precedence over everything for two weeks.''

''Do you know anything about the murderer?''

''His name was Ross Rasmus, an artist. He specialized in painting *mushrooms*. Can you swallow that? He must have been crazy to begin with! He daubed his confession on a wall with red paint.''

''Which wall?''

''I don't think anyone ever mentioned which wall.''

The chances were, Qwilleran reasoned, that the artist went back to his studio, where he kept his paints, and daubed it on his own wall. That would be 14-B. Keestra Hedrog might know something about it. ''Was there any speculation about motive?'' he asked Matt.

''Well, they were lovers, you know. That was pretty well-known. She liked to discover young talent—young male talent. Everybody figured she discovered a successor to Ross Rasmus, and he was jealous. The autopsy turned up evidence of drugs. He was stoned when he did it.''

''What was the weapon?''

''I don't believe the actual weapon was ever identified.''

''The reason I ask: The penthouse has a lot of his paintings on the walls, each with a knife included with the mushrooms. It's a Japanese slicer, and there's one exactly like it in the kitchen.''

''Oh, yeah,'' said Matt. ''There's plenty of those around. My wife has one. She's into stir-fry.''

They munched their sandwiches in silence, Qwilleran wishing he had some horseradish. After a while he said, ''The artist's body landed on some guy's car. He was quoted in your story. Do you remember the name?''

''Gosh, no, I don't. That was two months ago.''

At that moment a young woman in boots and a long skirt wandered over to their table, and Matt introduced her as Sasha Crispen-Schmitt of the *Morning Rampage*.

Qwilleran rose and said cordially but not truthfully that he had read her column and enjoyed it.

''Thanks. Please sit down,'' she said, looking at his moustache. ''I've heard about you. Don't you live up north in a town with a funny name?''

''Pickax, population three thousand. And if you think that's funny, we also have a Sawdust City, Chipmunk, and Brrr, spelled B-r-r-r. Will you join us for coffee or a drink?''

''Wish I could,'' said Ms. Crispen-Schmitt, ''but I have to get back to the office for another *paralyzing* meeting. What are you doing down here?''

''I just wanted to spend one winter away from ten-foot snowbanks and wall-to-wall ice.''

Matt said, ''He's staying at the old broken-down Casablanca.''

''Really?'' she said. ''I lived there for a while myself. Why did you choose that grungy place?''

"They allow cats," Qwilleran said, "and I have two Siamese."

"How do you like the building?"

"It's interesting, if you're a masochist."

"What floor are you on?"

"Fourteen."

"Well, it's better if you're high up."

"Not when both elevators are out of order at the same time," Qwilleran told her.

"Isn't Fourteen where they had a murder a couple of months ago?"

"So they tell me."

"Well, look, I'd love to stay, but . . . maybe we can have lunch while you're here."

"By all means," said Qwilleran. When she had walked away, he said to Matt, "Attractive girl. Married?"

The reporter nodded. "To one of our sportswriters."

"Shall we have dessert, Matt? Today's special is pumpkin pie with whipped cream. I wonder if it's the real thing. One gets spoiled living half a mile from a dairy farm."

The waitress who had not brought his horseradish was now unable to say whether the whipped cream was actually from a cow.

"If you don't know, it probably isn't," Qwilleran said. "Bring me apple pie with cheese. Is it real cheese? Never mind; I'm sure it isn't. Bring me frozen yogurt."

After coffee and dessert they left the Press Club, Matt to return to police headquarters and Qwilleran to ride the Zwinger bus to the Casablanca.

"Thanks," said Matt. "I enjoyed the lunch."

"My pleasure," said Qwilleran. "And say, would you do me a favor? Check your story on the Bessinger murder and see whose car was damaged in the parking lot, will you? Then give me a ring. Here's my number."

It was quiet around the Casablanca in the early afternoon. Before climbing the crumbling steps he had a look at the parking lot. The Purple Plum was safe in slot #28, but what he really wanted to check was the row of parking spaces adjacent to the building. They were numbered 1 to 20, and directly above them was the parapet of the terrace from which Ross had jumped. Slots 21 to 40 were on the west side of the lot. Both rows were inadequately lighted after dark; a single floodlight was mounted on the side of the building midway between front and back—only one light for a very large lot. It was another management economy.

Qwilleran could not say why, but his hand went to his moustache. This luxuriant facial feature was notable not only for its size but for its response to various stimuli. Reactions of doubt or apprehension or suspicion were always accompanied by a tremor on his upper lip. He pounded his moustache with his fist as he entered the building.

Upstairs he found another envelope under his door, and he groaned, presuming that Isabelle had been there again, but this time it was a heavy ivory-colored envelope with his name inscribed in very proper handwriting. Perhaps it was from Winnie Wingfoot, he thought hopefully as he tore it open. The message, obviously written with a fountain pen and not a ballpoint, read as follows: "Would you do me the honor of dining with me tonight at seven o'clock?—Adelaide Plumb." In the lower left-hand corner she specified RSVP and gave a telephone number.

Somewhat deflated, Qwilleran called to accept.

Ferdie Le Bull answered. "Okay, I'll tell her," said the houseman. "She's having her nap. It'll be chicken hash tonight. D'you like chicken hash? I don't call that real food, but she always has chicken hash on Thursday."

"Whatever the menu, Ferdinand, please convey my message: Mr. Qwilleran accepts with pleasure."

Hanging up the phone he called out to the Siamese, "You guys will eat better than I will tonight . . . Where are you?"

Koko was sitting quietly in the foyer, gazing out the French doors to the terrace, waiting patiently for the pigeons that never came in for a landing. Yum Yum was asleep on the waterbed; she slept entirely too much since arriving at the Casablanca, Qwilleran thought.

In preparation for his soirée with the Countess he threw some shirts and socks into a shopping bag and ventured down to the basement laundry room for the first time. As Old Red slowly descended he read the following notices on the bulletin board:

WANTED TO BUY—guitar—Apt. 2-F.
FREE KITTENS—Apt. 9-B.

The Cat Who Lived High

REWARD! Who stole cassettes from parking lot?
See mgr.

At the fourth floor Old Red came to a grinding stop, and a woman carrying a laundry bag started to board the car. Catching sight of the moustached stranger with a shopping bag, she started to back off but apparently decided to take a chance. There was no eye contact, but roguishly Qwilleran started to breathe heavily, causing her to edge closer to the door. He was feeling playful following his stimulating lunch at the Press Club and his brief dialogue with the Countess's absurd butler. When the elevator reached the bottom with a crash, the other passenger scuttled off the car, and he followed her with deliberately heavy footfalls.

The laundry room was large and dreary with one row of washers and another row of dryers, many of them labeled out of order. The peeling masonry walls had not known a paintbrush for perhaps sixty years. At that time—when family laundresses did the washing, ironing, and mangling—a cheerful environment was not thought necessary. Now the somber workplace was enlivened by a veritable gallery of prohibitions and warnings neatly printed with red and green felt markers and lavished with exclamation marks:

NO SMOKING! NO LOUD RADIO!
NO HORSING AROUND!!!
HAVE RESPECT FOR OTHERS!
CANADIAN COINS DON'T WORK!

NOT RESPONSIBLE FOR LOST WASH!
STAY WITH YOUR THINGS!!!
BALANCE YOUR LOAD!!!

Machines were churning and spinning, and one thumped noisily; not everyone had balanced his or her load. Several persons were patiently staying with their things: an old man jabbering to himself, the woman with two small children— speaking in their native tongue— another woman in a housedress and sweater, glowering at a student with his nose in a textbook who had not balanced his load. Qwilleran studied the signs for instructions:

TOO MUCH SOAP MESSES UP MACHINES!!
DON'T FEED THE MICE!!!
MOTHERS WITH BABIES—
NO DIAPERING ON MACHINES! USE RESTROOM!!

Although no stranger to laundromats, Qwilleran found sadistic pleasure in asking his fearful fellow passenger from Old Red how to use the washer, explaining in a graveyard voice that he was new in the building. She obliged without looking at him, then moved away quickly.

He balanced his load, inserted a coin, and studied the posted messages for further inspiration, no doubt from the motherly Mrs. Tuttle:

BE A GOOD NEIGHBOR! CLEAN LINT TRAP!
DON'T HOG THE DRYERS!!
NO LIQUOR! NO LOITERING!

The Cat Who Lived High

THIS IS NOT A SOCIAL HALL!!!
ONLY ONE PERSON AT A TIME IN THE RESTROOM
OR IT WILL BE LOCKED!!!

The benches were hard and backless and not likely to encourage loitering, but Qwilleran sat down and scanned the newspapers he had brought along until—from the corner of his eye—he caught a flash of red. Rupert had sauntered into the room and was surveying it for violations.

Qwilleran beckoned to him and asked, ''May I ask a question, Rupert? Why are there no pigeons on the terrace? My cats like to watch pigeons.''

''Them dirty birds!'' said the custodian in disgust. ''Lady that lived there before, she used to feed 'em, and the parkers in the lot raised holy hell. Don't let Mrs. T catch you feedin' 'em or she'll be after you with a rollin' pin!''

Qwilleran resumed reading Sasha Crispen-Schmitt's column in the *Morning Rampage*, a shallow recital of gossip and rumors. When another tenant entered the room carrying a laundry basket, he made the mistake of looking up. It was Isabelle Wilburton, wearing a soiled housecoat.

She came directly to him. ''Sorry if I offended you last night.''

''No harm done,'' he said, returning to his newspaper.

She loaded one of the washers, and he wondered if she would remove her housecoat and throw it in, but she was still decently clothed when she sat down beside him on the uncomfortable bench.

169

"I get so lonely," she said. "That's my trouble. I don't have any friends except the damned rum bottle."

"The bottle can be your worst enemy. Take it from one who's been there."

"I used to have a wonderful job. I was a corporate secretary."

"What happened?"

"My boss was killed in a plane crash."

"Couldn't you get another job?"

"I didn't . . . I couldn't . . . The heart went out of me. I'd been with him twenty years, ever since business school. He was more than a boss. We used to go on business trips together, and a lot of times we'd work late at the office and have dinner sent in. I was so happy in those days."

"I suppose he was married," Qwilleran said.

Isabelle heaved an enormous sigh. "I used to shop for gifts for his wife and children. When he died, everybody felt sorry for them. Nobody felt sorry for me. Twenty years! I used to have beautiful clothes. I still have the cocktail dresses he bought me. I put them on and sit at my kitchen table and drink rum."

"Why aren't you drinking today?"

"My check hasn't come yet."

"Did he leave you a trust?"

She shook her head sadly. "It comes from my family."

"Where do they live?"

"In the suburbs. They have a big house in Muggy Swamp."

"Apparently you haven't sold your piano."

"Winnie Wingfoot looked at it, but she can't make up her mind. Do you know Winnie?"

"I've seen her in the parking lot," Qwilleran said.

"Isn't she gorgeous? If I had her looks, I'd have a lot of friends. Of course, she's younger. Could you use a piano?"

"I'm afraid not."

"Is that your washer? It stopped," Isabelle informed him.

Qwilleran transferred his clothes to a dryer and returned to the bench. "Aren't you friendly with your family?"

"They won't have anything to do with me. I guess I embarrass them. Do you have a family?"

"Only a couple of cats, but the three of us are a real family. Did you ever think of getting a cat?"

"There are lots of them around the building, but . . . I've never had a pet," she said with lack of interest.

"They're good company when you live alone—almost human."

Isabelle turned away. She looked at her fingernails. She looked at the ceiling.

Qwilleran said, "Someone on Nine is offering free kittens."

"If I just had one friend, I'd be all right," she said. "I wouldn't drink. I don't know why I don't have any friends."

"I can tell you why," he said, lowering his voice. "I had the same problem a few years ago."

"You did?"

Although he had a healthy curiosity about the

secrets of others, Qwilleran was loathe to discuss his own personal history, but he recognized this was an exception. "Drinking ruined my life after I'd had a successful career in journalism."

"Did you lose someone you loved?" she asked with sympathy in her bloodshot eyes.

"I made a bad marriage and went through a shattering divorce. I started drinking heavily, and my ex-wife cracked up. Two lives ruined! So then I had a load of guilt added to my disappointment and resentment and murderous hate for my meddling in-laws. I lost my friends and couldn't hold a job. No newspaper would hire me after a couple of bad incidents, and I didn't have any convenient checks coming in the mail."

"What did you do?"

"It took a horrifying accident to make me realize I needed help. I was living like a bum in New York, and one night I was so drunk I fell off a subway platform. I'll never forget the screams of onlookers and the roar of the train coming out of the tunnel. They hauled me out just in time! Believe me, that was a sobering experience. It was also the turning point. I took the advice that had been given me and got counseling. The road back was slow and painful, but I made it! And I've never again touched alcohol. That's my story."

Isabelle's eyes were filled with tears. "Would you like to have dinner at my place tonight?" she asked hopefully. "I could thaw some spaghetti."

"I appreciate the invitation," he said, "but I have an important dinner date—so important," he added with an attempt at drollery, "that I'm washing my shirt and socks." He was relieved to see his dryer stop churning. Putting his shirts on hangers and throwing his socks and undershorts in the shopping bag, he escaped from the laundry room.

His telephone was ringing when he unlocked the door to 14-A. The caller was Matt Thiggamon. "Sorry to take so long," he said. "I got the guy's name. It's Jack Yazbro."

"Spell it."

"Y-a-z-b-r-o."

"Thanks a lot, Matt."

"Any time."

Qwilleran lost no time in going downstairs to the desk. "Mrs. Tuttle," he said, "I want to compliment you on the way you run this building. I've seen you handle a variety of situations in a very competent manner and deal with all kinds of tenants."

"Thank you," she said with her hearty smile, although it was partially canceled out by her intimidating gimlet stare. "I do my best but I didn't think anyone ever noticed."

"Even your signs in the laundry room are done with a certain flair."

"Oh, my! That makes me feel real good. Is everything all right on Fourteen?"

"Everything's fine. The skylight doesn't leak. The radiators are behaving. The sunsets are spectacular. Too bad this building is going to be torn down. Do you know when?"

She shrugged. "Nobody tells me a thing! I just take one day at a time and trust in the Lord."

"One question: Do you happen to know where Mr. Yazbro parks his car?"

"Wait a bit. I'll look it up in the rent book." She leafed through a loose-leaf ledger. "I remember he changed his parking space a while back. He always liked to park against the building, but . . ."

"But what?" Qwilleran asked when she failed to finish the sentence.

"Something fell on his car, and he asked to be changed."

"Do things often drop on cars parked near the building?" he asked slyly.

Mrs. Tuttle glanced up sharply from the ledger. "We used to have trouble with pigeons. Don't you go feeding them, now! Here it is—Mr. Yazbro. He was in #18. Now he has #27." She slapped the book shut.

Twenty-seven, she said.

"Thank you, Mrs. Tuttle. Keep up the good work!"

Qwilleran made a beeline for the parking lot. He had been parked in #27 when someone tampered with his tires. Now there was a minivan parked there. The slot had been vacant during the afternoon. Yazbro had just come home from work—that is, if the minivan belonged to Yazbro. It was impossible to be certain considering the disorganized parking system. He recorded the license number on a scrap of paper and returned to the front desk, waving it at Mrs. Tuttle.

"Sorry to bother you again," he said, "but is this Mr. Yazbro's license number?"

174

She consulted the ledger again, and the two numbers tallied. "Is anything wrong?" she asked.

"There certainly is! Yazbro is the snake who let the air out of my tires yesterday, and I'd like to discuss it with him. What's his apartment number?"

"He's in 4-K. I hope there won't be any trouble, Mr. Qwilleran. Do you want Rupert to go up with you?"

"No, thank you. It won't be necessary."

ELEVEN

RIDING OLD RED up to Yazbro's apartment on
Four, Qwilleran had plenty of time to plan his
confrontation with the man who had deflated his
tires. He had dealt with villains before, and he
knew how to bring them to their knees without
incurring hostility. He was a good actor and could
always carry it off. The trick was to open with
friendly small talk, throw in a little prevarication,
and then catch them off-base with an accusation
and a warning that was sinister but not too threatening. He knocked on the door of 4-K with au-

thority but not belligerence; that was another important detail. Then he waited. He knocked again.

A voice from within shouted, "Who zat?"

"Your neighbor, Mr. Yazbro," he replied in an ingratiating voice.

Qwilleran, standing six feet two and weighing a solid two twenty, did not consider himself a small man, but the giant with bulging muscles and aggressive jaw who answered his knock—totally filling the doorway, grasping a beer bottle by the neck, and stripped to the waist—made him feel like a pygmy.

"Mr. Yazbro?" he asked with poise that was admirable.

"Yeah."

"Do you drive a minivan and park in #27?"

"Yeah."

No one had ever called Qwilleran a coward, but he knew the better part of valor, and he was a master at inventing the quick lie. "I believe you left your parking lights on," he said agreeably. "Just thought you'd like to know." Then, without waiting to hear Yazbro's grunts of rage, he walked casually to the elevator and pressed the UP button for Old Green. The giant soon followed, rattling his car keys and muttering to himself, and pressed the DOWN button for Old Red.

"We've had a lot of rain lately," Qwilleran said pleasantly.

"Yeah," said Yazbro, as Old Green opened its door and transported Qwilleran, inch by groaning inch, to Fourteen.

The Siamese met him at the door. "Time for dinner?" he asked them.

A reply of sorts rattled in Koko's throat: "Rrrrrrrrrrrr."

"Does that mean you want roast raccoon rare . . . or ragout of rabbit?"

"Rrrrrrrrrrrrr," Koko gargled, and Qwilleran opened a can of red salmon, reflecting that he might have to take the cat to the veterinarian for a laryngoscopy.

While they devoured the salmon with rapt concentration, he analyzed Koko's current behavior. Besides making ugly noises in his throat, he prowled restlessly and followed Qwilleran everywhere, patently bored. It was understandable. Yum Yum was sleeping a lot and providing little companionship; there were no pigeons for entertainment; and Qwilleran himself had been absent a great deal or preoccupied with matters like Scrabble or the Grinchman & Hills report.

"Okay, you guys," he said. "Let's have some fun." He produced the new leather harnesses, jiggling them tantalizingly.

Koko had been harnessed before and was eager to buckle up, but Yum Yum resisted the collaring and girdling. Although usually susceptible to blandishments, she disregarded remarks that the blue leather matched her eyes and enhanced her fawn-colored fur. She squirmed; she kicked; she snapped her jaws. When Qwilleran tugged the leash, she refused to walk or even to stand on her four feet. He tugged harder and she played dead. When he picked her up and set her on her feet, she toppled over as if there were not a bone or muscle in her body and lay there, inert, not moving a whisker.

"You're an uncooperative, unappreciative, impossible wench!" he said. "I'll remember this the next time you want to take possession of my lap."

Meanwhile Koko was prancing about the room, dragging his leash. He was a veteran at this. Some of his greatest adventures had happened at the end of a twelve-foot nylon cord. Now he made it clear that he wanted to explore the terrace.

"It'll be cold," Qwilleran warned him.

"Yow," Koko replied.

"And there are no pigeons."

"Yow!"

"And it's getting dark."

"YOW!" Koko said vehemently, tugging toward the exit.

On the terrace he led the way impatiently, pulling Qwilleran toward the front of the building and then all the way back to the rear. At one point the cat stopped abruptly and turned toward the parapet. Qwilleran tightened his hold on the leash as Koko prepared to jump on the stone baluster. Teetering on the railing with his four feet bunched together, he peered over the edge. Holding the leash taut, Qwilleran also looked over the railing. Directly below was parking slot #18, the number painted on the tarmac in faded yellow paint.

"Incredible!" said Qwilleran.

"Rrrrrrrrrrrr," said Koko.

"Let's go inside. It's chilly."

Koko refused to move, and when Qwilleran

grabbed him about the middle, his body was tense and his tail curled stiffly.

Why, Qwilleran wondered as he carried the cat back indoors, did Ross walk, run, or stagger a hundred feet down the terrace in order to jump on Yazbro's car? Even more mystifying was the next question: How did Koko know the exact spot where it happened?

Back in the apartment he found Yum Yum asleep on the waterbed—harness, leash and all. Gently Qwilleran rolled her over, unbuckling the strap and drawing the collar over her head. Without opening her eyes she purred. And why not? She had won the argument. She had had the last word.

"Just like a female!" Qwilleran muttered.

It was time to dress for dinner with the Countess, and he brought his dark blue suit and white shirt from the closet, marveling that he had worn suits twice in two days. In Moose County he had worn them twice in three years, once for a wedding and once for a funeral. To his funeral suit he now added a red tie to elevate its mood. A striped shirt would have had more snap, but sartorial niceties were not in Qwilleran's field of interest.

This social event was one he hardly approached with keen anticipation. Nevertheless, years of carrying out unattractive assignments for tyrannical editors had disciplined him into automatic performance of duty. Also, there was the prospect of a book on the Casablanca—a coffee-table book in folio format with large photographs on good paper. The K Fund would underwrite it.

This was the afternoon, he remembered, that the Klingenschoen board was scheduled to meet, Hasselrich presenting the Casablanca proposition with quivering excitement and anecdotes about spinach timbales. As if his thoughts were telepathic, the phone rang at that moment, and Hasselrich was on the line, advising him that the board had voted unanimously to foot the bill for saving the Casablanca, leaving the amount entirely to Qwilleran's discretion.

"This may not be the last," said the attorney. "A resolution was passed to pursue similar ventures in the public interest as a means of enhancing the Klingenschoen image."

Qwilleran consulted his watch. The invitation was for seven o'clock, and it was not yet six. He telephoned Mary Duckworth. "Are you busy? Do you have a few minutes? I'd like to drop in for a briefing before I ascend to Art Deco heaven in the rosewood chariot. Also, I have good news!"

"Yes! Come along," she said. "Ring the bell. The shop's closed."

In his dark blue suit, with a raincoat over his arm, Qwilleran rode down on Old Green. A red-haired woman boarded the car at Nine, and he could feel her staring at him. He straightened his shoulders and concentrated on watching the floor indicator. Since some of the lights were inoperative, the car descended from eight to five to two to one. In the lobby Mrs. Tuttle looked up from her knitting with a smile of admiration. Two old ladies in quilted bathrobes squinted at him without scowling. It was the dark suit, he decided; he should wear it more often instead of waiting for another funeral.

As he strode down Zwinger Boulevard toward the Blue Dragon, he was stopped by a woman walking a Dalmatian. "Excuse me, do you know what time it is?" she asked.

"My watch says six-ten."

"You're new in the neighborhood."

"Just visiting," he said as he saluted courteously and went on his way.

Next it was Mary Duckworth's turn to exclaim. "You look tremendously attractive, Qwill!" she said. "Adelaide will be swept off her feet! She phoned me today—first time she has ever called— and said how much she enjoyed your company. She thanked me for taking you to tea."

"It's only because I play Scrabble."

"No, I think she liked your moustache. Or it was the Bosc pear. Whatever it was, you've kindled a light in the old girl's eyes."

"From the appearance of the old girl's eyes," Qwilleran said, "she has cataracts. Why doesn't she have surgery?"

"It may be that she doesn't want to see any better than she does. Did you notice that the windows have frosted glass? She wants time to stand still, circa 1935. But she can see the playing cards well enough—and the game board! . . . What's your good news?"

They sat in the shop, Qwilleran in a genuine Chippendale corner chair and Mary on a Chinese ebony throne inlaid with mother-of-pearl.

He said, "The Klingenschoen Fund has given

me carte blanche for the Casablanca preservation.''

''Wonderful! But I'm not surprised. After all, it's your own money, isn't it? My father says that's no secret in financial circles.''

''It won't actually be mine for another two years. But that's neither here nor there. The crucial question is: Will I be able to convince the Countess to sell?''

''The way things look,'' said Mary, ''you should have no problem. Are you looking forward to the evening?''

''I find the prospect challenging but the environment depressing, like a glamorous old movie palace that hasn't shown films since World War Two.''

''You must remember,'' she said, ''that an interior acquires a certain patina after sixty years, and the Plumb apartment is museum quality. There's a large vase in the drawing room, decorated with flowers and nude women. I don't know whether you noticed it—''

''I noticed it.''

''That piece alone is worth thousands of dollars on today's market. It's a René Buthaud.''

''Spell that.''

''B-u-t-h-a-u-d. We have a shop in Junktown that specializes in Art Deco, and the lowest price tag is in four figures.''

''I've been meaning to ask you, Mary,'' he said. ''How long have you known the Countess?''

''I didn't meet her until I joined SOCK and Di

Bessinger enlisted me for backgammon, but I've heard the Adelaide legend all my life."

"And what might that be?" Qwilleran's curiosity caused his moustache to bristle.

"Not anything you'd want to put in your book, but it was common gossip in social circles in the Thirties, according to my mother."

"Well, let's have it!"

"This is a true story," she began. "Soon after Adelaide made her debut she became affianced to a man who was considered a great catch, provided a girl had money. He was penniless but handsome and charming and from good stock. Adelaide was the lucky girl and the envy of her set. Then . . . the economy collapsed, the banks closed, and Harrison Plumb was in desperate straits. He had never been financially astute, my father said, and he had thrown away millions on the Art Deco renovation. But now half the units of Casablanca were vacant, and the remaining tenants lacked the cash to pay the rent. The building had been his passion for thirty years, and he was about to lose it. Suddenly three astounding things happened: Adelaide broke her engagement; her father was solvent once more; and one of her Penniman cousins married the jilted man."

"Are the obvious deductions true?" Qwilleran asked.

"There's no doubt about it. Adelaide bartered her fiancé for millions to save the Casablanca and save her dear father from ruin. And in those days a million was a lot of money."

"That says something about Adelaide, but I'm

not sure what," Qwilleran remarked. "Was it noble sacrifice or cold calculation?"

"We think it was a painful, selfless gesture; right afterward she dropped out of the social scene completely. Sadly, her father died within months, and the Casablanca never regained its prestige."

"How old was she when this happened?"

"Eighteen, I believe."

"She gives the impression of being satisfied with her choice. Who handles her financial affairs?"

"After her father's death her Penniman relatives advised her to invest his life insurance and exploit the Casablanca. Naturally the Pennimans are now advising her to sell—"

"—to Penniman, Greystone & Fleudd, of course. And you expect me to buck that kind of competition? You're a dreamer."

"You have a strong ally, though, in her love for the building and for her father's memory. You can do it, Qwill!"

Huffing into his moustache, he stood up to leave. "Well, wish me luck . . . What's that thing?" He pointed to a small decorative object.

"It's art glass—a pillbox—Art Deco design, probably seventy-five years old."

"Would she like it?"

"She'd love it! Even more than the Bosc pear."

"I'll buy it," he said.

"Take it, with my compliments." Mary removed the price tag. "I'll put it in a velvet sack."

With the velvet sack in his pocket, Qwilleran

paid his second visit to the Plumb Palace on Twelve. As he waited for the elevator at the bronze door, the feisty Mrs. Button came hobbling down the hall with her cane.

"My! You do look handsome!" she said in a high, cracked voice. "My late husband always looked handsome in a dark suit. Every Thursday evening he would put on his dinner coat and I would put on a long dress, and we would go to the symphony. We always sat in a first-tier box. Are you going up to play cards with Adelaide? Have a lovely evening."

Mrs. Button hobbled as far as the front door, then turned and hobbled back again—one of several ambulatory invalids who took their prescribed exercise in the hallways of the Casablanca. Qwilleran thought, If the building reverts to its original palatial character, what will happen to the old people? And the students? And Isabelle? And Mrs. Tuttle and Rupert?

Pondering this he rode up to Twelve in the rosewood elevator and was admitted by Ferdinand, looming huge in his coral-colored coat. "It's not gonna be chicken hash," were the houseman's first words. "It's gonna be shrimp. I dunno why. It's always chicken hash on Thursday."

The hostess came forward with hands extended and head tilted prettily to one side. She had been tilting her head prettily for so many years that one shoulder was now higher than the other. Yesterday Qwilleran thought her posturings and obsessions were ludicrous; today, having heard the Adelaide legend, he found her a pathetic figure, despite her turquoise chiffon hostess gown with floating scarfs and square-cut onyx and diamond jewelry.

"So good to see you again, Mr. Qwillen," she said.

He sat in the Bibendum chair, and Ferdinand served heavily watered grapejuice in square-cut stemware. Qwilleran raised his glass in a toast. "To gracious ladies in enchanted palaces!"

The sad little Countess inclined her head in acknowledgment. "Have you had an interesting day?" she asked.

"I spent the day looking forward to this evening and selecting this trinket for you." He presented the velvet sack.

With cries of delight she extracted the Art Deco pillbox. "Oh, thank you, Mr. Qwillen! It's French Modern! I shall put this in my boudoir."

"I thought it would be in keeping with the stunning ambiance you have created. Is that a René Buthaud vase on the mantel?" he asked, flaunting his newly acquired knowledge.

"Yes, and it means so much to me. It contains the ashes of my dear father. He was such a handsome and cultivated gentleman! How he loved to take me to Paris—to the opera and museums and salons!"

"Did you meet Gertrude Stein?"

"We attended her salon. I was a very young girl, but I remember meeting some dashing young men. I think they were writers."

"Hemingway? Fitzgerald?"

She raised her hands in a gracefully helpless

gesture. ''That was so long ago. Forgive me if I don't remember.''

At that moment Ferdinand made his menacing appearance and announced in a muscle-bound growl, ''Dinner's served.''

It was served on square-cut dinnerware on a round ebony table in a circular dining room paneled in black, turquoise, and mirror, its perimeter lighted with torchères. The entrée was shrimp Newburgh, preceded by a slice of pâté and followed by that favorite of the Twenties, Waldorf salad. Then Ferdinand prepared bananas Foster in a chafing dish with heavy-handed competence and a disdainful expression meaning that this was not real food.

During dinner the conversation lurched rather than flowed, their voices sounding hollow in the vaultlike room. Qwilleran was relieved when they moved to the library for coffee and Scrabble. Here he proceeded to amaze his hostess by spelling such high-scoring words as ZANY and QIVIUT, and once he retripled. She was a good player and she seemed to relish the challenge. She was a different woman at the game table.

At the end she said, ''This has been a most enjoyable evening. I hope you will come again, Mr. Qwillen.''

''Enough of formality,'' he said. ''Could you bring yourself to call me Qwill. It's good for seventeen points.''

''I must correct you,'' she said merrily. ''Fourteen points.''

"Seventeen," he insisted. "I spell it with a QW."

"Then you must call me Zizou, my father's pet name for me. It's worth twenty-three!" Her laughter was so giddy that Ferdinand made an alarmed appearance in the doorway.

"May I beg a favor of you, Zizou?" Qwilleran asked, taking advantage of her happy mood. "Yesterday I mentioned writing a book about the Casablanca. Would you consent to having your apartment photographed?"

"Would you take my picture, too?" she answered coyly.

"By all means. Sitting on the sofa, pouring tea."

"That would be quite exciting. What should I wear?"

"You always look beautiful, whatever you wear."

"Do you have a camera?"

"Yes, but not good enough for this. I'd hire an architectural photographer. He could take some striking views of these rooms."

"Would he photograph all of them?"

"All that you wish to have photographed."

"Oh, dear! I wonder if my dear father would approve."

Qwilleran launched his proposal. "He would approve enthusiastically, and there is something else that your father would want you to do. He would realize that buildings, like people, get tired in their old age. They need rejuvenation. If he were here, he would know that the Casablanca is badly in need of repair, from the roof to the basement.''

Shocked at the suggestion, the Countess fluttered her hands about her jewelry. ''I find my suite quite—quite satisfactory.''

''That's because you don't venture beyond your magnificent copper doors, Zizou. This may be painful for you to contemplate, but your palace is in bad condition, and there are people who think it should be torn down.''

She stiffened. ''That will never happen!''

''Some of the people who play bridge with you are asking to buy the building, are they not? If you sell to them, they'll tear it down. To save the Casablanca you need a partner—someone who appreciates the building as much as you do.'' (Careful, he thought; it sounds like a marriage proposal. Ferdie Le Bull was around the corner, listening.) ''You need a financial partner,'' he went on, ''who will put money into its renovation and restore it to its original beauty. Your father would approve of a partnership. When he built this palace in 1901, he had an architect for a partner. A financial partner would be the beginning of a new life for the Casablanca.''

The expression in her clouded eyes told him that the concept was beyond her comprehension. Her brain was geared for grand slams and retriples. Her face was a blank. She was withdrawing.

As if sensing a crisis, Ferdinand made his clumsy entrance. ''Want me to bring the tea?''

Once more the Countess cocked her head prettily and said in her debutante voice, ''Would you like a cup of camomile tea before you leave, Mr. Qwillen?"

"No, thank you," he said rising. "It has been an enjoyable evening, but I must say good night, Miss Plumb." He bowed out, and the glowering houseman showed him to the door.

Nibbling at his moustache, Qwilleran rode down to the main floor in luxury and rode up to Fourteen in the dismal clutches of Old Green. Ignoring Koko's greeting at the door he went directly to the telephone and called Polly Duncan.

"I crashed!" he announced without preamble. "I broached the subject of restoration to the Countess and hit a stone wall."

"That's too bad," she said soothingly but not earnestly.

"She's been out-of-touch for sixty years. She doesn't know what's happening and doesn't want to know. One can't reason with her."

"Perhaps you should consider this setback a signal from your tutelary genius, telling you to forget the Casablanca and come home."

"I can't give up so easily. The K Fund okayed the investment today, and it would be embarrassing—"

"Sleep on it," Polly advised. "Tomorrow it will be clear what you should do, but I wish you would seriously consider coming home. Today on the radio they reported a shooting in an office building down there. A man killed a lawyer and his secretary."

"That was a disgruntled law clerk who had been fired," Qwilleran explained.

"Next time it could be a disgruntled motorist who doesn't like the way you change lanes on the freeway," she said sharply. "You have a duty to play it safe, like English royalty."

"Hmff," Qwilleran grumbled. He took time to groom his moustache with his fingertips before changing the subject. "How's everything with you?"

"I may have some good news, Qwill. There's a chance that old Mrs. Gage on Goodwinter Boulevard will rent her carriage house."

"What about Bootsie?"

"She doesn't object to cats. How are the Siamese?"

"Yum Yum is rather lethargic and Koko is acting strangely," he said.

"They're homesick for Pickax," Polly said cunningly, adding weight to her argument. She knew he would return for the cats' well-being if not for his own. "What else did you do today?"

"I had lunch at the Press Club, but the service was terrible, and the food isn't as good as it used to be. I took Koko for a walk on the terrace, and I did some laundry in the basement of the building."

They rambled on like comfortable old marrieds until Polly ended the conversation with, "Think about what I said, dearest, and call me about your decision." She knew that Qwilleran liked to limit his long-distance calls to five minutes.

"*A bientôt.*"

"*A bientôt.*"

His frustration was subsiding, and he was about

to relieve it further with a large dish of ice cream, when he received an urgent phone call from Amber, asking if he had seen the night edition of Friday's *Morning Rampage*. "You're in Sasha Crispen-Schmitt's column!" she announced.

"I haven't seen the paper. Read it to me."

"You won't like it," she said, and then read: " 'Guess who's staying at the Casablanca in the penthouse apartment of the late Diane Bessinger! None other than Jim Qwilleran, former *Daily Fluxion* writer who inherited untold millions and moved to a small town that no one ever heard of. Would anyone care to put two and two together? Our guess: Qwill is here to bankroll the preservation of the Casablanca, which so many local bigwigs want to tear down. Get your ringside tickets for the Battle of the Bucks!' "

TWELVE

EARLY FRIDAY MORNING Qwilleran called Mary
Duckworth. "Have you seen the *Morning Rampage*?" he asked abruptly.

"I've just finished reading about you. I loathe
that kind of journalism! Where did they get their
information?"

"I was lunching with a *Fluxion* reporter at the
Press Club, and Sasha what's her name came to
our table. The guy told her I'm staying at the
Casablanca. In retrospect I'm convinced her appearance at our table was not accidental. It some-

how leaked out that the Klingenschoen Fund is interested in backing SOCK, and she was snooping for information.''

Mary said, ''I wonder what effect the item will have.''

''No doubt the developers will step up their campaign. The city might find an excuse for condemnation proceedings. Or—and this is a wild supposition—Adelaide's Penniman cousins might conspire to find her mentally incompetent. With their unholy influence in this town, they could swing it! But here's the real setback, Mary. I got nowhere with Adelaide last night, although the evening started well. After Scrabble we were on first-name terms. Then I started to talk business, as diplomatically as I could, and she retired into her shell. It's like trying to save a sailor from drowning when he doesn't know his boat is leaking.''

''What can we do?''

''I'd like to discuss it with Roberto. He used to be her attorney, you told me. Surely he learned how to get through to her. Can we pry him loose from his kitchen long enough for a conference?''

''Sunday evening is his night off.''

''Then let's get together on Sunday. You line it up. Let me know when.''

Qwilleran was in a bad humor. He paced the floor for a while, accidentally stepping on a tail or two, before deciding that ham and eggs would improve his disposition. But first he tuned in the radio station that offered round-the-clock news and weather. He learned that the thirty-seventh youth had been shot in a local high school and the temperature would be mild with high humidity resulting in increased smog.

On the way out of the building he was passing the manager's desk when a commotion at the rear of the main floor indicated that something or someone was being brought down on the freight elevator. He watched while ambulance attendants whisked a covered body to the front door.

"Who's that?" he asked Mrs. Tuttle.

"Mrs. Button, the dear soul."

"She talked to me last night, and she was in fine shape."

"That's the way it goes. The ways of the Lord are mysterious. Have you decided whether you'd like cleaning help, Mr. Qwilleran? Mrs. Jasper is available on Mondays."

"Okay, send her up," he said.

"Oh, look what we have here!" Old Green had arrived at the main floor, and Isabelle Wilburton stepped out of the car, cradling a kitten in her arms—white with orange head and tail.

"Isn't this the cutest, funniest thing you ever saw?" she gushed.

"He's so sweet! What are you going to call him?" asked Mrs. Tuttle.

"It's a girl. I'm going to call her Sweetie Pie. I got her from the people in 9-B."

"How old is she?"

Qwilleran edged away from the desk and went out to breakfast.

Putting the Countess out of his mind, he spent most of the day writing a column on the Casablanca for publication in the *Moose County Something*. The problem was: How to make the subject credible to north country readers when he could hardly believe it himself. While working, he evicted the Siamese from the library, an unfriendly act that aroused the indignation of Koko. The cat prowled outside the closed door muttering his new intestinal "Rrrrrrrrrr" as if he were about to regurgitate. After listening to the unsettling performance for half an hour, Qwilleran yanked open the library door.

"What's your problem?" he demanded.

Koko ran to the end of the foyer, where the French doors led to the terrace, but it was not the outdoors that interested him; it was the bloody butcher block painting. Standing on his hind legs with his head weaving from left to right like a cobra, he uttered his gagging guttural.

"Frankly, I feel the same way about it," Qwilleran said. Not only was the subject matter nauseating but the canvas was hung in a makeshift way, off-center and too low. With suspicion teasing his upper lip, he lifted the painting down from its hanger.

Immediately Koko stretched to his full length and sniffed the mushroom-tinted wall. Compared with the adjoining walls it looked freshly painted. Qwilleran, examining it closely, detected some unevenness enough to feel with his fingertips, and when the cat started prancing in circles with his back arched and his tail bushed, it was time to take the matter seriously. Qwilleran removed the shade from a table lamp and used the bare bulb to sidelight the wall surface. His suspicions were confirmed. The oblique light accentuated some crude daubing under the recent paint job. Large block letters in three ragged lines spelled out:

FORGIVE
ME
DIANE

There was a signature: two Rs, back to back.

So this was the confession! The management, in preparation for Qwilleran's arrival, had painted over it and hung a picture for further camouflage. Did Koko smell fresh paint? Or did he know it concealed something of interest? He was adept at detecting anything out of order or out of place.

"You're a clever fellow," he said to the cat, who bounded away to the kitchen and looked pointedly at his empty plate. As Qwilleran was giving him a treat, the telephone rang, and he took the call in the library. It was a familiar voice from Moose County.

"Hey, Qwill, I've just been reading about you in the out-state edition of the *Rampage*," said Arch Riker.

"Dammit! I didn't want the competition to know why I'm here," Qwilleran replied. "My story is that I'm here to write a book on the Casablanca, which is more or less true, and to get away from the severe winter up north."

"Skip the book and send us some copy," said the editor.

"I'm working on it. I was interrupted a few minutes ago by our resident investigator. He dredged up some evidence in connection with a murder-suicide incident in this apartment."

"What murder? What suicide? You didn't tell me anything about a crime."

"It was a lovers' quarrel, so they say, but when Old Nosey starts sniffing around in that significant way of his, my suspicions start working overtime."

"Now, back up, Qwill. Don't go charging into something that doesn't concern you," Riker warned him. "Just bear down on completing your original mission and hightail it back here while the roads are still open. We've been lucky so far—no snow—but it's on the way down from Canada. I wish they'd export more cheese and less weather."

Qwilleran said neither yes nor no; he disliked being told what to do. "If you talk to Polly, don't mention the murder," he said. "She worries, you know. She thinks murder is contagious, like measles."

When he concluded the phone call, Koko was sitting tall on the desk, looking hopeful, yearning for attention, and Qwilleran felt sorry for him. In the old days they had invented a game with the unabridged dictionary, which amused them both. "Okay, let's see what you and I can do with Scrabble," he said to the cat, as he scattered the tiles over the surface of the card table. "You fish out some letters, and I'll see if I can make a word."

Koko looked down at the assortment of small squares in his nearsighted way and did nothing until Qwilleran pawed at the tiles himself. Then the cat got the idea and withdrew E, H, I, S, A, P, and W. In a matter of seconds Qwilleran had spelled WHIPS.

"Those letters add up to thirteen points," he explained, "and the ones I didn't use add up to two. That's thirteen to two in my favor. If you want to score high, you have to choose consonants like X and Q and not too many vowels."

As if he understood, Koko proceeded to improve his game, and the score was a near-tie when it was time for Qwilleran to quit and dress for the evening. "Nothing personal," he said to the cat, "but I found the game more stimulating with the Countess."

He taxied downtown and dined at a middle-eastern restaurant before heading for the vernissage at the Bessinger-Todd Gallery. In the canyons of the financial district the Friday night hush was disturbed by a commotion around the gallery as cars pulled up one after the other. Three valets in red jumpsuits were kept hopping, and the hubbub within the building could be heard out on the sidewalk. Guests were pouring through the front door into an exhibit space already packed with art lovers, although art was not their prime interest. They milled about, drinking champagne, and shouting to be heard above the clangor of the music, while the musicians increased their volume in order to be heard above the din of voices. The center of attention seemed to be a young man with shoulder-length blond hair, who stood head and shoulders above all the rest.

Qwilleran saw no one he knew, apart from Jerome Todd and the sour-faced critic from the *Daily Fluxion*. He was not interested in the bar, and the buffet was engulfed by hungry guests, four deep. As for the art, he saw nothing he would care to hang on the walls of his remodeled barn, if he had one. The focal point of the exhibition was a trio of large canvases depicting ravenous eaters devouring fast food, obviously by the same artist who had painted the spaghetti orgy in 14-A.

On the balcony, away from the press of bodies, he found a more intimate collection of ceramics, blown glass, stainless steel sculpture and bronzes, as well as more breathing space. He was particularly curious about some ceramic discs displayed on small easels. Looking like limp piecrust, paper-thin, they were embellished with wavy sheaves of paper-thin clay and fired in smoky mushroom tones.

As he studied them with baffled interest, a hearty voice behind him said, ''I'll be damned if it isn't the best-looking moustache east of the Mississippi!''

He turned to see a tall, gaunt woman with straight gray hair and gray bangs, and he recognized the city's dean of potters. ''Inga Berry!'' he exclaimed. ''What a pleasure!''

''Qwill, I thought you were dead until I read about you in today's paper. Is it true what they said?''

"Never believe anything you read in the *Morning Rampage*," he cautioned. "Will you explain these things to me?" He pointed to the ceramic discs.

"Do you like this goofy stuff?" she asked with a challenging frown. Inga Berry was known for her large-scale ceramic pots thrown on the wheel and intricately glazed.

"They appeal to me for some obscure reason," he said, "probably because they look like something to eat. I wouldn't mind buying one."

The potter pounded his lapel with her fist. "Good boy! These are my current indiscretions in clay. I call them floppy discs."

"What happened to your spectacular pots?"

She held up two misshapen hands. "Arthritis. When your thumbs start to go, you can't throw pots on a wheel, but these things I can do with a rolling pin."

"Congratulations on your indiscretions. How do you get the appetizing effect?"

"Smoke-fired bisque."

"Your glass is empty, Inga. May I bring you some champagne?"

She made a grimace of distaste. "I can drink a gallon of this stuff without getting a glow. Let's get out of this madhouse and get some real hooch." She pushed back her bangs with a nervous hand.

Qwilleran shouldered a way through the crowd, the potter following with a slight limp. "Good show, Jerry!" she called out to Todd as they left, and Qwilleran threw the proprietor a complimentary hand signal that was more polite than honest.

Out on the sidewalk Inga said, ''Whew! I can't stand crowds anymore. I must be getting old. The Bessinger-Todd openings never attracted a crowd like this before all the lurid publicity.''

''Do you have a car, Inga?'' he asked.

''I came on the bus. A car's too much of a problem in the city, especially at my age.''

''Then we'll take a taxi . . . Valet! Cab, please.''

''I'm going on eighty, you know,'' said Inga, smoothing her ruffled bangs. ''That's when life begins. Nothing is expected of you, and you're forgiven for everything.''

''Are you still teaching at the arts and crafts school?''

''Retired last year. Glad to get out of that cesspool of twaddle. When I was young we had something to say, and we were damn good at saying it, but today . . .''

Qwilleran handed her into a taxi. ''How about going to my place at the Casablanca? I happen to have some bourbon.''

''Hot diggity! You're speaking my language. I spent some giddy hours at the Casablanca in the Thirties. The rents went down, and a lot of artists moved in and gave wild parties—beer in the bathtubs and nude models in the elevators! Those were the days! We knew how to have fun.'' When the cab pulled up in front of the building, she said, ''This place will be gone soon. I signed a petition for SOCK, but it won't do any good. If the Pennimans and the city fathers get their heads together and want the building torn down, it'll disappear overnight.''

''You ride the elevator at your own risk,'' he warned as they boarded Old Green.

''Do you still have your beautiful cats?''

''More accurately, they have me. At this moment Koko knows we're on the way up to Fourteen, and he'll greet us at the door. Did you ever see the Bessinger apartment?''

''No, but I've heard a lot about it. Her murder was something I can't get through my noodle. She was a good woman. I don't know about her private life, but she was always honest and fair with artists, and that's more than I can say about most dealers. And more than I can say about her husband.''

''I didn't know she was married, although I think the obituary mentioned daughters.''

''Oh, sure! She and Jerome Todd were married for years in Des Moines. They divorced after they came here.''

''Apparently it was amicable.''

''Yes and no, according to scuttlebutt. To tell the awful truth, I never knew what she could see in Todd. He's such a cold fish! But they stayed together as business partners. She took care of the talent; and he was a good businessman—good for himself, that is; not so good for the artists he represents.''

Old Green finally stumbled up to the top and stopped with a bang as if it had hit the roof, and when Qwilleran unlocked the door to 14-A and switched on the foyer lights, Koko walked to greet them with stately gait and lofty ears.

"Hello, you swanky rascal," said Inga. "Look at that noble nose! Look at that tapered tail! Talk about line and design! Where's the other one?"

"Probably asleep on the waterbed."

The potter gazed around the foyer with an artist's eye. "Pretty posh!"

"Wait till you see the gallery!" Qwilleran opened the French doors and turned on the track lights that illuminated the mushroom paintings, the conversation pit, and the well-stocked bar. "We'll have our drinks in the library, but I wanted you to see the artwork."

Inga nodded. "I knew Ross when he was in art school, before he got into mushrooms and found himself. Those paintings are worth plenty now . . . What's the cat doing?" Koko was burrowing under the dhurrie in front of the bar.

"Merely expressing his joy at seeing you again, Inga." He was loading a tray with bourbon, mineral water, glasses, and an ice bucket. "Go into the library and look at the art books while I get ice from the kitchen."

When he carried the tray into the library, Inga was exclaiming over the collection. "If they have an estate sale, I'll be the first in line. That's the only way I can afford books like these."

Qwilleran poured the drinks. "There won't be any bargains, Inga. The murder will give all of this stuff a juicy provenance, and the prices will skyrocket."

"Disgusting, isn't it?" she said. "Murder used

to be shocking. Now it's an opportunity for prof-
iteering.'' She raised her glass. ''Here's to the
memory of two good kids. I don't understand
how Ross could do it.''

''The autopsy showed drug use.''

She shook her head woefully. ''I can't picture
Ross as a druggie. He was kind of a health nut,
you know. He didn't go in for weight lifting or
jogging or anything like that, but he had definite
ideas about food. He was the next best thing to a
vegetarian.''

''What about his relationship with Lady Di?''

''Ah, there's the fly in the soup!'' Inga said.
''From what I hear, that's what broke up her marriage.''

''They say Ross's motive was jealousy. Di had
found a new protégé.''

Inga scowled into her gray bangs. ''Rewayne
Wilk. He was there tonight.''

''Spell it,'' Qwilleran requested.

''R-e-w-a-y-n-e W-i-l-k. Big blond with long hair
and a cleft chin. Maybe you saw his three mas-
terworks. He calls them *The Pizza Eaters*, *The Hot
Dog Eaters*, and *The Wing Ding Eaters*. All I can say
is . . . Van Gogh did it better with potatoes.''

''May I freshen your drink, Inga?''

''I never say no.''

''I suppose you've heard about Ross's confession painted on the wall,'' he said as he poured.
''I found it today. It had been painted over, but
the lettering shows through faintly.''

''Where? Let me see it.''

They went to the end of the foyer, Koko trotting ahead as if he knew their destination. Qwilleran removed the butcher block painting and sidelighted the wall with a bare lamp bulb.

Inga said, "It looks like he used pigment right out of the tube, and his brush was a #12 bright, but he spelled her name wrong. Poor kid! He had talent and a future, and he threw them both away."

"Speaking of wasted lives," Qwilleran said, "do you know Adelaide Plumb?"

"We've never met, but I've known about her for years."

"Do you know the story about her—how she sold her fiancé for millions to save the Casablanca?"

"It wasn't her idea," said Inga. "She did it under duress."

"What are you implying?"

"Her father set it up! That's not the conventional wisdom, but I happen to know that it's true. I was around in the Thirties, don't forget . . . What time is it? Here I am, babbling like an idiot, and it's time for me to go home. I live at the Senior Towers, and if I'm not in by eleven o'clock, they check the morgue."

"I'll take you home," Qwilleran said.

"Just call me a taxi."

Firmly he said, "Inga, I'm not letting you out of my sight until I deliver you to the Senior Towers and get a signed receipt."

"Well, I guess this is one of the perks when

207

you're eighty," she said, patting her gray bangs smugly.

Koko followed them to the door. "Back in a few minutes," Qwilleran promised, and when he returned, the cat was waiting expectantly. He led the way into the library and massaged the Scrabble box eagerly with his front paws.

"No games tonight, old boy," said Qwilleran. "We have matters to discuss."

Koko sat on the library table, tall and alert, as Qwilleran opened the covers of several large art books. Then he opened a desk drawer and examined the bracelet that Koko had found behind a sofa cushion.

"Inga is right," he said, addressing the cat. "Lady Di signed herself D-i-a-n-n-e on her bookplates. The Van Gogh was a gift from Ross, and he inscribed it 'To D-i-a-n-n-e from Ross.' The bracelet he gave her was engraved with the same double N. Why would he paint D-i-a-n-e on the wall?"

"Yow!" said Koko encouragingly.

"And why would he sign his so-called confession with his professional logo? He was 'Ross' on the bracelet and 'Ross' in the gift book." Qwilleran patted his moustache. "It looks to me as if the suicide was a hoax. Someone drugged him and threw him off the terrace, then went into his studio and got a tube of red paint."

"Rrrrrrrrrrrrrr," said Koko.

"Tomorrow we'll have a talk with Lieutenant Hames and let him figure out who really killed Lady Di, and who dumped her lover from the rear end of the terrace, where the floodlight doesn't reach.''

The cat slapped the table with his tail—twice.

''There may have been two of them involved in the crime.''

FOURTEEN

Author's note: There is no Chapter 13 in this book.

EARLY SATURDAY MORNING Qwilleran placed a telephone call to the Homicide Squad and left a message for Lieutenant Hames. When the phone rang a few minutes later, he was prepared to greet the detective but heard instead the soothing voice of Polly Duncan.

"Where were you last evening?" she began. "I tried to reach you."

"What time did you call?"

"At eleven, when the rates dropped."

To taunt her he replied, "I was taking a woman home. I met her at an art gallery, and we came here for a few drinks."

There was a worried pause. "Who was she?"

"An artist."

"Did you just . . . pick her up?"

"No, we'd met before. You don't need to worry, Polly. She's eighty years old and crippled with arthritis. Why were you trying to reach me?"

"To tell you that I read about you in the *Morning Rampage*. The library subscribes, you know. But mostly to thank you for the beautiful handbag. It's the nicest I've ever owned! That was very thoughtful of you, dearest, although it only makes me miss you more."

"I wanted you to know I'm thinking of you, in spite of being surrounded by female flashers and arthritic octogenarians and eccentric heiresses." He made no mention of Winnie Wingfoot, although he moistened his lips as her image flashed through his mind. "How's the kitten with a hollow leg?"

"Absolutely incorrigible! Last night I brought home two little lamb chops for my dinner, and as soon as I unwrapped them, he swooped in and dragged one down to the floor."

"Any news about the carriage house?"

"Yes, Mrs. Gage is letting me have it with the idea that I'll keep an eye on the big house while she's in Florida. So you can have your apartment, Qwill, if you come home. What did you decide?"

"I have eighteen more restaurants to try before I can return to face Moose County goulash."

"Oh, Qwill! It's not that bad! Where did you have dinner last night?"

"At a middle-eastern place downtown—hummus, pita, kabobs and tabbouleh."

"Alone?"

"Alone, and I have a receipted guest check to prove it."

After more affectionate banter Polly said, "Do be careful, dearest. If anything happened to you, it would break my heart, you know that."

"I'll be careful," he promised.

When he went out to breakfast, he discovered that Saturday morning was carnival time in the Casablanca lobby as the tenants turned out to shop for groceries, do laundry, pay the rent, pick up their dry cleaning, stock up on videos for the weekend, return books to the library, jog around the vacant lots, and do all the other busywork that occupies working people and students on their day off. Even the old and infirm were circulating; the two elderly women who usually drifted through the halls in quilted robes were fully dressed, explaining to everyone that they were being taken to visit a friend in a nursing home. Mrs. Tuttle was busy handling complaints and writing rent receipts. Rupert was directing a youth who was trying to mop the floor. Napoleon and Kitty-Baby were dodging feet.

After picking up a few treats for his roommates at a neighborhood deli, Qwilleran returned to the building and was heading for the elevator when he encountered the person he least wanted to meet. Surprisingly, Isabelle Wilburton presented a neat and appropriate appearance in a white blouse and khaki skirt. On previous occasions he had seen her in a spotted housecoat or a cocktail dress or a fur coat or less. She was carrying her kitten, nestled in a blue towel.

"Mr. Qwilleran, I took your advice," she said. "Isn't she adorable? Her name is Sweetie Pie."

"She's an appealing little cat," he agreed, "and she'll be good company for you."

"Would you like to have dinner with us tonight? I'm cooking a pot roast. I hope it will be good. I haven't really cooked anything for ages."

"I appreciate the thought," he said, "but I've already accepted another invitation."

"How about tomorrow night?" she asked hopefully.

"Unfortunately I've agreed to keep Sunday open for a meeting with the officers of SOCK. You see, I'm writing a book on the historic Casablanca."

"Oh, really? I could tell you a lot about that. My grandparents had an apartment here back in the 1920s, when it was so exclusive. My grandmother used to tell me stories about it."

"I'll keep that in mind. Thank you for the suggestion," he said, inwardly recoiling. "Has the mailperson been here?"

Isabelle waved an envelope. "Yes, the mail just came in." She appeared quite happy about it. No doubt the envelope contained her subsistence check.

Qwilleran went to the mailroom and found the door blocked by Ferdie Le Bull, his imprinted T-shirt stretched across his enormous chest. He confronted Qwilleran with the menacing scowl that was his idea of social grace. "When you gonna take the pictures?" he demanded.

"Of Miss Plumb's apartment? Whenever she gives her approval."

"Any time's okay. She never goes out."

"All right. I'll notify the photographer, and he'll call you to make an appointment."

"She's all het up about it," said the houseman. "Is he gonna take my picture, too?" He passed a hand over his bald head.

"Probably."

"Does he play bridge?"

"You'll have to ask him," said Qwilleran.

Encouraged by this positive development he determined to go ahead seriously with the book. As he waited for the elevator he visualized about thirty-percent text and seventy-percent black-and-white photos: views of the opulent lobby and Palm Pavilion, pictures of celebrities, old cars, and residents in nostalgic fashions—from Edwardian to Flapper Era to Early Thirties. In the center, a color section would feature overall shots of the Art Deco rooms as well as close-ups of the rare vase containing Harrison Plumb's ashes, the Cubist rugs and pillows, a tooled copper screen inset with ebony, tables with angular legs, club chairs with voluptuous curves, and walls of framed French art photos of the 1920s. It was all lush and otherworldly. The frontispiece would be Adelaide

St. John Plumb with her plucked and penciled eyebrows and her marcelled hair, sitting on the overstuffed sofa and pouring tea, looking like a living relic of the Casablanca's dim past.

For the text he would like to interview old-timers; surely there were such persons tucked away in odd corners of the building, living in faded splendor. It was a pity that Mrs. Button had not survived a little longer. Even Isabelle Wilburton might have to be interviewed.

As he pondered the possibilities, the door of Old Red opened, and the white-haired manager of Roberto's restaurant stepped from the car, accompanied by a pale-faced man who was much younger. He was the fellow with a bandage where his right ear should be.

Charlotte Roop was looking buoyantly happy. ''Oh, Mr. Qwilleran!'' she cried. ''I want you to meet my friend, Raymond Dimwitty . . . Ray, this is Mr. Qwilleran who I've told you so much about.''

Not believing what he had heard, Qwilleran said, ''I didn't catch the last name. Spell it for me.''

''D-u-n-w-o-o-d-y,'' said the man.

Qwilleran made heroic attempts not to stare at the ear patch as they exchanged polite words.

Charlotte said, ''We always go out to lunch on Saturday and then to a movie. There's a discount if you go early, and I don't have to be at the restaurant until four.''

''I hope you have an enjoyable afternoon. You

have good weather for it," Qwilleran said courteously.

Old Red had gone up without him, and now he waited for Old Green, wondering how this unlikely couple had met: Charlotte with her fluttery, spinsterish manner and white hair like spun sugar, a woman well past retirement age, and Raymond Dunwoody with his ear patch and blank expression, a man not over forty-five. When the elevator arrived and opened its reluctant door, a cheerful passenger with a laundry basket, on her way up from the basement, crowed, "Oh, wow! We have somebody rich and famous living here now!" This was followed by a gusty laugh.

"If I were rich and famous, I wouldn't be living at Ye Olde Broken-down Casablanca," Qwilleran said with forced geniality that concealed his irritation. He disembarked at Three and walked the rest of the way up to Fourteen, silently cursing Sasha what's her name for revealing his financial status. He enjoyed the role of a retired journalist; he did not enjoy the role of a millionaire. Briefly, he considered moving to the Penniman Plaza until he remembered that hotels did not accept cats.

On the way upstairs he heard an ambulance siren winding down in front of the building. Another casualty! Who was it this time?

Arriving at 14-A he found a newspaper clipping under his door with a note from Amber scrawled in the margin: "Did you see this?" It came from the business page of Saturday's *Morning Rampage*—an interview with one of the principals of Penniman, Greystone & Fleudd. Rexwell Fleudd stated that the proposed Gateway Alcazar was fifty percent leased, and ground would be broken sooner than expected. A one-column head shot of the developer showed a long narrow face with high cheekbones and blow-dried hair. Qwilleran crumpled it in disgust and tossed it in the wastebasket.

Immediately the delicate thud of velvet paws could be heard, bounding out of the bedroom, and Yum Yum, the sleeping beauty, made a nosedive into the wastebasket to retrieve the crumpled clipping. The crumpling of paper was a sound she could hear in her dreams. Qwilleran took it away from her, not wanting her to chew it and ingest printer's ink. As he did so, he had another look at that arrogant face and wondered where he had seen it before.

Yum Yum was peeved, and to assuage her ruffled feelings he stroked her fur and paid her a few lavish compliments on her pulchritude, her sweetness of disposition, and her nobility of character. She purred—and went back to bed.

Why does she loll around so much? he asked himself. Is it the smog? Or some kind of stress?

Meanwhile, Koko was waiting for action on the Scrabble table, and he won the first few draws so handily that Qwilleran changed the rules to permit proper nouns, slang, and foreign words. Even with a handicap the cat won, but the man had the satisfaction of spelling such words as IXION, MERCI, CIAO, and SNAFU. Toward the end of the game he spelled a word that proved to be prophetic: OOPS.

As it happened, he intended to spend the afternoon at the library, and on his way downtown he stopped at the Penniman Plaza for lunch. The coffee shop was on the mezzanine, and he was stepping on the upward-bound escalator when he heard a cracked voice directly behind him crying, ''Help me!''

He half-turned and caught a glimpse of a dirty white beard. At the same moment someone grabbed his arm. What happened next seemed to be in slow motion: his hand reaching for the handrail . . . the handrail moving beyond his grasp . . . his body sinking backward . . . his feet continuing to move upward . . . the steps behind him rising to meet his spine . . . the whole escalator ascending relentlessly as he lay on his back, riding to the mezzanine feetfirst.

The absurdity of his position stunned him momentarily until screams from onlookers recalled the episode on the subway tracks and marshalled his wits. In a matter of seconds he had to swing his legs around in the narrow space, maneuver his feet lower than his head, scramble to his knees, stand up. Just as the moving steps telescoped into the floor above, he was upright, and hands were helping him step onto terra firma.

''Are you hurt, sir?'' a security man asked.

''I don't think so,'' Qwilleran replied. ''Only a trifle surprised.''

''Let me take you to the manager's office, sir.''

''First I want to sit down and have a cup of coffee and figure out what happened.''

''You can get coffee right here in the bar, sir.

Are you sure you're all right?'' The uniformed guard conducted Qwilleran into a dimly lighted lounge. ''I'll notify the manager, sir. He'll send someone down.''

''Mr. Qwilleran! What happened?'' the bartender called out. He had a reddish moustache, and Qwilleran recognized the jogger from the Casablanca.

''I don't know exactly.''

Another security guard arrived on the scene. ''I was down there. I seen it. One of them kooks that wanders around—kind of unsteady on his feet—wanted to get on the escalator, and I told him not to. He grabbed this man's arm.''

''I rode up feetfirst,'' Qwilleran explained to the bartender. ''I've gone feetfirst into worse situations than this, but I'll admit this was a peculiar sensation.''

''You need a stiff drink. What'll it be?''

''My days as a stiff drinker are over, but I could use a strong cup of coffee.''

''Coming right up.''

Qwilleran sipped the brew gratefully while security personnel hovered about to prevent his escape, pending the arrival of a hotel official. He said to the bartender, ''You know my name but I don't know yours.''

''Randy. Randy Jupiter. I remember reading your column when you wrote for the *Fluxion*—the reviews about restaurants, I mean. I clipped every one and then checked them out on my day off. You were always right on!''

Qwilleran smoothed his moustache. Having his

column clipped was his favorite kind of compliment. ''A lot of new eating places have opened since then,'' he said. ''I've been away for three years.''

''They sure have! It looks like nobody stays home and cooks anymore. How long are you going to be here? I could recommend a few good ones.''

''My plans aren't definite. I'm here to write a book on the Casablanca, and it will depend on what luck I have with research.''

''The *Rampage* said you're going to buy the building,'' Jupiter said with a grin.

''No one believes the *Rampage*. Stick with the *Fluxion*, boy.''

''Didn't you say you're on Fourteen?''

''In 14-A.''

''That must be the Bessinger apartment. I've never seen it, but I hear it's something else.''

''It's unique,'' Qwilleran agreed.

The assistant manager appeared, and Qwilleran assured her he was not hurt and saw no reason to hold the hotel responsible. He willingly supplied the personable young woman with the information she needed for her report and accepted vouchers good for dinner and dry cleaning. When the transaction was completed the bartender said to Qwilleran, ''That's not too shabby.''

''She might have offered to go to dinner with me. Then it would be worth the indignity of riding up feetfirst. How long have you lived at the Casablanca?''

"Just a few months. Do you like jazz?"

"I was a jazzhound in college but I haven't done much listening lately." Qwilleran felt comfortable with the bartender. It was his private theory that men with large moustaches tend to gravitate toward other men with large moustaches. Likewise, fat men get together. Men with beards or long hair like to talk to men with beards or long hair.

Jupiter said, "I've got a super collection of old jazz artists. Any time you want to hear some great sounds like Jelly Roll, the Duke—"

"Do you have Charlie Parker?"

"I have everything. Just knock on my door. I'm in 6-A."

"My apartment has a fantastic stereo system and spectacular acoustics," Qwilleran said. "Perhaps you'd like to bring some recordings upstairs."

"I'd go for that."

"I'll get in touch with you."

"Call me here or at home." Jupiter scribbled two phone numbers on a cocktail napkin.

"Okay. Now I'm ready for lunch."

Lunch at the Penniman coffee shop was agreeably uneventful. Qwilleran also welcomed the scholarly silence of the library's history department, where he selected photos and signed an order for copies to be made.

Back at the Casablanca, 14-A was equally quiet. Too quiet! Koko seemed preoccupied as he waited for the mincing of the roast beef from the deli, and Yum Yum did not report at all until Qwilleran went to the bedroom and said, ''Would Cleopatra consent to rise from her divan and repair to the dining salon for a light repast?''

He should have known that Koko's distracted demeanor was the countdown before the blast-off.

FIFTEEN

KOKO'S ABNORMAL BEHAVIOR during the preparation of his dinner meant that mischief was hatching in that fine brown head. But Qwilleran had other matters on his mind, such as: what to wear for his dinner engagement at Courtney Hampton's apartment. Amber had specified that dress would be casual. Remembering the clothing salesman's supercilious gibe (''Just in from the country?''), he deliberately chose to wear his cashmere pullover, a garment that would impress anyone who knew the price of sweaters. At the appointed time he walked downstairs to the eighth floor and knocked on Amber's door. When she opened it he caught a glimpse of a room piled high with cardboard cartons and shopping bags.

"How recently did you move in?" he asked as they walked down the hall to the front of the building.

"I've been here two years, but it seems I never get around to unpacking," she said with a humorously hopeless shrug. "Now—let me tell you about Courtney's place, so it won't come as a total shock. He has one of the big old apartments, and he puts on the dog when he entertains, even hiring a woman to cook and a man to serve. But he doesn't have any furniture!"

"If the food is good, I'm prepared to eat off the floor," Qwilleran said. "Incidentally, I have yet to see an apartment in this building other than the penthouse and the Art Deco extravaganza on Twelve."

"I meant to ask, how did you get along with the Countess?"

"Very well. We played Scrabble, and I let her win a little."

"You men are so gallant—when you lose."

A pair of topiary trees flanked the entrance to 8-A. "He only puts them out when he's having company," Amber explained as she clanged the door knocker.

"I hope he also takes in the brass knocker when he goes to bed," Qwilleran said. "Someone stole my plastic rubbish container last night."

The door was opened by an emaciated gray-haired man in a white duck coat—someone Qwilleran had seen in the lobby, or on the elevator, or possibly in the laundry room. Not far behind him was the host, wearing a coolie suit in black silk and making gestures of Oriental welcome.

"Well, look at you!" Amber exclaimed.

"Just in from the rice paddy?" Qwilleran asked.

They entered a large room with dark walls lighted only by candles, Amber remarking, "I see Mrs. Tuttle cut off your electricity again."

Courtney reproached her with flared nostrils. "What you see here," he said to Qwilleran, loftily, "is one of the original suites, occupied for sixty years by a bachelor judge. All I did was paint the walls Venetian red. The black walnut woodwork and the hardwood floors are original. I apologize for the lack of furniture. Special-order items take an *unconscionably* long time."

"They're growing the trees," Amber said.

As Qwilleran's eyes became accustomed to the dim light, he realized he was in a room at least fifty feet long and bare enough to be a ballroom. In one corner was a compact seating arrangement: two couches right-angled against the wall, covered with fringed Spanish rugs and heaped with pillows of some ethnic origin. The couches were actually army cots, he later decided. For a cocktail table there was a large square of thick plate glass supported by concrete blocks, and under it was a worn Persian rug, the only floor covering in the room. Three long-stemmed white carnations in a tall crystal vase looked aggressively contemporary. In candlelight the corner was almost glamorous.

"You have a new rug," Amber observed.

"A semi-antique Tabriz, my dear—this month's acquisition from our friend Isabelle."

She explained to Qwilleran, "He means Isabelle Wilburton. He's systematically stripping the poor woman's apartment."

"I am keeping the poor woman *afloat*," Courtney said with hauteur. "Last month's acquisition was that painting over the sideboard—American, of course—probably of the Hudson River school. A curator from the art museum is coming here tomorrow to identify it incontrovertibly." The misty landscape in an elaborate gilded frame was hanging above a sideboard composed of two large, wooden packing cases, on which stood a silver teaset. "Would we all like a margarita?"

"Qwill doesn't drink," Amber announced.

"Evian?" asked the host.

"Evian will do," Qwilleran said, "if you don't have Squunk water."

The other two gave him a brief questioning glance. No one outside of Moose County had ever heard of Squunk water. Then Courtney turned to the white-coated server. "Hopkins, bring us two margaritas and an Evian for the gentleman." The white coat disappeared into the gloom at the far end of the room, and the host went on. "Originally the suite consisted of this drawing room plus a large bedroom totally without closets plus a *huge* bathroom. *Where* did they hang their clothes in 1901? And *what* did they do in the bathroom that required so much space? Fortunately the judge added closets and a kitchenette.''

Amber said to Qwilleran, "You should see Court's previous apartment. It was like a cell at Leavenworth."

"*Courtney!*" he corrected her with a frown.

The drinks and a silver bowl of macadamia nuts were served by Hopkins, moving as if in a trance.

Qwilleran asked, "How was your card game Wednesday night?"

"Not too excruciating, although I could manage nicely without the camomile tea and caraway seed cake. The Countess was my partner. Considering that she acts like a ghost of the 1920s, she's a *killer* at the bridge table."

"Who else was there?" Amber asked.

"Winnie Wingfoot and that *pushy* Randy Jupiter. He probably *bribed* Ferdie to include him," Courtney said with a curled lip.

"I think Randy has a lot of personality," Amber said in his defense.

"*Too much* personality. I don't trust that kind. And he *jogs.*"

"You're such a snob, Court."

"*Courtney*, please!"

"At least Randy is friendly and alive," she persisted. "Most of the people in this building are half dead."

The host said, "That reminds me, guess who died today?"

"Okay, twenty questions," Amber said. "Was it a man?"

"No."

"Then it was a woman. Did she wear a hearing aid?"

"No."

"Was she in her eighties?"

"No."

"In her seventies?"

"No. You'll never guess, Amber."

"Did she live on Seven?"

"No."

"Did she break her hip last year?"

"Give up, Amber. Give up! You'll never guess," said Courtney. "According to Madame Defarge—who sits behind her bulletproof window, knitting and counting bodies—it was *Elpidia* that they carried out."

"What!" cried Amber.

"Who's Elpidia?" Qwilleran asked.

"The Countess's personal maid," she said. "What happened, Courtney?"

"They say it was food poisoning, but I think it was an O.D. Being personal maid to the Countess would drive *anyone* to pills."

Qwilleran said, "I never saw the maid or the housekeeper."

"The maid was kind of weird, but the housekeeper's nice," Amber informed him. "She's Ferdie's mother. She has her own apartment on Two, but Ferdie lives in."

"She commutes daily to Twelve, where she bakes her *famous* caraway seed cake," Courtney added. "Incidentally, I've asked Winnie to drop in for a drink before she goes out for the evening . . . Have you met Winnie, Qwill? May I call you Qwill?''

''By all means . . . I haven't met Ms. Wingfoot but I've seen her. A beautiful girl!''

''When I look at Winnie,'' Amber said, ''I want to go home and take an O.D. myself.''

The door knocker resounded, and Qwilleran's pulse quickened. He smoothed his moustache and jumped to his feet as Hopkins admitted the satin-clad model. She glided into the room, glittering and dragging a fur jacket.

''Winnie, my angel,'' said the host, ''this is Qwill Qwilleran, who is going to buy the Casablanca.''

''Not true,'' said Qwilleran, taking the hand that was extended languidly in his direction.

''Our paths have crossed,'' said Winnie. ''In the car park, under inauspicious circumstances. I trust your difficulties were satisfactorily resolved.''

''Thanks to your prompt assistance, Ms. Wingfoot.''

''Winifred,'' she corrected him.

''Would you like a margarita, angel?'' the host asked.

''It would pleasure me immensely.''

She sat on the army cot next to Qwilleran, who was aware of a heady scent and long silky legs.

''The weather turned out to be quite pleasant today,'' he said, knowing that it was a dumb remark.

''Quite revivifying,'' she said.

''Did you buy Isabelle's piano?'' Courtney asked her. ''She told me you were looking at it.''

''I have it under consideration.''

''Do you play?'' Qwilleran inquired.

''Yes, rather well,'' she replied, bestowing a sultry glance on his moustache.

Courtney said, ''Mrs. Button died this week, and Madame Defarge says there's going to be a tag sale. I hope it's true. I have my sights on a small Rubens Peale.''

Hopkins materialized from the dark end of the room with a tray of margaritas.

Amber said, ''Isabelle has adopted a cat, and I may have to break down and get one myself. I had another mouse last night.''

''If you would clean up your apartment, Amberina dear,'' said Courtney, ''you would solve your problem. The little things are *incubating* in those eighty-four shopping bags . . . When is the Bessinger estate going to be liquidated, Qwill?''

''I have no idea. I'm just subletting while I work on a book about the Casablanca.''

Courtney explained to Winnie, ''Qwill is a noted journalist.''

''How delicious!'' she said.

''I'm hoping to interview old-timers who remember something about the early days. Any recommendations?''

''Mrs. Jasper!'' said Courtney and Amber in unison.

''She did housework in the Casablanca way back when,'' Amber said, ''and she can tell you all kinds of stories.''

Winnie, upon finishing her drink, uncrossed her incredible legs and rose, saying, "I regret I must wrench myself away from this stimulating group, but I have a dinner date."

As the host escorted her to the door, Qwilleran remarked quietly to Amber, "I imagine she has no trouble getting dinner dates."

"I'm in the wrong business," she whispered.

Courtney lighted candles at the dark end of the room, where planks were laid across columns of concrete blocks to form a long narrow table. "Hopkins, tell Cook we wish to serve now," he said.

The seats were upended orange crates, each with a velvet cushion weighted at the four corners with tassels. "Watch out for splinters," Amber warned Qwilleran.

For a table centerpiece white carnations were arranged with weeds from the parking lot. Pewter service plates and goblets were set on the bare boards, and there were four tall pewter candlesticks.

"Where did you steal these?" Amber asked, and Courtney reproved her with a withering glance.

The soup course was cream of watercress, followed by crabcakes with shitake mushrooms, baby beets in an orange glaze, and wild rice. A salad of artichoke hearts and sprouts was served on Lalique plates as a separate course, and the meal ended with a chocolate soufflé. Not bad, Qwilleran thought, for a crate-and-block environment.

Amber said to him, "Every year on the Fourth of July Courtney gives a party on the roof with picnic baskets full of chicken and wine and cherry tarts. The roof is a super place to watch the fireworks."

"How do you get up there?"

"There's a stairway from Fourteen. The door says No Admittance, but it's never locked. It's a nice place to sun in the summer."

Qwilleran said, "As an expert on the Casablanca scene, perhaps you could answer some questions, Courtney. How come Rupert never seems to do any work? He just hangs around."

"Actually he's a security guard," said the host, "and he has an *arsenal* under that ill-fitting jacket."

"How about this guy Yazbro on Four?"

"He's a furniture mover with one claim to fame: Ross's body landed on his car, and he got his name in the paper. Shall we have coffee in the lounge area? And would we all like to hear some Noel Coward?" He moved toward a stack of strawberry crates containing cassettes and compact discs.

"Play the tape of your own show, Courtney," said Amber. She turned to Qwilleran. "He's producing an original musical called *The Casablanca Cathouse*, and the opening number is a blast!"

"I'm doing the book and lyrics, but I haven't found a composer yet," said the impresario. "Keestra is doing the choreography. You may have heard, Qwill, about Keestra Hedrog and her Gut Dancers. She lives in 14-B."

"Are they belly dancers? I've heard some strange bumps coming through the wall."

"They're non-disciplinary, non-motivational interpreters of basic sensibilities," Courtney explained patronizingly.

"Play the opening number, Court," Amber urged.

"*Courtney!*" he rebuked her. "You'll have to imagine the music."

The tape started to unreel, and his voice, with an affected British accent, announced, "Presenting a musical in two acts by Courtney Hampton. *The Casablanca Cathouse*—Act one, Scene one." The lyrics followed:

*There's a spot that has been libeled as an odious
    address
Because it's old and battered and the lobby is a
    mess.
True . . .
The roof may leak, the hallways reek,
The elevators fail to rise, the ceilings drop before
    your eyes,
But it's really not as squalid as you'd guess.
The window sills may start to rot, the taps run
    dry (both cold and hot),
And occasionally the kitchen sink develops a
    peculiar stink,
But it's really not as nasty as you think.
Yes . . .
The Casablanca Cathouse is a marvelous place to
    live,
Tenants getting more exclusive all the time!*

*The strippers from the Bijou were evicted the
     first night.*
*We've lost the drunken deadbeats who had that
     bloody fight.*
*There's a madam on Eleven, but she seems a bit
     all right,*
And the window washer fell and gave up crime.
Yes . . .
*The Casablanca Cathouse is a MARVELOUS
     place to live!*
The mice are getting smaller every year.
*We're just a tad Bohemian with a decadent kind
     of chic.*
*We pass each other in the halls and never, never
     speak.*
*Whenever we get mugged, we simply turn the
     other cheek.*
To be normal, good, or rational is queer.
Oh . . .
*We've got intriguing clutches of folks with canes
     and crutches,*
And lonely wraiths and elderly voyeurs,
*And male and female flashers and flocks of aging
     mashers,*
And gorgeous broads in diamonds and furs.
Yes . . .
*The Casablanca Cathouse is a MA-A-
     ARVELOUS place to live!*
All others by comparison seem dead.
It has a reputation as a seedy sort of spot.
*No one runs for Congress, and no one owns a
     yacht,*

But things are getting better since Poor Old Gus
  was shot,
And the helicopter's always overhead!

There was a long pause, Courtney pressed a button, and he and Amber looked expectantly at their guest.

"It'll never play Broadway," Qwilleran said, "but you might do a season on the Casablanca roof."

"The plot," the author explained, "is based on the Bessinger murder."

Qwilleran was staring into space. He cupped a hand around his moustache. He jumped to his feet. "I've got to get upstairs! Excuse me," he blurted, heading for the door. "Great evening! Great dinner!" He was out in the hall when he finished his explanation, and he ran upstairs to Fourteen. A tremor on his upper lip warned him of trouble.

As he unlocked the door to 14-A, he heard water running and splashing. He dashed down the bedroom hall, flipping wall switches as he went. When he reached the master bedroom he found the floor wet. *The Waterbed!* he thought . . . No, the gushing and splashing came from the bathroom. He turned on the light. The floor was flooded! The washbowl was overflowing; the faucet was running full force; and there on the toilet tank sat Koko, surveying his achievement.

SIXTEEN

WHEN QWILLERAN RUSHED into 14-A and found the bathroom flooded and the culprit sitting on the toilet tank, he had no time to analyze motives. He tore off his shoes and socks, threw bath towels on the floor, then squeezed them out—a performance that Koko found diverting. Qwilleran growled into his moustache but realized the futility of a reprimand. If he said "Bad cat!" Koko would merely gaze at him with that no-speak-English expression.

The mopping job finished, he took the towels

to the basement to put in the dryer, but the laundry room was locked for the night. It gave him time, however, as he rode down on sluggish Old Red and up again on laggard Old Green, to think about Koko's misdemeanor. The cat had rubbed his jaw against the lever-type faucet. It was obviously neurotic behavior; he was bored and lonely and wanted to attract attention. With Yum Yum in her indolent mood, Koko missed the chasing, frolicking, wrestling, and mutual grooming sessions that are so important to Siamese pairs.

It's my fault, Qwilleran said to himself; I dragged them to the city when they wanted to stay in the country.

Koko was waiting for him when he returned with the pail of wet towels. "I'm sorry, old friend," he said. "Tomorrow's Sunday. We'll spend the day together. We'll find something interesting to do. If the weather permits, how would you like to go for a walk on the roof?"

"Yow," said Koko, squeezing his eyes.

He gave the cats a bedtime snack—a morsel of smoked salmon from the deli—and was getting into his pajamas when he had reason to pause and listen. Something could be heard crawling under the floor.

"That's no mouse," he said aloud. "That's a rat!"

The cats heard it, too, Koko scurrying around with his nose to the floor, and even Yum Yum sniffing in a lackadaisical way.

Qwilleran strode to the housephone in the

kitchen and rang the manager's night number. Rupert answered.

"Rupert! This is Qwilleran on Fourteen. We've got rats up here under the floor! . . . Rats! That's what I said. R-a-t-s! Yes, I can hear them under the floor in the master bedroom. The cats hear them, too . . . Oh! Is that so? . . . Hmmm, I see. That's too bad . . . Well, sorry to bother you, Rupert. Good night."

He returned to the bedroom. "It's a plumber in the crawl space," he informed the Siamese. "He's investigating a leak. Water's dripping down into the Countess's bedroom. Does that make you feel guilty, Koko?"

The cat laundered a spot on his chest with exasperating nonchalance.

If it had happened to any apartment but that of the Countess, Qwilleran reflected, the management would have waited until Monday.

True to his word he spent Sunday with the Siamese, first grooming them both with a new rubber-bristled brush he had found in a pet shop. Then he read aloud to them from *Eothen*, Yum Yum falling asleep on his lap during the chapter on the Cairo plague. Around noontime he strapped the harness on Koko and took him for a walk—out of the apartment, across the elevator lobby, through the door marked No Admittance, up two flights of stairs, and out onto the roof, Koko marching with soldierly step and perpendicular tail.

It was glorious on the rooftop. There was a dramatic view of the downtown skyline and the river curving away to the south. The cat sniffed the breeze hungrily and tugged on the leash; he wanted to walk to the edge. Qwilleran had other ideas; he pulled Koko to the skylight and peered down into the penthouse apartment. Although the glass was clouded with age, certain panes had been replaced in recent times, and it was possible to see the long sofa, the large paintings, and some of the potted trees. At night, with the gallery lighted, anyone on the roof could look down and see whatever was happening in the conversation pit.

Qwilleran thought, What if . . . ? What if someone on the roof had witnessed the murder of Di Bessinger and knew the true identity of the murderer? Why wouldn't he come forward with the information? Because he would fear for his own life, or because he would recognize an opportunity for blackmail? But that was the way it happened in mystery novels, not in real life.

The skylight held no attraction for Koko, who preferred to walk on the low parapet that edged the roof. Together they made one complete turn around the perimeter before going downstairs for the next activity, which was Scrabble.

Hardly had the game started when the telephone rang. Qwilleran hoped it might be Winnie Wingfoot; he had a hunch she would follow up their brief acquaintance of the evening before. Instead, it was the disappointing, reedy voice of Charlotte Roop.

"Are you busy, Mr. Qwilleran? I hope I'm not interrupting anything."

"I was just thinking of going for a walk," he said, "but that's all right."

"I wondered if I could go up and see your beautiful pussycats a little later on, if it wouldn't be too much of an imposition."

She had shown no interest in the Siamese when they lived on River Road. "Sure," he said without enthusiasm. "What time would be convenient?"

"Well, I'm due at the restaurant at four, and if I went up there about three thirty . . ."

"That's good," he said, thinking that she would be unable to stay long. "I'll expect you at three thirty. I'm in 14-A."

"Do you mind if I bring my friend?"

"Of course I don't mind." What else could he say?

To Koko he said, "Your old pal Charlotte is dropping in at three thirty. Try to act like a gentleman." During their previous acquaintance, which had been brief, the cat had gone out of his way to shock and embarrass the woman. Charlotte was easily shocked and embarrassed in those days.

They went back to their Scrabble. Koko was partial to the letter O, and Qwilleran was building words like FOOT, ROOF, TOOT, and DODO when the telephone rang again. This time he was sure it was Winnie Wingfoot, but it was Isabelle Wilburton, and she was inebriated.

"Watcha doin'?" she asked in a sleepy voice.

"I'm working at my desk," he said coolly.

"Mind if I . . . come up?"

"I'm afraid this is not a good time to visit. I'm concentrating on a problem."

"Wanna come down here?"

"I've just told you, Miss Wilburton, that I'm extremely busy and cannot leave my work at this time," he said with a touch of impatience.

"Why don'cha call me Isabelle?"

"All right, Isabelle. As I said, I can't interrupt what I'm doing."

"Don'cha like me?"

He had a great desire to hang up, but he said as graciously as he could, "It's not that I don't like you; it's simply that you are calling at an inopportune time."

"Don'cha wanna see my cat?"

"I've seen your cat, Isabelle. I saw her in the lobby yesterday. She's a nice little kitten and I told you so."

"Wanna come and have dinner?"

He tried to speak kindly. "Perhaps you don't remember, but I told you yesterday that I have a dinner meeting with the officers of SOCK."

"Nobody wants to eat with me," she whined. "I don't have any friends. I'm gonna jump off the roof."

"Now, wait a minute, Isabelle. Don't talk like that. You have a good life ahead of you. How old are you?"

"Forty-two. Forty-three. Don't remember."

"Do you remember the conversation we had in the laundry room? I had the same experience when I was your age, so I know how you feel and what you're going through. I also know you can get help, the way I did, and start enjoying a good life again. There are groups you can join, where you'll meet people who have the same problem as yours.''

"Don't have any problem. Just don't have any friends. No reason to live anymore. Gonna go up on the roof and jump off.''

"Isabelle, the last time I saw you in the lobby you were carrying your kitten in a blue blanket, and you seemed very happy. What's the name of your kitten?''

"Sweetie Pie.'' Her speech was slurred.

"Is she good company?''

There was no answer. He thought he heard a glug and a swallow.

"What do you feed her?''

"Stuff out of a can.''

"Do you play with her? Kittens like to play. You should tie a twist of paper on a string and swing it around—let her jump for it and chase it.'' It was an asinine conversation, but he was trying to distract her from her grisly intention. "Where does she sleep?''

"On my bed.''

"Is she a happy cat?''

"Guess so.''

"Does she purr a lot?'' He hoped that something would capture her interest.

"I dunno.''

"Kittens need love and attention. They like to be brushed, too. Have you tried brushing her?'' Qwilleran mopped his brow. Why was he perspiring? Why was he working so hard? She wasn't even listening.

"Wanna come down . . . have a drink?" she mumbled.

"Have you had anything to eat today, Isabelle?"

"Gonna jump off the roof . . . end it all."

"Listen, Isabelle, you can't do that. Think of Sweetie Pie! She needs you! What would she do without you? She's just a helpless kitten."

"Gonna take her with me."

He paused for an instant. Then, "Hold the line a minute, Isabelle. Don't hang up! I'll be right back!"

Hurrying to the kitchen he rang the housephone. "Isabelle Wilburton's threatening to jump off the roof!" he shouted. "I've got her on the phone!"

"Keep her on the line," Mrs. Tuttle said. "I'll go up to her apartment."

He rushed back to his phone in the library but heard only a dial tone. Was she on the way to the roof—with the kitten? Running out of the apartment and slamming the door, he sprinted up two flights of stairs, three at a time; there was no one up there. He waited for a while, but Isabelle didn't appear. Could she have arrived before him? Impossible! Yet he looked over the edge apprehensively. A wind had sprung up, and he stepped inside the stairwell for protection.

What am I doing here at the Casablanca? he asked himself. It had been nothing but stress in the last week: cranky elevators, cold showers, runaway radiators, the Gut Dancers, trouble in the parking lot, the crazy Countess, and now Isabelle! After ten or fifteen minutes he was sure she had been intercepted, and he started downstairs. At the bottom of the second flight he received a harsh surprise. The steel door shutting off the stairwell was locked!

At first he refused to believe it. Then he realized that Mrs. Tuttle had sent Rupert up to lock the door and foil the would-be suicide. He banged on the door with a fist, hoping that Keestra Hedrog would be spending a quiet Sunday afternoon at home and would hear him. The only response was a muffled ''Yow!'' from behind the door of 14-A. Koko knew he was in trouble, but a lot of good that did!

Qwilleran returned to the roof and looked over the edge, doubting that he could signal for help from that height. There was no one in the parking lot, Sundays at the Casablanca being as quiet as Saturdays were hectic. He circled the roof, hoping to see a pedestrian walking a dog on Zwinger Boulevard, or a jogger behind the building, or someone throwing rubbish into the dumpster. There was no one in sight, and it was getting cold.

Slowly he started down the two flights to Fourteen. In the stairwell he could hear the machinery in the elevator housing, as well as a certain familiar clanking and banging that meant Old Red or Old Green was approaching Fourteen. He ran down the stairs and was pounding on the door and calling for help when the elevator arrived.

''Oh, dear!'' said a timid voice. ''Who's that?''

"I'm locked in the stairwell! Get the manager to open the door!"

"Oh, dear! This is Charlotte, Mr. Qwilleran. We were just coming to see you . . . Raymond, go down to the desk and tell them. I'll stay here."

There were sounds of an elevator descending.

"How did you get locked in there, Mr. Qwilleran?" asked the reedy voice that now sounded so welcome, so comforting.

"You'll never believe my story," he said on the other side of the door. "I'll tell you when I get out."

"Roberto is expecting you for dinner tonight. He said to send you up to his apartment when you arrive."

"Am I holding you up? I don't want you to be late for work."

"Oh, no, it's only twenty-five minutes to four. I'm sure Raymond will get someone right away."

Qwilleran had always found conversation with Charlotte to be strained, even without a heavy door between them, and he was relieved when the elevator made its noisy arrival and Rupert unlocked the door.

"Nobody told me you was on the roof," he said.

"Nobody knew. Thanks, Rupert. I wasn't looking forward to spending the night in the stairwell. You'll have to let me into 14-A, too. I forgot my key."

Standing by were Charlotte Roop and her friend with the ear patch. Qwilleran felt momentarily grateful to both of them, and he felt a flash of sympathy for Dunwoody, wondering why he wore such a noticeable badge of his deformity. Perhaps he could not afford a prosthetic ear.

"Come in," he said. "Welcome to the garden spot of the Casablanca."

The two entered, gazing in wonder.

"Were you never here before?" he asked.

"No," said Charlotte. "I never was."

"Where did it happen?" Dunwoody asked.

"Where did what happen?"

"The murder."

"I don't know," Qwilleran said untruthfully. He opened the French doors to the gallery. "This is the former swimming pool, now a combination living room and art gallery. Won't you go in and sit down? Be careful going down the steps. I'll try to find the cats."

Awestruck, the couple wandered into the sky-lighted wonderland of potted trees and gargantuan mushrooms.

Qwilleran found Yum Yum in the bedroom, dozing on the waterbed, and he found Koko in the bathroom, sitting in the turkey roaster—just sitting there. "No comment, please," he said to the cat. When he returned to the gallery with an animal under each arm, his visitors were huddled close together on the twenty-foot sofa like babes in the wilderness.

"Here they are! This one is Koko, the male, and this is Yum Yum, the female," he said, aware of the inanity of the statement.

"What kind are they?" asked Dunwoody.

"Siamese. Very intelligent."

Yum Yum demonstrated her intelligence by scampering up the stairs, through the French doors and back to the waterbed. Koko scratched his ear with a hind foot, a trick that required him to cross his eyes and show his fangs—the least attractive pose in his entire repertory.

"May I offer you a drink?" Qwilleran asked.

"Nothing for me," said Charlotte.

"Wouldn't mind a beer," Dunwoody said, his impassive face showing a glimmer of interest.

Excusing himself, Qwilleran went to the kitchen and returned with a tray. "Just in case you want to change your mind," he said to Charlotte, "here is a glass of white grapejuice." He refrained from saying that it was Koko's private stock; the notion would have offended her. Dunwoody reached for his glass of beer gingerly; it was doubtlessly the only beer he had ever drunk from Waterford cut crystal. "Cheers!" Qwilleran said grimly as he raised his own glass of grapejuice.

"Unusual room," said Dunwoody.

"The entire apartment was created from a former restaurant called the Palm Pavilion. The building has an interesting history. I'm thinking of writing a book about it."

Charlotte said to her friend, "Mr. Qwilleran is a brilliant writer." They both gazed on him in wonder.

"Are you also in the restaurant business?" Qwilleran asked the man.

"No, I work for the city."

"He's an engineer," said Charlotte proudly.

"How do you like living in the country, Mr. Qwilleran?"

"Now that I've adjusted to the fresh air, safe streets, and lack of traffic, I like it."

"I've always lived in the city. So has Raymond, haven't you, dear?" She turned and beamed at her companion.

Qwilleran resisted a desire to look at his watch. "How long have you lived at the Casablanca?"

"Ever since they tore down our old building on River Road. Raymond moved in . . . when did you move in, dear?"

"Four months ago."

"It's convenient to our work," she explained.

"That's a definite advantage," said Qwilleran.

"The bus stops in front." This was Dunwoody's contribution.

The three looked at each other, Qwilleran trying desperately to think of something to say. It was the longest ten minutes in his memory.

Dunwoody spoke again. "What's that cat doing?"

Koko was burrowing under the dhurrie in front of the bar.

"Stop that, Koko!" Qwilleran scolded. He dragged the cat from under the rug and straightened it to cover the bloodstain. "It's a bad habit he's picked up. Another beer, Mr. Dunwoody?"

"It's time for me to go to work," said Charlotte. "Come, Raymond. Thank you, Mr. Qwilleran."

"My pleasure, I assure you. It's fortunate that you happened along when you did." He had been

248

so relieved to see them arrive, and now he was so relieved to see them leave!

His guests climbed out of the conversation pit, murmured their goodbyes, and left the apartment. If Qwilleran had been a drinking man, he would have poured a double scotch. Instead he scooped a large dishful of Neapolitan ice cream for himself and a spoonful for the Siamese. They lapped up the vanilla but showed their disapproval of the chocolate and strawberry by pawing the air in sign language that said, "Take it and bury it!"

Considering the events of the afternoon, Qwilleran was glad when it was time to dress and go to dinner at Roberto's. Out came the gray suit again, and at six thirty he walked to the Blue Dragon to pick up Mary Duckworth.

On the way to the restaurant she said, "Will you explain something, Qwill? Last Monday you told me you didn't play table games, and three days later you were beating the Countess at Scrabble."

"It astounds me, too, Mary. First, Yum Yum found that blank tile, and then Koko found the Scrabble box, so I read the instructions and decided to give it a try. If I happened to win, it was beginner's luck," he said modestly. "Incidentally, there are several tiles missing in the Scrabble set. I wonder what happened to them."

"Di had a cat who used to steal them and push them under the refrigerator," she said.

"I didn't know she had a cat."

"A Persian named Vincent—after Van Gogh, you know."

"What happened to him?"

"Her ex-husband took him. Vincent lives at the gallery now."

"Did she like Scrabble, or did she play to humor the Countess?"

"She was an avid player. It was a Sunday night ritual. I used to make a foursome occasionally."

"Were you there . . . on the Sunday night . . . when she died?"

Mary nodded. "That's a painful memory. When I left the party around eight o'clock, everything was fine."

Qwilleran had another question to ask, but they had arrived at the restaurant, and two other couples were preceding them up the steps, creating congestion in the foyer where Charlotte was official greeter.

"We'll go right upstairs, Charlotte," said Mary.

SEVENTEEN

THE EGGPLANT-COLOR carpet of Roberto's restaurant continued up the stairs to his apartment. "You'll find that his taste has changed radically, Qwill," said Mary, raising the eyebrows that were so accustomed to being raised. "In Italy he discovered International Modern!" As a purveyor of Chippendale and Ch'ien-lung, she obviously disapproved.

"I like Modern, myself," he said. "I've liked it ever since I sublet Harry Noyton's apartment at the Villa Verandah."

"Noyton's place was Victorian Gothic compared to what you are about to see," she replied.

The carpet ended at the top of the stairs, and the floor from there on was a glossy expanse of amber marble. Here and there on this mirrorlike surface stood constructions of steel rods or tubes combined with geometric elements of glass or leather, apparently tables and chairs. Roberto made his entrance from the far end, where Qwilleran supposed he did his actual living in a baronial snuggery furnished with cushioned couches and red velvet.

This attorney who preferred to be a chef was an impressive figure of a man, his shoulders rounded from bending over lawbooks and the chopping board. In dress he was still conservative, and he still had a slow, judicial manner of speech punctuated by thoughtful pauses, but he used his hands more eloquently, something he had not done before living in Italy for a year.

"Good . . . to see you again," he said. There was no effusive Continental embrace; that would be too much to expect from the former Robert Maus.

"Roberto, this is a great occasion," Qwilleran said. "It's been three years since we last met, but it seems like three decades. Let me tell you that your restaurant is handsome, and the food is superb."

"I have learned a few things," said the host. "Sit you down. We shall have an apéritif . . . and some private conversation . . . and then go down to dinner."

Qwilleran selected an assemblage of rods and planes that seemed least likely to assault his body and found it not only surprisingly substantial but remarkably comfortable. The other two members of the party seated themselves at some distance from each other and from Qwilleran. Space was part of the design in this cool, calm, empty environment.

"The service downstairs," Qwilleran went on, "is excellent. Where do you find such good waiters?"

"Law students," said the restaurateur. "I tell them to consider our customers . . . as the ladies and gentlemen of the jury."

"I'm glad you've hired Charlotte Roop as your manager. She seems very happy and not quite so strait-laced."

Mary said, "You can't give all the credit to the job. She has a male companion, probably for the first time in her life."

"I know," said Qwilleran. "I've met him. Does anyone know what happened to his ear?"

"Dynamite explosion," said Roberto. "The poor fellow . . . is lucky to be alive."

"He's had extensive plastic surgery," Mary added.

They discussed the metamorphosis of Junktown, Zwinger Boulevard, River Road, and the city in general. Then Roberto said, "I understand you have a problem, Mr. Qwilleran . . . concerning the Casablanca."

"I do indeed, and it has nothing to do with ways and means, since the Klingenschoen Fund has agreed to underwrite the restoration. The obstacle is Miss Plumb herself. I thought I had established a rapport with her, but as soon as I mentioned the possibility of a restoration, she dropped the curtain. Perhaps you know how to get through to her. After all, you were her attorney for—how many years?''

Roberto took a deep breath and emphasized his words with the hand gestures of desperation. ''Twelve years! Twelve frustrating, thankless years. I much prefer to be . . . stuffing tortellini.''

Mary said, ''How does she react to your proposal to write a book, Qwill?''

''I doubt whether she grasps the concept, but she likes the idea of having her picture taken. Leaving the book aside, there is one aspect of this entire project that alarms me. SOCK has powerful opponents, and now that the news has leaked that SOCK has a source of funding, they may take desperate measures. All they need to do is pray for Miss Plumb's demise, you know, and their goal is accomplished. If their prayers are answered, Providence might deal her a sudden heart attack or a cerebral hemorrhage or salmonella poisoning.''

''A rather . . . ghastly . . . hypothesis,'' said Roberto.

''Did you know that her maid died suddenly yesterday?''

''Elpidia?'' Mary asked in surprise.

''Elpidia. Food poisoning, they said. Was it the chicken hash? Or did she sneak some chocolates intended for the Countess?''

Roberto said stiffly, "If you suspect attempts on Miss Plumb's life . . . I see no foundation whatever . . . for your line of reasoning."

"A great many interests would benefit from the Countess's death: the developers, the banks, the city treasury . . ."

"But we are talking about reputable businessmen and civic leaders . . . not the underworld."

"I know the Pennimans and the Greystones are fine old families, patrons of the arts, and all that, but who is Fleudd?"

Roberto and Mary exchanged glances but neither ventured a reply. Mary said, "Qwill's hunches have been right in the past, Roberto, even when they seemed farfetched."

"I'm not making any accusations," Qwilleran said. "I'm just throwing out a few questions. Who, for example, is the grotesque houseman who works for the Countess? Can he be trusted?"

"Ferdinand," Mary said earnestly, "is a very loyal and helpful employee, no matter how absurd he may appear. His mother has been housekeeper for the Countess for years."

"And who handles her legal affairs now that you're out of the picture, Roberto? Who drew up her new will after the Bessinger murder?"

"My former law firm."

"Why did they steer her bequests to miscellaneous charities? Are they unsympathetic to the Casablanca cause?"

Mary said, "They were obviously influenced by the Pennimans—"

"What I am saying is this," Qwilleran interrupted. "The cards are stacked against us. Ordinarily I don't give up easily, but now I'm convinced that the Casablanca restoration is hopeless. What concerns me is the safety of that pathetic little woman on the twelfth floor. What can be done to protect her?"

Roberto was frowning and withdrawing in a display of incredulity.

"You may think my suspicions unfounded," Qwilleran went on, "but you said the same thing three years ago on River Road, and you remember what happened there!"

"Qwill may be right," Mary said.

"I would also like to submit that the ruthless forces endangering the Countess have already committed two murders in pursuit of their goal."

"What . . . are you . . . saying?" Roberto demanded.

"I have reason to believe that Bessinger, as heir to the Casablanca, was murdered by someone hired to eliminate her, and Ross Rasmus was framed."

"What evidence do you have?"

"Enough to discuss with a friend of mine at Homicide." Qwilleran smoothed his moustache confidently. "At this particular moment I'm not at liberty to reveal the nature of the evidence or the identity of my source." He had no intention of telling this unimaginative dealer in torts and tortellini about the significant bristling of his moustache or Koko's propensity for unearthing crimes.

At that juncture a waiter appeared and announced that their table was ready, and Roberto ushered them downstairs, obviously relieved to terminate the disagreeable topic of conversation.

In the restaurant, surrounded by other diners—one of whom was a man in a dinner jacket, a man with a long thin face and high cheekbones—they talked about Italian food, the antique show in Philadelphia, and life in Moose County, and at the end of the meal Roberto said, "The matter you mentioned upstairs, Mr. Qwilleran . . . allow me to give it some thought."

As Qwilleran escorted Mary Duckworth back to the Blue Dragon, he was carrying a foil packet wrapped in a napkin. They walked in silence for a while—past a woman walking a Great Dane, past the citizens' patrol swinging flashlights. Then he said, "Tell me about the night she was killed. Who was there playing Scrabble earlier in the evening?"

"It was a holiday weekend," Mary said, "and she had invited a lot of people in for snacking and grazing at five o'clock. Roberto refused to go. He is quite opinionated about food, as you know, and he abhors snacking and grazing. So I went alone. Ross was there, of course. And Ylana Targ, who writes the art column for the *Fluxion*. And Jerome Todd. And Rewayne Wilk, Di's latest discovery; he paints disgusting pictures of people eating. And there were some other artists." She mentioned names that meant nothing to Qwilleran. "And there was that *pill*, Courtney Hampton, whom I cannot stand! Di thought he was terribly clever. And there were some others who live at the Casablanca.''

"How long did the party last?''

"It started thinning out at eight o'clock, and I left. Di wanted me to stay for Scrabble, but I had promised to meet Roberto for dinner. He has become a good and dear friend.''

Qwilleran told himself that these two stuffed shirts deserved each other. He said, "No one answered my question when I asked about Fleudd. Who is he anyway?''

"He's supposed to be an idea man. Penniman & Greystone took him in a few months ago. They were always rather conservative, you know, and Fleudd is supposed to shake them up.''

"Was the Gateway Alcazar his idea?''

"I suppose so.''

"Does he eat at Roberto's often?''

"I don't know. I've never seen him there.''

"Well, he was there tonight.''

Qwilleran stroked his moustache as they said goodnight in front of the Blue Dragon, and he made a mental note to call Matt Thiggamon in the morning.

EIGHTEEN

EARLY MONDAY MORNING Qwilleran received a phone call from Homicide, but it was not Lieutenant Hames on the line. It was the nasal voice of his partner, Wojcik, a by-the-book cop who lacked Hames's imagination and had a lip-curling scorn for meddling journalists and psychic cats.

"Wojcik here," he snapped. "You called Hames. Anything urgent?"

"I owe him a lunch, that's all. Is he around?"

"Out of town for a couple of days."

"Thanks for letting me know. I'll call him later."

It was a promise Qwilleran was destined not to keep.

For the cats' breakfast he minced baked shrimp stuffed with lump crabmeat and placed the plate on the floor. *"Gamberi ripieni alla Roberto,"* he announced, "with the compliments of the chef. *Buon appetito!"* The Siamese plunged into their breakfast with gusto. Their current behavior might be abnormal, but there was nothing wrong with their gustatory connoisseurship.

As he watched them devour the repast with gurgling murmurs of ecstasy, there was a knock at the door. Before he could respond, a key turned in the lock, the door opened, and a gray-haired rosy-cheeked woman in a faded denim smock bustled into the foyer.

"Oh, you still here? Mornin' to you. I be Mrs. Jasper," she said. "Mrs. Tuttle said I were to clean on Mondays."

"Happy to have you. I'm on my way out to breakfast, so I won't be in your way. Do you know where everything is?"

"That I do! I cleaned for Miss Bessinger, and I handle everythin' careful, like she said, and clean the rugs with attachments, them bein' hand-made. *You moved one!"* she exclaimed with a frown, as she peered into the gallery where the dhurrie covered the bloodstain.

"I prefer to have it there," Qwilleran said. "Will you water the trees? They haven't had any attention for a week."

"Water trees, change beds, put sheets and towels through laundry, turn on dishwasher, push vac around, and dust a bit," she recited. "I don't do windows." She marched into the kitchen and poked her head into the dishwasher, which was empty.

"I take my meals out," Qwilleran explained. "That's the cats' plate on the floor. There may be some cat hairs around the apartment. I have two Siamese."

It hardly needed mentioning. Koko was circling the woman with intense interest and sniffing her shoes.

"No bother. Miss Bessinger had a Persian, and I have a tom of my own, though his tomcattin' days be over. You've seen Napoleon, like as not. We live on the main floor, and he be a sociable critter."

She headed for the gallery with the vacuum cleaner and attachments, which Qwilleran offered to carry. Her regional speech reminded him of certain longtime residents of Moose County. "May I ask where you came from originally, Mrs. Jasper? You're not city bred."

"Aye, I come from a small town up north, name of Chipmunk. My paw had a potato farm."

"I know Chipmunk very well," he said. "I live in Pickax City."

"Aye, Pickax! Paw used to drive the wagon to Pickax to buy feed and seed. Sundays we went fishin' at Purple Point. Once we see'd a minstrel show at Sawdust City. It were good livin' up there, it were. A body felt safe. On the radio this mornin' they was three people shot to death at the Penniman Hotel, and a man in a car shot another driver on the freeway. It warn't like that in Chipmunk!''

''When did you leave Moose County?'' Qwilleran asked as he plugged in the vacuum for her.

''I were fifteen year old. I be seventy-six next birthday but more strong and able than some young ones be. On the farm I hoed potatoes and kept chickens and milked the cow and growed vegetables for the table—afore I were ten year old.''

''Why did you leave Chipmunk?''

''I were itchin' to see the big city, so my paw let me come and live with my aunt Florrie. She were a cook for some folks livin' here, and she got me a job as a housemaid. Worked here seven year afore I married my Andrew and raised a family. He were a mailman. Three boys and two girls we had, and one born dead. I cooked and cleaned and washed and ironed and made everythin' they wore on their backs till they growed up and moved away. Then I went back to housekeepin' for folks, and when my Andrew died—that good man!—I moved in here, main floor, and kep' right on workin'.''

''Was Miss Bessinger nice to work for?''

''Aye, she were very tidy. Some folks is terrible messy, but not her! It were a great pity what happened.''

''Did you clean for the man next door also?''

''Aye. He were messy, but he were a nice man. Come from the country, he did. Them tubs of dirt on the porch—he growed tomatoes, corn, and beans out there last summer, and the hellycopter were always flyin' over, disturbin' the peace. Didn't know corn plants when they saw 'em."

"Were you shocked to hear he had murdered Miss Bessinger?"

"I were that! I were up late that night, watchin' TV, and I heard screamin' outside the window and then a big bang. That were when he landed on a car. I looked out, but it were dark back there. Then the police and ambulance come, and I went out in the hall—everybody out there in their nightclothes and Mrs. Tuttle tellin' them to go back to bed. It were awful! No one knowed she were lyin' dead upstairs."

Mrs. Jasper turned on the vacuum cleaner, putting an end to her monologue, and Qwilleran went in search of the Siamese. Yum Yum was on the waterbed, gazing into middle distance; Koko was prowling restlessly, talking to himself in guttural rumblings and curling his tail into a corkscrew—something he had never done before. Qwilleran called the desk and inquired about an animal clinic.

"Are the kitties sick?" Mrs. Tuttle asked.

"No, just acting moody, and I want to have them checked."

"The nearest vet is out River Road eight miles." She gave the name and number of the clinic. "You have to call for an appointment. How is Mrs. Jasper doing?"

"She's a vigorous woman for her age."

"Don't know where she gets her pep. She'll

talk your ear off, too, if you let her. Hope there's nothing wrong with the kitties."

He called the clinic and said he would like the doctor to examine two Siamese.

"What is the nature of the problem?" asked the receptionist.

"We're from out of town, and since arriving in the city the cats have not been themselves. I want to be sure there's nothing radically wrong with them. They're very important to me."

"In that case we could squeeze you in this afternoon—say, at four o'clock. What are their names?"

"Koko and Yum Yum. My name is Qwilleran. I'm at the Casablanca."

"We have a lot of patients from there."

"See you at four."

It was another promise he would not keep.

Before going to breakfast he tuned in the radio—not only for the weathercast but to corroborate Mrs. Jasper's report about three murders at the Penniman Plaza. Oddly, the shooting on the freeway was mentioned, but there was no word about the triple killing at the hotel. His mounting curiosity led him to the Plaza for breakfast. On a newsstand he picked up a copy of the *Morning Rampage* and found that the paper had not covered the incident. Not all the homicides in a large city are reported in the press—of that he was well aware—but when three persons are shot to death in a large downtown hotel with deluxe pretensions, it should be front-page news.

At the coffee shop he ordered a combination of

steak, eggs, and potatoes that would have been called a Duck Hunter's Breakfast in Moose County; at the Penniman Plaza it was the Power Brunch. He waited until the waitress had poured his third cup of coffee before he asked her about the triple killing. She had no idea what he was talking about.

On the way out of the building he stopped at the bar. It opened at eleven, and Randy Jupiter was in the process of setting up. Qwilleran perched on a barstool. "I hear you had some excitement here over the weekend, Randy."

"We did? I've been off since Saturday afternoon."

"There were three murders in the hotel. Didn't you hear about it?"

The bartender shook his head.

"It was on the radio."

"Are you sure? It could've been some other hotel." Jupiter glanced quickly around the bar and then wrote "can't talk" on a cocktail napkin. He said, "The coffee's brewing. Want a cup?"

"No, thanks," said Qwilleran. "I had three in the coffee shop." He slid off the stool. "If you're still interested in a jazz session, how about tonight?"

"Sure! Any requests?"

"Your choice, but no screaming trumpet. It sends the cats into fits. I like sax myself. Shall we say eight o'clock?"

Before stepping onto the escalator Qwilleran checked the vicinity for possible hazards, then rode slowly down on the moving stairs, reflecting that the radio station he had tuned in, as well as the *Morning Rampage*, were Penniman-owned. For information on the triple murder he would have to wait for the *Daily Fluxion* to hit the street, or for the bartender to arrive with his jazz recordings, or for Hames to come back to town.

Returning to 14-A he found Mrs. Jasper in the kitchen, with Koko watching her every move.

"The boss, he be tellin' me what to do," she said. "Now I'll take the towels and things down to the laundry and have a bit of lunch afore I come up again."

Qwilleran went into the library to peruse his notes gleaned from photo captions at the public library. Koko followed and leaped to the library table, where he took up his post on the volume of Van Gogh reproductions. He could have chosen Cézanne, Rembrandt, or one of the other masters, but he always elected to sit on the Van Gogh, complacently washing up. It occurred to Qwilleran that Vincent, the Bessinger Persian, might have elected to sit in that spot while waiting to steal a Scrabble tile.

From his notes he could reconstruct the romantic past of the Palm Pavilion. Harrison Plumb had celebrated his daughter's birthday with a musicale featuring a string quartet from the Penniman Conservatory. The Wilburtons hosted a reception for a visiting professor of anthropology who was lecturing at the university. The Pennimans entertained the French ambassador. Mr. and Mrs. Duxbury gave a dinner for the governor. No amount of restoration and no amount of Klingenschoen money, he had to admit, would ever recall the magic of the Casablanca's first quarter of a century. It could only be captured in a book, with pictures and text, a thought which reminded him to line up the photographer. He called Sorg Butra's number and was informed that the photographer was out of town on assignment. Qwilleran left a message for Butra to call him.

It was a call he would never receive.

When Mrs. Jasper returned with her laundry basket, he flagged her down at the library door, saying, "When did you first come to work at the Casablanca, Mrs. Jasper?"

"Just afore the 1929 Crash. That's when folks was jumpin' off the roof. It were terrible."

"Come in and sit down. Do you remember the names of any people you worked for?"

She sat on the edge of a chair with the basket on her lap, her rosy cheeks glowing. "I only worked for one family, and they was just two of 'em—father and daughter. He were a nice man with a little moustache. Mr. Plumb were his name."

"His daughter still lives here!"

"Aye, on Twelve. Miss Adelaide. Her and me was the same age."

"Here, let me take that basket. Make yourself comfortable," he said with a sudden surge of hospitality. "Would you like a cup of coffee?"

"I just had a nice cup o' tea downstairs, thankee just the same."

"What kind of work did you do for the Plumbs?"

"I were backstairs maid. I had a room of my own—imagine!—and me just a young girl from Chipmunk. They hired a lot of help in them days. We had a good time."

"What was Adelaide like when she was young?"

"Oh, she were a sassy girl, that one! Mr. Plumb spoiled her somethin' terrible. Bought her an automobile for her birthday, and the houseman used to drive her up and down Zwinger Boulevard like a princess. I remember her comin'-out party and the dress she wore—all beads and feathers and way up above her knees. That were the style then. After that the young men came callin' and bringin' chocolates and flowers. First thing we knowed, she were engaged to the handsomest of the lot." Mrs. Jasper shook her head sadly. "But it were too bad the way it worked out."

"What happened?"

"Well, now, the weddin' were all set, invitations and all, weddin' dress ordered special from Paris. Then somethin' happened suddenlike. Mr. Plumb were upset, and Miss Adelaide were poutin', and the help was tiptoein' around, afraid to open their mouth. I asked Housekeeper and she said Mr. Plumb were short of money. Next thing, he sold the automobile and let some of the help go, and Miss Adelaide stayed in her room and wouldn't come out, no matter what. Housekeeper said Mr. Plumb made her break her engagement. After that he got sickly and died." Mrs. Jasper leaned forward, wide-eyed. "It be my notion that Miss Adelaide poisoned him!"

Qwilleran, who had been lulled into a reverie by the singsong quality of the woman's voice, fairly jumped out of his chair. "What makes you think so?"

"She talked to me chummylike, us bein' the same age."

"What did she tell you?"

"Oh, she hated him for what he did! That were what she told me, stampin' her feet and throwin' things and screamin'. She were spoiled. Always got what she wanted and did what she wanted. I wouldn't put it past her to poison her own father."

"How would she get her hands on poison?"

"There were rat poison in the basement. The janitor had it in his cupboard with a big skull and crossbones on it."

"Come on, Mrs. Jasper," Qwilleran chided. "Can you picture the belle of the Casablanca prowling around the basement to steal rat poison?"

"Not her. It were the houseman, to my way o' thinkin'. He were a young man what looked like a movie star, and she smiled at him a lot. Housekeeper said no good would come of it."

"Very interesting," said Qwilleran, huffing into his moustache. He had a sympathetic attitude that encouraged confidences, true or false, and persons in all walks of life had poured out their secrets, but servants' gossip hardly qualified for the Casablanca history.

"Aye, it were interesting," Mrs. Jasper went on. "After Mr. Plumb died and she got the insurance money, the houseman bought hisself an automobile! Where would a young whippersnapper get money for an automobile in them days?''

"How many times have you told this story, Mrs. Jasper?''

"Only to my Andrew after we was married, and he said not to talk about it, but the Countess be old now, and it don't matter, and I always wanted to tell somebody.''

"Well, thank you," he said. "It's after three o'clock now, and I must take the cats to the doctor.''

"I'll water the trees and then I be through," said Mrs. Jasper.

Qwilleran paid her and said he would see her the following Monday—another promise he would be unable to keep.

Both of the Siamese were on the waterbed. "Everyone up!" he called out cheerfully. "Get your tickets for a ride in the Purple Plum!" He made no mention of the clinic, and yet they knew! No amount of coaxing would convince them to enter the carrier.

First he tried to push Koko through the small door, beginning with the forelegs, then the head, but the cat braced his hind legs against the conveyance, straddling the door and lashing his tail like a whip. Even employing all his cunning, Qwilleran still could not engineer four legs, a head, a lashing tail, and a squirming body into the carrier simultaneously. In frustration he abandoned the project and had a dish of ice cream, and when he returned to the scene some minutes later, both animals were huddled in the carrier contentedly, side by side.

"Cats!" Qwilleran grumbled. "CATS!"

He carried the coop from the apartment and rang for the elevator.

"Don't shriek when the car is in operation," he cautioned Yum Yum. "You know what happened last time." He held his breath until Old Green landed them safely on the main floor.

"Bye-bye, kitties," called Mrs. Tuttle, looking up from her knitting as they passed the bullet-proof window.

The two old women in quilted robes had their heads together as usual, scowling and complaining. "Moving out?" one of them croaked in a funereal voice.

"No, just going to the doctor," he replied. It was a mission he never accomplished.

A brisk breeze was blowing down Zwinger Boulevard, whipping around the Casablanca and whistling through the cat carrier, and Qwilleran removed his jacket and threw it over the cage. As fast as possible he zigzagged through the parking lot, sidestepping the potholes. Not until the obstacle course was half negotiated did he look up and realize that slot #28 was vacant. The Purple Plum had vanished.

NINETEEN

QWILLERAN TORE BACK into the building with two confused Siamese bumping around inside the carrier. "Mrs. Tuttle!" he called out at the desk. "My car is gone! It's been stolen!"

"Oh, dearie me!" she said, not as perturbed as he thought she should be. "Did you lock your doors? Someone had cassettes stolen, but he left his doors—"

"I always lock my doors!"

"Was it a new car?"

"No, but it was in excellent condition."

Rupert, hearing the commotion, sauntered over and leaned on the counter. "Don't pay to keep a nice car."

Mrs. Tuttle offered to call the police.

"Never mind," Qwilleran said in annoyance. "I'll go upstairs and call them myself. I just wanted you to know." Although he had no affection for the Purple Plum, he resented having it stolen.

Riding up in Old Green he said to the occupants of the carrier, "You two will be happy about this development. Now you don't have to go to the doctor."

He telephoned the clinic and canceled his appointment. "My car has been stolen," he explained.

"I've had two stolen," said the receptionist comfortingly. "Now I drive an old piece of junk."

Next he called the precinct station, and a bored sergeant took the information, saying they would try to send an officer to the building.

Then he called Mary and broke the news.

"I sympathize," she said. "I don't own a car anymore. I take taxis or rent a car when I need transportation."

"They're sending an officer over here."

"Don't count on it too much, Qwill."

Suddenly he was enormously hungry. He fed the cats hurriedly and went out to dinner, riding down on Old Red. When it stopped at Four, Yazbro stepped aboard, squinting at Qwilleran with a glimmer of hostile recognition.

"My car has just been stolen," Qwilleran said to enlist the man's sympathy.

Yazbro grunted something unintelligible.

"It was parked in #28, next to your slot. Was it there when you left this morning?"

"Di'n't notice."

Qwilleran went to the deli for an early dinner. All he wanted was a bowl of chicken soup with matzo balls, a pastrami sandwich two inches thick, a dish of rice pudding, and some time to sort out his feelings about life in the big city. The Press Club was not what it used to be. The staffers at the *Daily Fluxion* were all new and uninteresting. There was no one whose company he enjoyed half as much as that of Polly Duncan and Arch Riker, not to mention Larry Lanspeak, Chief Brodie, Junior Goodwinter, Roger MacGillivray, and a dozen others. The Casablanca itself was a disaster, and the Countess would never agree to sell to the Klingenschoen Fund. And the last straw was the theft of his car.

Even the prospect of writing a book on the Casablanca was losing its appeal. At this moment he had only one reason to stay. He wanted to have lunch with Lieutenant Hames as soon as the detective returned to town. He wanted to tell him about Koko's discoveries: first the bloodstain, then the bracelet, and finally the confession on the wall. He would relate how the cat found the exact spot where the artist was said to have jumped from the terrace. Then he would advance his theory that special-interest groups were resorting to criminal means to clear the way for the

Gateway Alcazar: knifing the heir to the Casablanca and throwing her lover from the terrace, after drugging them both. But in attempting to frame Ross they had used an unlikely signature on his alleged confession and had misspelled Dianne. Furthermore, one tenant heard screams as the body plummeted to earth. As a newsman Qwilleran had seen suicides jump off high buildings and bridges, and they jumped in desperate silence.

He walked home slowly and found the crumbling front steps a disgrace, the lobby grim, the tenants depressing, and Old Red an affront to human dignity. Koko met him at the door as usual and trotted to the library as usual, where he took up his position on the Van Gogh volume as usual, tensing his tail like a corkscrew.

"What are you trying to tell me?" Qwilleran asked him. "Was that Vincent's favorite perch?" The thought crossed his mind that Vincent had witnessed the murder, and he had an irrational desire to visit the Bessinger-Todd Gallery once more.

When he phoned, he was answered in a hurry. "Is the gallery still open?" he asked. "This is Jim Qwilleran at the Casablanca."

"I've just locked the door. This is Jerry Todd. What can I do for you?"

"I never had a chance to talk with you about artwork for my barn, and I may be leaving soon."

"If you want to come over, I'll wait," the art dealer suggested.

"Be right there."

Qwilleran ran downstairs, thinking it quicker and easier than taking the elevator. He hailed a cab and arrived at the gallery within minutes.

Todd unlocked the door. "That was fast."

"I see you've sold a lot of things since Friday night," said Qwilleran, observing the empty walls.

"Very successful opening," the dealer said cheerfully, pinching his nose in the odd way he had. "*The Pizza Eaters*, *The Wing Ding Eaters* and *The Hot Dog Eaters* all went to one buyer, a fast-food chain. They wanted them for their corporate headquarters. It will occupy an entire floor of the Gateway Alcazar. Did you see anything you liked at the opening?"

"Nothing suitable for a barn, to tell the truth."

"Perhaps you should consider contemporary tapestries if you're going to have a lot of wood surfaces. We have one artist who does abstract weavings in nature themes. I can show you pictures of her work." He produced an album of color slides.

Qwilleran, who truthfully had no plans to convert his barn, was captivated. "How large are they?"

"She takes commissions to order, including some huge tapestries for hotel lobbies. You'd never guess it, but she's just a tiny little thing. Here's her picture."

The artist had a roguish pixie face that appealed to Qwilleran. "Your suggestion is certainly something for me to consider," he said. "I'll get back to you after I consult my architect."

"Architects approve of her tapestries. They complement rather than compete with the architecture, and her perception of dimension is outstanding. She shows great sensitivity with threads, and of course she dyes her own colors."

At that moment a mushroom-tinted Persian walked into the room waving a plumed tail. "Is that Vincent?" Qwilleran asked.

"Yes, that's Vincent. He was Dianne's cat and I adopted him. They don't allow pets where I live, but he's happy in the gallery, and customers like him," said Todd, pinching his nose. Vincent circled the two men with dignity and oscillating tail.

"Did he experience any psychological trauma as a result of the Labor Day incident?"

"Apparently not. She always locked him up in the bedroom when she had company. He liked the waterbed, so he didn't object. In fact, when he came to live at the gallery, I bought him a cat-size waterbed."

"You did? Where did you buy it? I have a cat who'd like a waterbed."

"From a mail-order catalogue. I can get the information for you if you're interested."

"I'd appreciate that. And by the way, when Vincent lived at the Casablanca, did he make a habit of sitting on any of the art books?"

"Not that guy! He always looks for the softest seat in the house!"

Qwilleran cleared his throat. "I have something to tell you, Mr. Todd, and I hope it won't be too distasteful. Since living in the penthouse I've found evidence that Ross did not commit the murder and did not take his own life.''

Todd gulped and pinched his nose. ''What kind of evidence?''

''That's something I can't discuss until I've talked with my friend at the Homicide Squad.''

''Oh, God! Does that mean the case will be reopened? We've had enough notoriety! Nobody knows me as a gallery director anymore; I'm the ex-husband of a murdered woman. I swear there are people who think I did it!''

In a kindly vein Qwilleran went on. ''I understand there was a cocktail party the evening before Labor Day. If you were there and can recall some of the other guests, it may help corroborate my suspicions.''

''I was there!'' Todd said grimly. ''Di had invited a lot of people including the girl from the newspaper, so I felt I should make an appearance. Ylana Targ. She writes the art column.''

''How late did you stay?''

''Till about ten o'clock. I wanted to leave earlier because one fellow had brought jazz records, and jazz drives me up the wall, but it started raining— a real cloudburst. The skylight started leaking, and we had to put pots and pans around to catch the drips.''

''Who was there when you left?''

''Ross, of course. Di and Ylana and Ross and another fellow from the building were playing Scrabble. A few others were in the living room, drinking and passing smokes around. I don't remember who they were.''

"The fellow who made a fourth for Scrabble—do you know his name, or what he looked like?"

"He was slick-looking . . . well-groomed . . . sort of like a male model."

"Well, I won't detain you any longer," Qwilleran said. "Thanks for staying open. I'll call you about the tapestries when I get back to Pickax. I think we can do business."

He returned home, changed into a sweatshirt, track-lighted the gallery, filled the ice bucket on the bar, and put a bowl of cashews on the cocktail table. "Care for a few rounds of Scrabble while we're waiting?" he asked Koko.

The cat was more than willing. (No wonder! Qwilleran thought. He always wins!) On this occasion Koko was choosing a preponderance of low-scoring consonants like R, S, L, T, and N, and Qwilleran was considering another change in the rules, when the velvet paw drew forth D, E, V, B, O, G, and J. Immediately Qwilleran spelled JOVE, which netted fourteen points, leaving only seven for Koko.

"By Jove!" he said to the cat. "I think we've got it!"

At that moment there was an awkward knock at the door. He swept the tiles into the Scrabble box and went to admit his guest.

The Penniman bartender was loaded down with cassette-caddies and LPs. "Relax!" he said. "I'm not planning to stay three days. I brought a whole bunch so you can take your pick."

"Come in. I've been looking forward to this."

"Man, this is not too shabby!" said Jupiter in

admiration as he perused the foyer. "And it opens right onto the terrace!"

"You've never been here before?"

"Never got invited."

"Wait till you see the sunken living room." Qwilleran opened the French doors. "The stereo is down in the pit. Here, let me take some of that load."

They carried the recordings into the gallery and piled them on the giant cocktail table. The guest stood in the middle of the pit with his hands in his pockets, staring in every direction. "I should think you'd get fed up with mushrooms."

"Don't knock them," said Qwilleran. "Since the scandal, they've become gilt-edged securities. They don't belong to me, of course. I'm just subletting. Let's have a drink. What's yours?" Hearing the rattle of icecubes, Koko made his imposing entrance through the open French doors. "Here comes the lord of the manor."

"Good-looking cat," said Jupiter. "Better than most of the rat catchers around this building."

It was almost as if Koko resented being lumped with rat catchers. From that moment on, he devised ways of tormenting the visitor. But first he had his saucer of white grapejuice.

Jupiter with his vodka on the rocks and Qwilleran with his club soda took seats on the long sofa, and the latter said, "They stole my car from the parking lot today."

"Par for the course," said the other with a shrug.

"You people around here are so damned casual

about car theft!'' Qwilleran complained. ''Even the old ladies in the lobby talk about muggings the way we talk about weather in Moose County.''

Koko jumped on the back of the long sofa and walked its length like a model on a runway. On the way back he stopped to sniff the guest's hair.

''Hey, what's going on back there?'' Jupiter said, slapping the back of his head.

''Sorry,'' said Qwilleran, pushing the cat off the sofa. ''He likes your shampoo . . . Now, can you tell me what happened at the hotel over the weekend?''

''It was in the *Fluxion* this afternoon, so it's no secret any more. Two men and a woman in a suite on the top floor were gunned down execution-style, so you know it's drug-related. The hotel always tries to put the lid on anything like that. They think it'll scare off the tourists and conventions . . . *Hey, what's he doing?*''

Koko was on the cocktail table, biting the corners of record jackets. Qwilleran sent him flying with a gentle backhand, and the cat spent the next ten minutes licking his damaged ego.

''How'd you get your big jazz collection, Randy?''

''I was lucky. I had an uncle who was a bebop drummer—never made it big, but he got me hooked, and then he died and left me all his records. D'you have any requests?''

''Well, I told you I like sax—Sidney Bechet, Jimmy Dorsey, Stan Getz, Charlie Parker, Coltrane. If I could play an instrument, that's what I'd like to play. It's almost like the human voice.''

''Okay, we'll start with Charlie . . . What's that thumping noise?''

''That's Keestra Hedrog and her Gut Dancers. They rehearse in 14-B every Monday night. I'll close the doors and it won't bother us.''

Koko was standing in the doorway, half in and half out of the room, and when Qwilleran climbed out of the pit and tried to close the double doors, the cat stood as if glued to the threshold. ''Are you coming in or staying out?'' Qwilleran asked.

Koko deliberated, unable to make up his mind, until a slight tap from a size twelve shoe sent him catapulting into the gallery—down into the pit, up onto the rim, circling it like an indoor track, picking up speed and flying across the cocktail table, scattering cassettes in all directions.

''Cripes! He's like a tornado!'' Jupiter said as he retrieved his collection.

''Sorry, he's wound up tonight for some reason . . . . Koko! You behave, or leave the room!''

The cat jumped to the top of the bar, among the bottles and decanters, where he could keep the visitor under surveillance, and the evening progressed uneventfully for a while.

Jupiter played a program that went from bebop to swing to Chicago jazz to big band to Dixieland to blues to rag. After his third drink he pantomimed a bebop drummer in sync with a recording, and the frenetic performance sent Koko burrowing under the dhurrie.

"Now what's he doing?" the man wanted to know.

"That rug covers the stain where Dianne Bessinger bled to death."

"No kidding!"

"I believe it was Labor Day weekend. How long have you lived here?"

"I moved in . . . let's see . . . Memorial weekend."

"Did you get to know Dianne or Ross?"

"No, they never came into the bar, and I don't go for this kind of stuff." Jupiter waved an arm around the gallery walls.

Qwilleran said, "Since moving into this apartment I've discovered some new twists regarding the murder. Did you know that there are prominent men in town who would profit by Dianne's death?"

"No kidding!"

"It's a fact."

Jupiter said he'd like another drink, and after pouring it Qwilleran said, "What's more, I happen to have evidence that Ross did not kill Dianne."

"You're kidding!" Koko had returned to the sofa-back and was sniffing the bartender's head again. His neck was reddening. He brushed the cat away like an annoying fly.

"Yes, there's no doubt in my mind that it was a frame-up. In fact, I have an appointment at the Homicide Squad tomorrow—to turn my information over to the detectives."

"How'd you find out?" The vodka was coloring Jupiter's face to match his moustache.

"I have a snoopy nature and a little experience in criminal investigation. There are tenants who heard screams just before Ross landed on Yazbro's car. Dianne's murderer tossed the artist over the parapet, after dragging him down to the dark end of the terrace." Qwilleran kept a sharp eye on his guest and saw his hand go into his sweater pocket. "Want any more ice?" he asked as he carried his own glass to the bar. Feeling secure behind the massive piece of furniture, he went on. "But here's the clincher: You see that skylight up there? Someone was on the roof when it happened. There was a witness!"

Jupiter struggled to his feet. Qwilleran thought, he's half-bombed! The man walked unsteadily to the bar and stood on the dhurrie, his hand still in his pocket. Wordlessly the two of them faced each other across the bar, until the heavy silence was broken by a clatter of glassware as something dropped between them. Koko had flown through the air, landing on the bar with arched back, bushed tail, flattened ears, and bared fangs.

Taking advantage of the distraction, Jupiter sneaked around the end of the bar, snatching a small tube from his pocket. As he raised it there was a *click* and a knifeblade shot out. Qwilleran, without taking his eye off the knife, grabbed a bottle by the neck. For one frozen moment they faced each other. At the same time a blur of fur passed between the two men, landing on the assailant's shoulder. A whiplike tail flicked twice.

There was a yell of pain, and the man put a hand to his eyes. The other hand wavered, and Qwilleran smashed down hard on the knife, then brought the bottle down on Jupiter's head. As he collapsed, Qwilleran kicked the knife away and stood over him with the bottle.

The French doors burst open! Two figures appeared on the level above. One of them had a gun.

"Hold it! I got you covered!"

Qwilleran started to raise his hands before he realized that the man with the handgun was wearing a red golf hat. The man behind him had the paunchy figure of Arch Riker.

"Call the police!" Qwilleran yelled.

Riker's ruddy face turned pale. "Qwill! You're supposed to be dead!"

TWENTY

"I NEED A DRINK!" said Arch Riker after the police and their prisoner had cleared out.

"First tell me what the hell you're doing here!" Qwilleran demanded of his friend.

"I came to feed the cats! And claim your remains at the morgue!"

"I don't get it."

Riker explained slowly and clearly. "The police here called Brodie in Pickax early this morning. They told him someone shot at you on the freeway. They said your car crashed and burned.

They said you were incinerated along with all identification. They traced the car to you through the license plates."

"Someone stole my car! That's what happened."

"Whatever. I picked up your dental records from Dr. Zoller and caught the first plane out of Pickax. The whole of Moose County is in mourning."

Qwilleran started for the telephone. "I'd better call Polly."

"Don't! She'll have a stroke. She thinks you're dead. I'll call Brodie and he can break the good news to her. Also, I should call my news desk and the radio station. If you're feeling generous, you can pour me a double scotch."

When the two men settled down in the library with their drinks, Qwilleran posed a question: "Was the episode on the freeway a random shooting? Or did they think they were taking a shot at me?"

"Why would anyone want to shoot you?"

"It's a long story."

Koko walked into the room with feline insouciance as if nothing had happened all evening. He jumped to the library table and sat on the Van Gogh.

"Where's Yum Yum?" Riker asked.

"In the bedroom, sleeping her life away. I've got to get the cats back to Pickax. Something here disagrees with them."

"If people are taking shots at you and threatening you with knives, you'd better get your own tail back to Pickax, friend. What have you been doing? Meddling again? Snooping where you have no business?''

''Do you want to hear the whole story, Arch? Or do you want to preach a sermon?'' Qwilleran asked.

He related the murder-suicide myth as reported in the newspaper and described Koko's several discoveries. ''Here's the bracelet,'' he said, drawing it from a desk drawer.

''What's the significance of the numbers?''

''It's obviously a private code between lovers. I think the numbers refer to the value of letters in a Scrabble set. The 1-1-4-1, for example, could stand for L-O-V-E. It could also stand for T-O-F-U, although I doubt that—''

''How do you know so much about Scrabble all of a sudden?''

''I've found out it's not a bad game, Arch. I also tried entertaining Koko with a kind of scratch-Scrabble because he was bored, and I kept spelling words that started a train of thought. HOAX, for example. I began to wonder if Ross had been framed. At first I suspected Dianne's ex-husband.''

''Pity us ex-husbands,'' said Riker. ''We're always the first suspects. I live in mortal fear that someone will murder Rosie.''

''The guy had a habit of pinching his nose, and I attributed it to guilt, but later I decided he was sensitive to cat dander.''

''I'm glad the ex-husband got off the hook.''

"There's more to the story, Arch. Do you want me to go on?"

"Please do. This is better than television."

"Okay. Then I realized that the developers who wanted to tear down the Casablanca had a strong motive for eliminating Dianne, and I began to suspect one of them—a guy by the name of F-l-e-u-d-d, pronounced Flood. Koko put the idea in my head—I won't tell you how, because you won't believe it. Anyhow, I checked it out with a guy at the *Fluxion* and learned that Fleudd has a past history of dirty tricks—nothing felonious, so far, just unscrupulous. So I thought, Suppose Fleudd had an agent in residence at the Casablanca who committed the double murder and tipped him off to my purpose here! The word AGENT turned up on the Scrabble board, and tonight I came up with JOVE—which is another name for Jupiter, right?"

Riker said, "You spelled HOAX and AGENT and JOVE because the ideas were already lurking in your subconscious."

"Be that as it may, when Jupiter came up here for a jazz session, I caught him in a couple of lies that suggested he had something to hide, so I tried a little prevarication of my own. After he'd had a few drinks and was losing control, I told him that someone on the roof had witnessed Dianne's murder through the skylight. That brought him out in the open, and if Koko hadn't whipped his tail at the crucial moment, I probably wouldn't be here talking to you."

"Yow," said Koko, who liked to hear his name mentioned.

"Speaking of tails, Koko is beginning to convey information by means of *tail language*, just as humans express emotions with body language. In the last few days he's been twisting his tail like a corkscrew."

"Are you trying to tell me that Koko knew the murderer was a bartender? If so, his tail's not the only thing that's screwy around here! What does a cat know about bar accessories?"

"Cats are gifted with senses that transcend human intelligence—a fact that's hard for us to accept—and Koko's senses are becoming more acute every year."

"You're really wound up tonight!" Riker held out his glass. "How about another touch? And then I'll turn in. This whole day has been an unnerving experience, and I've got to catch an early plane tomorrow. How about you? What have you decided about the Casablanca?"

"I'm giving it up. I'll hang around long enough to turn my evidence over to Lieutenant Hames, and then I'll rent a car and drive the cats back to Pickax . . . See you in the morning, Arch. The guestroom is down the hall, first door on the right. Just throw the cats' cushion off the bed."

Qwilleran, having made his decision to forget the Casablanca and go home, slept well that night. He slept well until about three o'clock in the morning, at which time he dreamed someone was pounding him on the stomach. When he opened his eyes, he was sitting and Koko was having a catfit—jumping on and off the bed, pouncing on his body, yowling and growling. When the cat ran from the room like a crazed animal, Qwilleran followed him down the bedroom hall, past the guestroom where Riker was snoring quietly, and into the foyer. There Koko clawed at the parquet floor, his tail tense and twisted. Next he was racing madly about, knocking things over, crashing into furniture.

Qwilleran listened. He could hear what was alarming the cat! It was a rustling, crackling, creaking under the floor!

Bolting back to the guestroom he yelled, "Arch! Arch! Get up! Get up! Quick! We're getting out of here!" Then he ran to the housephone and rang the night number. "Ring the fire bell!" he shouted. "Get everyone out! Get the Countess out! Fire between Twelve and Fourteen!"

Riker appeared in the foyer, groggy with sleep. "What? . . . What? . . ."

"No questions! Throw on some clothes!" Qwilleran pushed Yum Yum into the carrier, and Koko followed her without bidding. "Don't pack! No time to lose!" He pulled on pants and a sweater over his pajamas and pointed Riker to the door. "Down the stairs! Take the cats and start down! Hurry!"

He delayed long enough to hammer at the door of 14-B.

"Who is it?" a voice screamed.

"Building's on fire! Get out fast!" he yelled, then dashed for the stairs. The fire bell had started its urgent clamor, and at the tenth floor tenants began stumbling into the stairwell, grumbling and questioning.

Qwilleran caught up with Riker and said, ''Give me the cats and you go ahead. Try to get a cab out in front.''

''What . . . ?''

''Don't ask. Just do it!''

On the main floor the tenants, clutching cats and other treasures, were in an uproar.

Qwilleran shouted to Mrs. Tuttle over the heads of the milling crowd, ''Can you get Miss Plumb out?''

''We phoned and Rupert went up there!''

The emergency door was open, and sirens could be heard, converging from all directions. Not stopping to recognize faces in the lobby, Qwilleran pushed through to the front door and found Riker flagging a cab. He put the carrier in the front with the driver and shouted, ''Penniman Plaza!'' before climbing into the backseat.

Angrily Riker said, ''Will you tell me what this is all about?''

''I don't know.'' Qwilleran pounded his moustache with his fist . . . *''Oh, my God!''*

A deafening explosion rocked the cab. A flash of light illuminated Zwinger Boulevard. Looking out the rear window they saw the Casablanca crowned with fire.

''Jeez!'' yelled the driver. ''Cracked my windshield!'' He started to pull over.

''Don't stop! There'll be fallout.''

Moments later, the roof of the cab was showered with debris. Sirens screamed. Red and blue flashing lights filled the street. At the hotel the security guards were out on the sidewalk, looking toward the west.

While the cab waited, Qwilleran ran in to the registration desk and came out with the word that the Airport Motel was the nearest facility that would accept pets. The driver headed for the freeway, and his passengers rode in silence, sickened by the enormity of the disaster and stunned by the thought of their near-extinction. All was quiet in the cat carrier.

Finally Qwilleran said, ''The noise I heard . . . the noise Koko detected . . . under the floor . . . It sounded like someone in the crawl space, setting a fire . . . I didn't have time to think . . . Now I realize they were planting a time bomb.'' His thoughts went to those whose lives had touched his briefly:

The Countess . . . Had they been able to dislodge her from her palace? Rupert with his handgun and Ferdinand with his muscle could overpower her, if not convince her, but they had only minutes to act. It was questionable that all three could escape.

Isabelle . . . She lived on one of the upper floors. Was she sober enough to recognize the danger? If not, her troubles were over.

Winnie Wingfoot . . . She also lived on Ten, but she had probably stayed out all night.

Keestra Hedrog . . . No cause for concern. She would fly to safety on her broomstick.

Amberina Kowbel . . . Poor, disorganized Amber! At least she would never have to unpack the eighty-four shopping bags and the mountain of cartons.

Courtney . . . He would get out all right, lugging his Hudson River painting.

But what about the nameless old ladies in quilted robes? And all the others with canes and crutches?

He said, "It would have been wrong, Arch, to evict all those people and revert the Casablanca to a ritzy enclave for the superrich."

"They're evicted now, that's for sure," said Riker.

The driver tuned in the round-the-clock news station on his radio. After a few words about a woman arrested for selling her children, and about the discovery of three bodies buried in Penniman Park, the announcer said: "Bulletin! An explosion rocked the near West Side at 3:18 this morning, destroying the top floors of the Casablanca apartment house. The cause has not been determined. Firefighters and rescue crew are on the scene, and survivors are being evacuated. The blast broke windows in Junktown, and debris fell on an area of several blocks. There is no report on the number of casualties at this time. Stay tuned."

The cause has not been determined, Qwilleran thought. He remembered Amber saying, "The city would love it if something terrible happened to the Casablanca." He remembered that Raymond Dunwoody worked for the city and had lost an ear in a dynamite explosion. Had he planted dynamite in the crawl space between Twelve and

Fourteen? If so, at whose behest? Qwilleran felt a tingling sensation in the roots of his moustache—the old familiar feeling that meant he was on the right trail. It was the man with an ear patch, he recalled, who had been the dinner guest of an affluent businessman at the Japanese restaurant; the generous host, Qwilleran now knew, was Fleudd. He had joined Penniman & Greystone in the spring, and Dunwoody had been living with Charlotte Roop for the last four months, no doubt relaying information about SOCK when she innocently discussed conversations she had overheard at Roberto's. Furthermore, it was Memorial Day weekend when Jupiter moved into the Casablanca. They were both undercover agents for Fleudd!

Riker broke the silence as they approached the motel. "I had enough sense to grab my credit cards, but I don't have my socks or my razor or my partial!"

"I'm in the same boat," Qwilleran said. "I have my wallet but I've lost everything else, including the cats' turkey roaster."

The clerk at the motel said, "We have a few rooms with waterbeds."

"Not for me," said Riker.

"I'll take one," said Qwilleran. "And do you have a disposable litterbox for the cats?"

Once situated in the room, he opened the door of the carrier and threw himself on the bed, while the Siamese inspected the room like veteran travelers.

In a matter of minutes someone kicked the

door, and Riker was standing there with two paper cups. "Turn on the TV! There's live coverage on 'All-night News' right after the commercials. And here's some free coffee."

An announcer in a parka—filmed against a background of fire trucks, ambulances, and police cars—was saying, "Firemen are still fighting the blaze at the Casablanca apartments following an explosion at 3:18 this morning. The blast, of unknown origin, destroyed three floors of the building, which is almost a hundred years old."

The camera zoomed to the top of the blackened, smoldering structure, while the voice-over continued: "Forty-two residents have been hospitalized with injuries, and many are missing. No bodies have been recovered. Jessica Tuttle, manager of the Casablanca, says it is impossible to tell how many persons were in the building at the time of the explosion."

The face of Mrs. Tuttle, grim and managerial, flashed on the screen with a microphone thrust in front of her. "We have about two hundred tenants," she said, "but we don't know who was in the building when it happened and who wasn't. We're grateful for the prompt rescue attempts. Everything's been handled very efficiently . . . No, I don't know what could have caused it. Perhaps the Lord is trying to tell us something."

A cracked voice off-camera shouted, "He's tellin' ya to tear the place down!"

The video cut to a Red Cross van and then a bus being loaded with refugees in nightclothes, some huddled in blankets. Voice-over: "Survivors are being bused to temporary shelters. Residents who were not on the premises at the time of the explosion are urged to telephone the following number to assist in the search for the missing . . .''

Qwilleran said, ''There's Mrs. Jasper with Napoleon, boarding the bus!'' She raised the cat's paw to wave at the camera. ''And there's Yazbro, the skunk who let the air out of my tires!''

A man in a red golf hat was helping elderly tenants into the bus. Then, as the camera panned the windows of the loaded vehicle, showing strained and frightened faces, Qwilleran caught a glimpse of plucked eyebrows, marcelled hair, and a head tilted prettily to one side. His sigh of relief was more like a groan.

He said, ''I wonder if poor Charlotte got out safely. I wonder if her 'gentleman friend' got out in time. If not, he's lost more than an ear on this job.''

''Yow!'' said Koko. He was sitting tall on the TV and washing up—just as he had sat tall on the volume of Van Gogh, licking his right paw and washing his mask, his whiskers, and particularly his right ear.

''Remarkable cat!'' Qwilleran murmured without elucidating to his skeptical friend.

''I've had all I can take,'' said Riker. ''I'm going to bed.''

As soon as he was out of the room the Siamese engaged in a sudden expression of joy, chasing each other wildly under and over the furniture; they knew they were going home. Qwilleran propped himself against the headboard and watched the steeplechase.

Eventually Yum Yum snuggled down on his lap. She had lost her apathy and moody aloofness. Had she been affected by the "opalescence" that hung over the city like a stifling blanket? Did she find it unsettling to live on the fourteenth floor (which was really the thirteenth)? Or was she simply using feline strategy to get her own way? Qwilleran stroked her soft silky fur and called her his little sweetheart, and she responded by raising a velvet paw to touch his moustache, all the while squeezing her eyes and purring deliriously.

As for Koko, he jumped on the bed and flopped down in an attitude of exhaustion. It had been a strenuous night. He had saved an estimated two hundred persons.